The critics love P9-CBS-945

FIRST YOU RUN

"A rollercoaster ride filled with heart-stopping suspense and a scorching hot romance which will keep you on the edge of your seat until you turn the last page."

—*Simply Romantic Reviews*

"St. Claire continues to exceed all expectations."

—*The Winter Haven News Chief* (FL)

"Nonstop, fast-paced, action-filled romantic adventure that will keep you on the edge of your seat from beginning to end. Filled with heart-stopping suspense and sizzling hot romance. . . . St. Claire's latest story leaves us wanting just one thing—more Bullet Catchers!"

—Romance Novel TV

"[The Bullet Catchers] series continues to improve with age, delivering taut plots with plenty of twists."

—*Romantic Times*

"Exciting, sexy as hell, romantic suspense. . . . You won't want to put the book down."

—Reader to Reader Reviews

THEN YOU HIDE

"St. Claire aces another one!"

—*Romantic Times*

"*Then You Hide* is nothing short of spectacular with the fast pace and the tension constantly mounting. I couldn't stop turning the pages as I just had to see what would happen next as the various twists and turns kept coming."

—Kwips and Kritiques

"This hide-and-seek novel moves at a rapid clip as it follows an extremely headstrong heroine."

—*Romantic Times BookClub*

"With snappy dialogue, appealing characters and a noteworthy plot, *Then You Hide* is a rewarding romantic suspense story."

—*Single Titles*

"A thrilling and engrossing read. The plot was filled with suspense, and kept me on the edge of my seat. The romance was hot."

—*Queue My Review*

TAKE ME TONIGHT

"Sexy, smart, and suspenseful, *Take Me Tonight* is an absolute must-read. . . . St. Claire really rocks."

—Mariah Stewart, *New York Times* bestselling author

"You actually have to put *Take Me Tonight* down every once in a while just to catch your breath."

—Romance Reviews Today

"Definitely one of St. Claire's best and not to be missed!"

—*Romantic Times*

THRILL ME TO DEATH

"Sizzles like a hot Miami night."

— Erica Spindler, *New York Times* bestselling author

"Sultry romance with enticing suspense."

—*Publishers Weekly*

"Fast-paced, sexy romantic suspense. . . . A book that will keep the reader engrossed in the story from cover to cover."

—*Booklist*

"Roxanne St. Claire's got the sexy bodyguard thing down to an art form. . . . [She] expertly entertains through the novel's emotional twists and sensual turns, rocketing us through a series of exciting events . . . one heck of a love story."

—Michelle Buonfiglio, LifetimeTV.com

KILL ME TWICE

"When it comes to dishing up great romantic suspense, St. Claire is the author you want. Sexy and scintillating . . . an exciting new series."

—*Romantic Times*

"*Kill Me Twice* literally vibrates off the pages with action, danger, and palpable sexual tension. St. Claire is exceptionally talented."

—*The Winter Haven News Chief* (FL)

KILLER CURVES

"A sleek, sexy, and very American romantic suspense novel. . . ."

—*Publishers Weekly*

"This book really grabbed me . . . refreshingly cool."

—*Orlando Sentinel* (FL)

FRENCH TWIST

"Great reading!"

—*Romantic Times*

"Intriguing suspense that crackles with sexual tension. . . ."

—*The Winter Haven News Chief* (FL.)

Also by Roxanne St. Claire

ROXANNE ST. CLAIRE

NOW YOU DIE

POCKET STAR BOOKS

New York   London   Toronto   Sydney

The sale of this book without its cover is unauthorized. If you purchased this book without a cover, you should be aware that it was reported to the publisher as "unsold and destroyed." Neither the author nor the publisher has received payment for the sale of this "stripped book."

Pocket Star Books
A Division of Simon & Schuster, Inc.
1230 Avenue of the Americas
New York, NY 10020

This book is a work of fiction. Names, characters, places, and incidents either are products of the author's imagination or are used fictitiously. Any resemblance to actual events or locales or persons, living or dead, is entirely coincidental.

Copyright © 2008 by Roxanne St. Claire

All rights reserved, including the right to reproduce this book or portions thereof in any form whatsoever. For information address Pocket Books Subsidiary Rights Department, 1230 Avenue of the Americas, New York, NY 10020

First Pocket Star Books paperback edition September 2008

POCKET STAR BOOKS and colophon are registered trademarks of Simon & Schuster, Inc.

For information about special discounts for bulk purchases, please contact Simon & Schuster Special Sales at 1-800-456-6798 or business@simonandschuster.com

Cover design by Carl Galian

Manufactured in the United States of America

10 9 8 7 6 5 4 3 2 1

ISBN-13: 978-1-4165-5244-4
ISBN-10:   1-4165-5244-8

This one is dedicated to Micki Nuding, whom I have greedily called "my" editor since book one. Ten times I've handed her my very best work, and ten times she's made it better. Her editorial touch is delicate and magical, her vision is clear and unerring, her enthusiasm (and the occasional tear) is the greatest of all payoffs for months of hard work. When I say I'd be lost without her, I'm not even kidding. She is my partner on every page, my advocate on every decision, and one helluva shoe shopper, too.

ACKNOWLEDGMENTS

ONCE AGAIN, I called in the experts and backup team. I acknowledge them all with deep gratitude and amazement that they put up with me. Most especially . . .

Novelist, friend, and totally connected Washington powerhouse Karna Bodman, who provided access to the U.S. Supreme Court, specifically the office of Justice Sandra Day O'Connor, to help ensure that my fiction didn't veer too far from fact.

Former New York City police officer Travis Myers, who sat next to me on a plane seeking peace and quiet and ended up becoming a source of inspiration and information, sharing way more than he needed to, giving me one too many ideas, and helping me understand the real impact of injury. And what a vocabulary!

A plethora of fantastic ladies in South Carolina, who never grew impatient during this or the two previous books. Nina Bruhns, Veronica Alderson, April Alsup, C. J. Lyons, Judy Watts, and so many of the generous writers of the South Carolina RWA chapters, as well as numerous Realtors and residents of Kiawah Island and Charleston. Thank you for being my eyes, ears, personal tour guides, and sounding board. If any of you write about Florida, I hope to return the favor.

Holly Simpson, PR director of the South Carolina Aquarium, who provided details, floor plans, seating suggestions, and fact checking, along with a nod to the entire Aquarium staff for their generous assistance. Everyone should go there!

Once again, a special shout-out to Roger Cannon, who was only minding his own business in a bookstore one day and now has to read entire passages of manuscripts to make sure I can handle a Glock, at least on the page. He's a hero and deserves some romance on the range.

Literary agent, cheerleader, voice of reason, and all-around woman of steel, Kim Whalen of Trident Media Group. I couldn't imagine doing this job without her keen sense of style, humor, and grace under pressure.

The wonderfully gifted art department under the leadership of Lisa Litwack, the ever-enthusiastic publicity department under the guiding hand of Jean Anne Rose, and all of the talented editorial, sales, and marketing professionals at Pocket Books. I feel the love and am honored to be part of the team.

The one and only fabulous, gorgeous, hysterical, inimitable Kresley Cole, whose voice on the other end of my phone got me through every scene, every chapter, every day of writing this book (and most others). I may have the handle, but *you* are the rock.

I always acknowledge my family of four—my husband, Rich; our children, Dante and Mia; and the world's most perfect pooch, Pepper, who stand by me and amaze me and love me and need me every day. But this time, I'd also like to acknowledge my sister, my three brothers, their spouses, and their children. While writing this book, we came together in a way few families ever get the chance to, and their collective wisdom, humor, sarcasm, and love inspired me more than I ever dreamed possible. My family tree is large, the branches are strong, and the fruit is sweet. I'm blessed to have them all. Now if I could just get that license plate.

PROLOGUE

Camille Griffin Graham State Penitentiary
Columbia, South Carolina
1984

EILEEN STAFFORD'S CELL door clanged open at six-thirty in the morning. Blinking sleep away, Eileen turned on her cot to meet the black-eyed gaze of the guard known as "Evil Eyes."

For one wildly insane moment, Eileen thought she was about to be set free.

Miss Stafford, the courts of South Carolina have carefully reviewed your case and realized that . . .

The fantasy ended with the clamp of handcuffs around Eileen's narrow wrists just before Evil Eyes elbowed her out of the cell. Hope was suffocated so instantly in this place, along with the frequent daydreams that kept her sane.

They walked in silence down a dim hallway and stopped at a desk, where Evil Eyes mumbled something to the guard, who responded with a look of surprise. Then the main doors opened and a blast of chilly autumn air snapped over Eileen, sneaking into her shackled wrists and up the ankles of her gray jumpsuit.

Hope gushed through her again. Why would they drag her out at this hour unless someone had finally discovered who *really* killed Wanda Sloane? Maybe a clue had been found, a witness had come forward . . .

Her slippers shuffled to keep up with Evil's long strides as they followed the concrete path from one gray structure to another in the dreary dawn light.

They finally stopped along the fenced-in edge of the property at a single-story building, with shrubs, fresh paint, and grime-free windows. This had to be the warden's office.

Against everything she had in her, another wave of hope swelled. Maybe . . . one of the girls . . .

No. Her daughters were forever gone to her, three seeds thrown to the wind, and all she could do was pray that wherever they were, they were cherished little seven year-olds who would never know what their birth mother did, or why.

The guard knocked hard, matching the sound of Eileen's heart.

She stole a glance at him. "What's—what's going on?"

She got a contemptuous look in response. "You have a visitor."

She *never* had visitors. Almost never.

Could it be a defense lawyer? A real one, instead of the pushover who'd been bought and then banished from Charleston?

The door was opened by a man she'd never seen before, short and stocky with glasses on his pockmarked nose.

"You can leave now," he told Evil Eyes, as he indicated for Eileen to come in. "*You* go in there."

Eileen glanced around. There was nothing but an entryway—no desk or guard, no other inmates. Just a linoleum floor and four doors.

She took a few steps to the one he'd indicated, catching a glimpse into another room as she passed. All it contained was a double cot with rumpled sheets.

Oh, Lord above, this was for conjugal visits.

Fear burned in her stomach and she felt lightheaded.

"That door," the man said impatiently. "He's ready for you."

"I'm sorry, I—"

"Go in the fucking room and shut up. He's ready for you."

Could *he* actually come here, buy this man's silence, and force her to have sex with him? After letting her take the blame for a murder he committed?

Of course he could. *He could do anything.*

Wordlessly, she stepped to the door, lifting her shackled, shaking hands to turn the knob. It opened with a creak, revealing another double cot—empty. She stepped inside and kept her eyes on the linoleum floor.

"Hello, Leenie."

It wasn't him, but it was someone she hated almost as much. She looked up into the hazel eyes and bushy brows she'd come to know so well during her trial. On the witness stand, he'd told lie after lie about the night he'd arrested her, about his "investigation" full of bogus evidence and ridiculous speculation, about the "confession" she gave him.

What could he possibly want now that she lived here without any chance of parole?

He leaned against the wall, his eyes cold.

"You can't say hello?"

"What do you want?" The words came out rough and low.

"You probably don't hear much from the world in here, so I dropped by to tell you that the state of South Carolina has officially launched a court of appeals."

Appeals? She couldn't help the tiny gasp that hissed through her teeth. A second chance?

He chuckled and shook his head. "You'll never guess who's one of the six justices handpicked to run that court."

No chance. "Big surprise." It fell right in line with his ambitions.

He laughed again and reached into the pocket of his pricey sports jacket. "Actually, I do have a big surprise for you, Eileen." He pulled out something white and square. "I want to show you a picture."

She lifted her chin. "Of what?"

"Not what. Who." He turned the white square over.

At first all she saw was green and red, a blur of ornaments, a sparkle of tinsel. Then her eyes focused. And welled with tears.

The child was tiny, fair, doe-eyed . . . and about six years old.

"Your daughter."

One of them. The thought steeled her. She still knew something he didn't: two more daughters had been born that dark night on a rural road up in Holly Hill.

She tore her hungry gaze from the picture, determined not to let him see what it did to her. "What about her?"

"She's recently been adopted."

She'd been adopted six years ago. Illegally, but adopted. "How recently?"

"Less than a month, since someone . . ." He raised a brow to underscore just who that might be. ". . . saved her from the foster home system and took her under his protective wing."

He had her? In his own home? Envy and fury whipped through her. It was bad enough he'd trapped her in this hell, but he had one of the girls? She forced a shrug. "Why are you telling me this?"

"A simple, straightforward warning, Eileen." He pocketed the picture. "If you decide to get chatty with anyone, she won't see next year's Christmas tree. And now that you know who controls the appeals process, you shouldn't waste her life like that."

"I'm wasting mine instead."

He grinned. "Exactly. And let's keep it that way . . . Leenie."

The nickname was intentional. A way for him to remind her that he spoke directly for her former lover, the son of a bitch who made her give up her most precious gift and then, as if that weren't enough, framed her for murder.

He left without another word and Eileen dropped onto the thin mattress.

One of six on the court of appeals already. He ultimately planned to get to the top, and everything was aligned to get him there including the necessary family connections.

As long as she rotted in Camp Camille for a murder he'd committed. And she would, for that child in the picture and her two sisters.

But . . . what if . . . someday, a long time from now, those girls sought the truth? What if one of them turned out to be her guardian angel who would drop down from above and demand that the world know she was innocent? Then he'd be forced to confess his crimes. Someday . . .

Eileen closed her eyes to indulge in the fantasies that kept her alive, but all she could do was sob with regret and remorse and the empty heart of a mother who loved her daughters so much, she gave up her life for them.

There was no such thing as a guardian angel. Only the devil, and he had all the power.

CHAPTER
ONE

Astor Cove, New York
The Hudson River Valley
Late Summer, 2008

LUCY SHARPE WOKE to the sound of gunfire. Steady. Distant. Infuriating.

She rolled out of bed and strode to the window, totally naked, completely awake, and royally pissed. Who the hell was taking target practice at three in the morning?

She peered at the training compound a half mile away, a few security lights casting yellow circles around the perimeter, but otherwise dark. Only one man had the nerve to do something like this.

Jack Culver. A master at worming his way into places he didn't belong.

She resisted looking at the empty bed behind her. Instead, she scooped up her satin drawstring pajama pants and stepped into them, then yanked the matching camisole over her head.

As she flipped her hair out from underneath the thin fabric, she snagged her G-23, checked the magazine, then headed out of her room. Barefoot, armed, and riled enough to scare the crap out of that son of a bitch, she padded down the long, dark hallway that separated her private living quarters from the rest of the ten-thousand-square-foot mansion.

At the top of the stairs, she paused at the library doors, considering a change in plans. Most nights when she couldn't sleep, she fought the demons by working, coordinating the resources of her successful security and investigation firm and focusing on problems she could solve. Present-day problems, not ancient ones that were out of her control.

But tonight wasn't most nights. And the demons weren't in her head, they were in her compound. One demon, anyway.

And this one was staying at the Bullet Catchers' guesthouse, invading the Bullet Catchers' war room, and infiltrating her carefully constructed, perfectly organized, highly efficient world. And using her firing range as his personal playground in the middle of the night.

How the hell had he managed it? She'd *fired* him. And yet . . . he'd managed to wrangle an invitation back. A temporary one, anyway.

Another gunshot echoed.

He wasn't even *allowed* to fire a gun. Downstairs she stabbed at the alarm pad in the kitchen and stepped outside into the night air, the temperature in the Hudson Valley suspended between the final dog days of August and the first nip of autumn.

The stone path was cool under her feet as she moved soundlessly, passing the guesthouse. This smaller version of her own Tudor mansion was dark for the night, the bodyguards and security specialists who were at headquarters for training or for assignment briefings all asleep now.

Another round popped. *Not all of them.* The shots were slower now, as if he'd switched to a .45 and the recoil—and that wounded trigger finger—had changed his rhythm. And the echo told her he was out on the straight range, behind the two-story live fire house they used for training.

Breaking every rule and pissing her off: that would definitely be Jack.

She stayed in the shadows, following a half-mile hilly path to the training compound. When she reached the classroom and simulation facility, she stealthily moved around the building.

She saw the target silhouettes, five of them static, others moving on a cable between them. She heard him rack the semiautomatic he had no right carrying, let alone firing, and then the shuffle of his foot as he took his stance.

She inched out and lifted her Glock, her eyes on the central moving target. When she smacked that silhouette right in the heart, he'd get the message to stop. She slipped her finger over the trigger just as the moon came out from behind a cloud, spilling silver light all over the range . . . and over Jack.

She couldn't look away. She could barely breathe.

His dark hair tumbled down to broad, bare shoul-

ders, the carved angles of his back shadowed and
smooth. He aimed his gun with steady, tensed arms,
his legs in a wide stance. He wore only jeans that were
slung low on his narrow hips and fitted over his hard,
curved backside.

She closed her eyes, leaning her warm face against
the cool cement wall, the image vivid in her mind.

But wait a second. Something was wrong with that
picture . . .

Jack was shooting left-handed.

She popped around the corner again to make sure.
Of all the arrogant, stubborn, stupid things. Did he
think she'd change her mind and let him carry if he
fired with his other—

The shot cracked and the moving target stopped
dead on its cable, shot to the heart.

All right, everyone gets lucky sometimes. Especially
Jack. She waited, her weapon down as she watched.

He fired. Hit the head. Fired again. Hit the heart.
Fired again. Hit the kidney. Fired again. Right between the eyes.

He lowered the gun, and his black hair caught the
moonlight as he gave a hoot of victory. The sound
reached into Lucy's gut and twisted something she did
not want to have twisted.

Not by a man she loathed, blamed for almost killing one of her best men, and had fired because of
it. Still, as much as she hated him, as much as she
vowed he'd never be a Bullet Catcher again, as much
as she regretted the one night she'd let him enter the
ultimate place he had no right to be—her body—she

couldn't fight the tendril of respect that curled around her heart.

He'd taught himself to shoot left-handed—and damn straight, too.

Did he really think that would change her mind? Earn his old job back?

Get real, Jack.

The only reason he was allowed here was because he had information that could help her on a case, and the briefing was early tomorrow morning. *Very* early.

Once more, she drank in the vision of his half-dressed body in the moonlight, then started home, moving as silently as she had on her way there.

Forget sleep. *That* was a lost cause.

She followed alongside the building, thinking about tomorrow's meeting and how Jack would undoubtedly—

A hand clamped over her face and she bucked backward, instantly raising her weapon only to have it knocked right out of her hands. She whipped her elbow around, aiming for the throat, but her attacker ducked at exactly the right instant.

She coiled to throw a kick, but he twirled her effortlessly and pressed her flat against the wall, pushing a shocked breath from her lungs.

Firm, confident hands pinned her against the wall. "Leaving so soon, Ms. Sharpe?"

"You bastard."

"I love you, too."

He was six-two and a hundred eighty pounds of solid attitude, but she could have fought him. "I have ten different moves that could fold you in half."

He laughed softly. "Sweetheart, you fold me in half by standing still."

Of course he'd turn it into a sexual tease. "If you don't get your goddamn hands off me, Jack, I'm going kick you so hard you'll still be limping tomorrow."

His expression was pure sin, white teeth gleaming, midnight eyes mocking. He took that same wide stance he'd had at the range, offering her direct access to his crotch. The move brushed his hips against her, the contact branding.

"Go ahead. Gimme your best knee."

Her body betrayed her with a white hot crackle of response.

"You are seriously pushing your luck, Culver."

His eyes narrowed and he pinned her, his chest against hers, his hips dangerously close. "What I'm pushing is you against the wall. Like it?"

"Unless you want me to hurt something you value, let me go."

"It's so damn hard . . ." He leaned in an inch, as if he might show her exactly *how* hard it was. ". . . to get your attention around here."

"That's because I'm working. I have a company to run, and you're interrupting the sleep I need to do that." She pressed harder against the building, determined not to give in to the impulse to do the opposite.

Just once. Here in the dark, alone. Just one more time to feel the hot steel of him.

"We'll talk in the morning, Jack. You'll have my attention at the meeting."

"But I have it now."

She shook some hair off her face so she could look right into his eyes. "You've got five seconds to back off."

"Then I'm gonna use them—"

"Four."

He stared at her, his eyes smoky and heavy lidded. "To ask a favor."

"Three."

"You know I'll go right down to the wire."

"You know I'll break your balls, just like that drug addict broke your trigger finger."

His look grew dangerously dark. "My *old* trigger finger."

"Yeah, I saw your new trick. Not impressed. As far as I'm concerned, your *only* trigger finger is injured for life. Regardless of the fact that you managed to get that expunged from your NYPD record, and lied about it to me."

His fingertip grazed the skin under her earlobe, sending a shiver from her neck to her toes.

"My trigger finger works just fine." He dropped his gaze, looking right at the one place where she couldn't hide her response. Her nipples jutted against the thin satin, twin peaks of reaction. "It's firing you up."

She gave him a solid push. "Stop it."

He backed up with a smile, keeping one hand on her shoulder. "Since you're here, let's talk."

"I'm going back to bed."

"I'll go with you." At her look, he grinned. "Up the path, I mean."

That's how Jack always operated. He inched his way into places, eased himself where he shouldn't be, and the next thing she knew, *wham*—he was taking matters into his own hands. "No."

"Then how about a little friendly competition?" He turned to pick up her gun. Handing it to her, he let their fingers brush. "My left hand against your right?"

He never took no for an answer. "I can't take advantage of you like that, Jack."

"Sure you can. Come on." He nodded his head toward the range. "It'll be fun."

Actually, it probably would be. Wrong on every level, but fun. "No."

"You're worried I'll beat you."

She snorted softly.

He leaned closer. "You'll like the prize."

Something unholy and unwanted rolled through her at the rumble in his voice. "Which is?"

"Oh, let's see. Let's make it interesting, but . . . safe."

Nothing was safe with him.

"How about . . ." He was already leading her toward the firing range. "The winner gets to do anything they want to the loser . . . above the neck."

She laughed. "Above the neck."

"Yeah." He guided her to the shooting berm. "You win, you can do anything you want to me above the neck. You can box my ears. You can pull my hair. You can—"

"I get the idea."

"Kiss me with tongue."

"We can't—"

"We could."

"—can't set up a Tyro course, because I only have one round."

He turned toward a prep area where he'd laid out several different weapons and magazines. "Got a Glock mag right here."

So he'd been planning this all along.

"I'll set up the Tyro," he said. "Three stages, three targets, twenty-four shots, ten yards."

"Fine." She slipped the extra ammo into the elastic waistband of her sleep pants and got into position. "I'm going to kick your injured ass and then slap your arrogant face. And then I'm going to bed." Alone.

At the opposite end of the range, the circular markers thunked into place. Without taking a breath, she stood, aimed, and fired eight times. She missed the third shot by a millimeter but made the rest.

He fired eight times. And missed nothing.

Neither said a word.

She shook her hand, shot until she had emptied the clip, reloaded, racked, and finished the next eight. She missed nothing.

He did the same, missing one.

"Tie game," he said. "Together, this time."

Her eyes locked on the target; she aimed the Glock. Next to her, he did the same.

"Shoot," he ordered.

They fired simultaneously, each shot echoing over the hills and disappearing into the night.

She missed one. He drilled a three-inch hole in the bull's-eye.

She lowered her weapon. "Nice work."

He shoved his weapon into the waistband of his jeans, then took her Glock, setting it with the others.

"Time to pay the piper," he said softly, turning back to her.

Anticipation rolled over her skin, leaving chills, and making her take a half step backward as he lifted his hands to her face.

She couldn't really say no if she wanted to.

"Above the neck, one can find . . ." Strong, warm fingers cupped her face, lifting it toward his. The twinkle in his eyes was the only evidence of humor; otherwise his expression was purely serious. Purely hot. "Many attractive things."

Against her will, she parted her lips. She could do this. She could kiss Jack Culver, take his tongue, feel his body, and walk away. She had control over everything—including her libido.

No one was *that* irresistible.

Her eyes drifted closed as he lowered his face, his breath on her mouth, his fingers just skimming her hairline. He didn't kiss her. Instead, he threaded his hands in her hair and slowly, gently combed through, sliding his fingers all the way to the ends with a sigh of raw appreciation.

"Are you done now?"

"Mmmm. No." He turned her face, his lips brushing her cheek. A stroke of her hair and a kiss on the cheek? Surely Jack wouldn't settle for that.

Disappointment, cold and sudden, dropped through her.

She stiffened and started to pull back as he placed his lips over her ear.

"All I want above your neck, Lucinda Sharpe, is your brain. That incredible, wicked, keen mind that puts others to shame."

She stayed very still, the sensations of his words in her ears whirling down to her toes.

"Do you know what I love most about your mind?"

The word *love* delivered a little jolt through her, but she didn't move. "I can't imagine."

"That it's open." He punctuated that with the tiniest flick of his tongue against her lobe, firing a few more sparks and deadening any common sense.

"Open?"

"Open to every possibility, no matter how outrageous or unbelievable or impossible it might seem when you first hear about it."

She inched around to face him, close enough to count every lash and every unshaved whisker, but far enough away to lessen his magnetic pull.

"What are you talking about?"

"I need you to have an open mind tomorrow when I present the evidence in the Stafford case." He paused, then leaned a little closer to whisper the rest. "No matter what I say."

"I always have an open mind."

"I'm going to be testing it."

She pulled away completely. "How?"

"You'll see."

All her synapses were firing now, her mind firmly back in focus.

"That's why you did this? You made all this noise that you knew would get me down here just to ask me to have an open mind?" She didn't believe it, not for a minute.

"Yep. Unless you want to go into the woods and make out."

"What do I have to have an open mind about? You have a theory about the murder?"

He stepped away to get her gun. "Here you go, Luce." He handed it to her, letting their fingers touch again. "You better get some sleep now. Be careful on your way back to the house. There are wolves all over this place." He winked and walked away, disappearing into the darkness.

Three hours later, Lucy was still at her desk poring over files and thirty-year-old transcripts from Eileen Stafford's trial, when her breath was stolen for the second time in one night.

She blinked at the picture, turned it upside down, and slid her gaze over to the list of names she'd been jotting down on a yellow pad.

"No damn wonder he wanted me to have an open mind." A wry smile pulled at her lips.

Jack was a lot of things: a tease, a flirt, an unrelenting, shameless, fearless smart-ass, who had his finger on all her hot buttons and loved to press them. He was also a brilliant investigator, and he could solve crime puzzles like no one she'd ever met.

But more than anything, Jack had a vigilante streak that had gotten him in a lot of trouble.

If he was right about this . . . what would he do about it?

She shuddered to think of the ramifications.

She wanted the truth, and then justice. Jack wanted retribution—period. That was the fundamental difference between them.

She flipped the picture again, looking at the names she'd written, especially at one she'd originally discarded.

Jack wanted much more than an open mind. He wanted access. And she was one of the few people in the world with the connections to investigate something of this magnitude.

Jack knew that, of course. He was using her.

Which made them even. Because that night a little over a year ago, when he'd made her forget every pain and every regret she carried, she'd been using him.

So she owed him one. And if he was right, this would make history. No, this would *change* history.

Jack knew all too well what she found irresistible.

CHAPTER
TWO

THE BULLET CATCHERS' pristine, polished, state-of-the-art war room was a complete train wreck.

Files, papers, maps, calendars, yellowed newspapers covered the table, with the granddaddy of Things That Pissed the Boss Off—a box of doughnuts—right in the middle of it all.

Jack watched the door to Lucy's office open slowly, ready to gauge her nonverbals to figure out if she had done what he expected her to do a few hours ago.

She didn't flinch. She didn't curl that perfectly bowed upper lip or raise a thank-you-very-much sarcastic brow over one of her almond-shaped ebony eyes. She didn't tunnel her fingers through her veil of black velvet hair, lingering in the single streak of white while she blew out a sigh of disgust at the mess.

All she did was take her seat at the opposite end of the massive table, quietly greet the others in the room, and fold her hands over a thick file folder that was as crisp and clean as her winter white silk jacket.

She didn't meet his gaze, though. So one of two things had happened after he left her. She'd either gone up to her tower and sweated all the fever out on tangled sheets—like he had. Or she'd gone to her office and surrendered to an entirely different need: the need to know everything.

His money was on her legendary curiosity. Although her libido wasn't anything to underestimate.

Had his plan worked?

He'd wanted to force her to the files, and coax her to where he needed her to go. Then she'd be predisposed to his preposterous idea. Better yet, she'd think it was her own.

Manipulating the Grand Manipulator was an art form, and sometimes, he was fucking Picasso.

"Good morning, Ms. Sharpe." He smiled at her.

"Jack." She didn't really look him in the eye. Not good.

He definitely got a few sideways glances from the others around the table. She'd brought in Roman Scott, a former NSA guy who could actually be a big help on this one. And Donovan Rush, a new kid she'd had in training for a while, who looked ready and eager to attack a big assignment.

Across the table was a husky guy named Owen Rogers who hid keen intelligence under his cool reserve. In for the ride as well was Lucy's assistant, Avery Cole, and Sage Valentine, Lucy's niece and the head of the ever-growing Bullet Catchers' investigation division.

Thank God there was no sign of the boy wonder

Dan Gallagher. If she kept Dan away from this, he had a shot at getting what he wanted.

If any of the others wondered why the hell Jack had been allowed back into their hallowed halls on a personal case, they were all too highly trained to show it. Without preamble, Lucy launched into a comprehensive briefing.

"For the past several months, Jack Culver has been working on a private case to help a woman locate three daughters she gave up in a black market adoption operation known as Sapphire Trail, back in 1977. The Bullet Catchers have been peripherally involved."

That was one way to describe it. Lucy's interest in the case had been ice cold in the beginning. Jack had convinced Adrien Fletcher, the only Bullet Catcher he still considered a friend, to help him find Miranda Lang. Fletch did so and in the process fell madly in love with her.

As a favor to Miranda, Lucy had agreed to apply her considerable resources to finding the other sisters as well, putting Wade Cordell on the trail of one and giving Jack everything he needed to find the other.

"We've had some luck in the searches," Lucy continued. "Wade located Vanessa Porter in the Caribbean, and reunited her with her mother just a few weeks ago."

And luckily Vanessa had been a match for the bone marrow that Eileen needed to stay alive.

Ever since he'd met Eileen through a different adoption search his one-man PI firm had been conducting, finding her daughters and a bone marrow match had been Jack's goals. But now that he'd accomplished that, he wasn't going to rest until one final detail of this woman's life was smoothed out.

He wanted to set her free, and to destroy the man who'd unjustly put her in jail. Unfortunately, Eileen refused to say who that was. She was convinced that "*he* could do anything," and that "anything" meant he'd hurt her daughters.

Based on what he knew so far, she was probably right.

"So, did you find the third daughter?" Roman Scott asked, looking up from his notes.

"Jack did." Lucy paused and glanced at Jack, giving him the lead.

"Her name was Kristen Carpenter," he said.

"Was?"

Jack answered Donovan's question with a nod. "She was killed while crossing a street in Washington, D.C., a few months ago. A hit and run, and big surprise here, they never caught the guy."

"Then both daughters are accounted for and under Bullet Catcher protection," Roman Scott said, jotting down a note. "And the third is deceased. What's the investigation, the hit and run?"

"The investigation is into the murder that the mother was convicted of," Lucy said. "She's been in prison since the girls were eight months old, and totally silent regarding her innocence."

"So why are we investigating?" Owen asked.

"Because she's innocent," Jack said simply. "She's been too scared and too sick to talk much, but I've picked up enough clues and I've been playing with the puzzle pieces, and the picture is—"

"Extraordinary," Lucy finished.

Oh, yeah.

"Let me give you some history to put it all in perspective," he said. "The murder in question took place eight months after Eileen Stafford had her illegitimate triplets and gave them all up for illegal adoption. During the second half of her pregnancy, she'd stayed hidden in her home in a suburb of Charleston, on an unpaid leave of absence from her job as a legal secretary at the county courthouse. When she returned to work, things had changed."

"In what way?" Avery asked.

"She'd been replaced, primarily in one courtroom and in one highly regarded judge's chambers, by a woman named Wanda Sloane."

"The victim," Lucy interjected for clarity. "Another attractive legal secretary."

"No one disputes the fact that they were jealous of each other, or that Wanda and Eileen were known to swap insults and gossip about the other," Jack continued. "Just typical workplace cattiness, by all accounts. But one night, not far from the courthouse, a witness saw a woman running from an alley and driving wildly out of town. Curious, the witness went into the alley, found Wanda Sloane's freshly shot body, and called 911 from a pay phone. Thirty minutes later, a cruiser pulled Eileen over racing out of Charleston. A Raven Arms .25 caliber pistol was on her front seat."

"Sounds pretty open and shut," Owen said.

"Except that the trial was quick, too quiet, and stunningly biased," Lucy replied, flipping through transcripts. "Evidence was tampered with and the key players, like her public defender, the eyewitness, and the judge, are all dead. A man who visited her in prison about fifteen years ago, the adopted father of one of the daughters, was murdered on his way home from South Carolina. The arresting officer was recently killed in his condo when it was burned to the ground. And Kristen Carpenter's death might not have been an accident."

"So do you have a list of suspects?" Owen asked in typical Bullet Catcher cut-to-the-chase fashion.

"A very short list," Jack replied. "One."

He could have sworn Lucy said "One" at the same time, but her voice was covered by her library door popping open, bringing all the conversation to a halt.

Dan Gallagher's crooked smile beamed over the crowd and settled on Lucy. "Hope I'm not too late, Juice."

Fuck. Despite an urge to smack the table, Jack hid any reaction to the new arrival or the obnoxious nickname, especially because a few faces turned to see if he would do exactly that.

"You are," Lucy said, indicating the empty chair on her right. "But since you came in through my office and I had the speaker on, I assume you're up to speed."

Dan winked at Avery as he took the seat. "No wonder we all work for her. She's always one step ahead of everyone." He reached toward a pile of file folders, then pulled his hand back from the mess. "Whoa."

"Here." Lucy handed him one of her perfectly arranged dossiers.

He flipped it open and narrowed green eyes on Jack. "Go on, Culver. Sounds like it's just getting interesting."

Jack pulled out a page from his chaotic files, all his focus on the word in the middle. Six letters. Two syllables. One brilliant, crazy, impossible idea that would make Gallagher snort and the rest of the table gasp. And Lucy?

He'd know in a second.

"At the time Eileen was working at the courthouse, there was a distinguished circuit judge there. For a year prior to her pregnancy, Eileen worked for him on a regular basis, spent many evenings in his chambers, and was seen outside of the courthouse with him on one occasion."

He looked up to see Lucy writing a notation. Dan leaned over to boldly read her notes, but got a warning look for the effort. *Score one.*

"This man, by virtue of his position and his marriage into one of Charleston's oldest and wealthiest families, had tremendous power and connections. He was then, and is now, respected, revered, and admired."

"Come on, you're killin' me," Dan interjected. "Who the hell is it and where's the evidence?"

Lucy put a hand on Dan's arm. "Let him finish." *Score two for the away team.*

"First, I think he's the most likely candidate to be the father of the triplets," Jack said.

"There is no evidence on file of the father," Avery said. "I studied those files after Miranda and Vanessa were found, and nothing indicates his identity."

"Actually, something does," Jack said. "And the evidence is on Miranda Lang and Vanessa Porter."

"Ah, yes," Dan said, a smile tipping. "The famous tattoos on their necks. Numbers, I believe we established in our last meeting on the subject."

Jack ignored the undercurrent of sarcasm in Dan's voice. "The babies were all tattooed, yes. The nurse who tattooed them told me in one interview that this wasn't all that unusual in the black market, and in the case of Eileen, she believed they were numbers."

There were a few surprised responses and some dubious looks, but not from Lucy. Her nod was imperceptible.

He took out the pictures of Miranda's tattoo and the one of Vanessa's laser scar where she'd had the tattoo removed.

"On Miranda, there is what appears to be a one and a four."

"Or someone with a sick sense of humor," Dan added. "Who wrote *hi* on a baby if you read fourteen upside down."

Jack looked up at him. "You're actually not too far off from my theory. Now look at Vanessa's tattoo. These two tiny squiggles we've assumed to be two sixes."

"What was on the third sister, the one who was killed?" Sage asked.

"Nothing on an ME's report, and the family had

her cremated immediately," Jack said. "We'll never have that piece of the puzzle."

Roman Scott leaned forward, tapping his finger on his chin. "Numbers, huh? A safety deposit box? Or what about an address? We should run every combination of those numbers for matching street addresses."

"We can. But consider something else." Jack ripped a clean sheet of paper from a legal pad and grabbed a marker from the table. On it, he re-created the *fourteen* from Miranda's neck. Then he took another page and drew the two curled sixes. "These," he said, "could be lower case *g*'s." He looked up at Lucy, saw the acknowledgment in her eyes, telling him she'd gotten this far last night. Had she made the final connection?

"Put them together and you could have . . ." He wrote the letters in large capitals. *H-I-G-G.*

"Or twenty-four other combinations," Roman added.

"True. But only the letters *H-I-G-G* spell out the first four letters of the name of the powerful, connected, wealthy circuit court judge who worked very closely with both Eileen Stafford and Wanda Sloane." Jack looked into Lucy's eyes and silently invited her to drop the bomb.

She leaned forward as though he'd pulled her by an imaginary string, her gaze on him. "Spessard B. Higgins," she said softly. "Also known as Higgie."

The name hung over the silent room, dropping a few jaws with its weight.

Predictably, Dan choked first. "*Higgie?* Are you kidding? The U.S. Supreme Court justice? That Higgie?"

"There is no other," Lucy said. "He worked very closely with Eileen in 1976 through 1978. After she returned from her leave of absence, they were never seen in the same room again prior to her conviction."

Dan stared at Lucy, then Jack, his look a mix of ridicule and disbelief. "That's what you've got? Some thirty-year-old alleged tattoos that upside down and sideways *might* spell the first four letters of the name of the man who is the closest thing we have to a living saint in the country?"

"There's more," Lucy said. "And of course we'll get even more."

"Yeah? Like what?" Dan asked. "You better get fingerprints, a signed confession, a murder weapon in his underwear drawer, and then put on bulletproof vests. Because that man is more popular than the pope."

"I believe there's enough evidence to merit a covert investigation conducted by the Bullet Catchers," Lucy replied.

Jack could have crawled over the files and kissed her.

Dan threw his dossier on the table in disgust. "Well you better hurry, Luce, because the chief justice just announced he has cancer. A nomination to the head seat could be right around the corner, and Higgie is at the top of the list."

"All the more reason he shouldn't get away with murder," Lucy said.

Jack gave Lucy a huge smile. "You are so correct, Ms. Sharpe."

She smiled right back, delivering a jolt of raw pleasure straight through him. "You did the work, Jack."

Dan looked from one to the other, his own smile wry. A lock of sandy hair tumbled over his forehead as he flipped the file closed. "Count me out."

"As a matter of fact," Jack said, "you were never counted in."

Dan stood slowly, then pushed his chair back in place. "Good. Because I don't want to be involved in the bloodbath we're going to take for going after an American icon on such loose speculation."

He walked to the main door. "Good luck, gang."

He left, and Lucy sat still for a moment, then closed her file. Jack's gut tightened. Dan had a lot of pull over her; she trusted him.

Lucy stood and indicated Jack take over with a wave of her hand. "Go over some more details with this team. I suggest we assign someone to each aspect of the case from Kristen's death to the paperwork you're missing from the black market adoptions at Sapphire Trail and—"

"Got it, Luce. I have a list ready."

"Excuse me, then." She stood and followed Dan's path, leaving an awkward silence in the room.

Who would win this round?

The man she admired, respected, trusted, and some said secretly loved? Or the man she loathed, avoided, doubted, and once, in a moment of weakness, screwed senseless on the floor of a hut in Malaysia?

Shit. There was no contest.

Dan was halfway down the stairs by the time Lucy caught up with him. He didn't slow his step, but crossed the hall and reached the door, forcing her to nearly run down the stairs in three-inch heels.

She slammed her hand on the door, blocking him and holding it closed. "What the hell do you think you're doing?"

"I could ask you the same thing, Lucy." A world of hurt and anger darkened eyes that were almost always smiling, always teasing, and always on her. "Do you have any idea what it could do to the Bullet Catchers if it got out that we were conducting a clandestine investigation of one of the highest ranking judges in the country? My God, Lucy, Higgie is so far above reproach that he . . . he . . ." He shook his head, at a loss. "He's untouchable."

"No one is untouchable, Dan, and he's no saint. I know the man."

"Of course you do, which is exactly why that gutter rat Culver is using you. What's his game? Trying to make a name for himself as a PI? Going after the biggest get in the history of justice? Jesus Christ, Lucy, do you forget what that guy *did* to me?"

Not for a day.

"He *accidentally* shot me," Dan said, before she could answer. "After he lied to you about his record, his injury, and his capabilities. He weaseled his way into the Bullet Catchers and then damn near took me out with a stray bullet."

He hadn't exactly weaseled, since he'd passed every test she had with flying colors, and she believed in her heart that the gunshot was a complete accident. Dan had even admitted he'd made a sudden and unexpected move. But she knew better than to argue that now. "He was fired for his actions."

"But now he's back, just as close to you as he could be, dangling the big one that he knows you could never, ever resist. How the hell did he convince you of his ridiculous theory that a Supreme Court justice is a murderer?"

"He didn't. I came to the same conclusion—and you would, too."

Dan blew out a disbelieving breath. "Based on what?"

"Jack asked me to have an open mind last night and I—"

"Last night?" As soon he said it, she realized her mistake. "You were at dinner with a client and me in the city last night until eleven o'clock. You saw him after that?"

She lifted her chin. "Don't do this, Dan. Don't let your emotions or your jealousy get in the way of what's important here."

"Jealousy?" He spat the word. "I'm not jealous of some has-been cop with a malfunctioning finger and even more malfunctioning instinct."

"Forget the messenger for a minute, Dan. What if Spessard Higgins killed that girl thirty years ago? What if he manipulated the trial and used his power to frame and then silence a woman who'd been his mistress? What if he killed Vanessa's father, and then paid someone to drive a car into Kristen Carpenter as a warning to her mother in jail? Could you sleep at night, knowing that man is at the helm of justice in this country, sitting on a public pedestal when he deserves to be locked up?"

"You're the one with sleeping problems, Luce. Not me. Hope this helps." He got the door open and walked out into the sunshine, looking up for a second to let it bathe his handsome face. Then he lifted a hand over his shoulder. "See ya."

She took a step and grabbed his arm. "What do you mean, see ya?"

"I've got some business in the city: a security analysis for paying clients. Remember them? You like that kind. Or used to."

"Stop it. You can't just walk out of this meeting because your feelings are hurt and you don't like something I'm doing."

He closed his eyes for a second, then turned to her. "Watch me."

"Excuse me?"

At her haughty tone, he gave her a half smile. "Don't pull rank on me now, Juice. I know you're the boss, you own the business, and you call the shots. I also know nobody else gets away with talking to you like that. But sorry, I just don't want to be involved in something that could be this detrimental to the company."

"The company or to you?"

"Lucy, if you're wrong, and this goes public, you'll lose everything we've—*you've*—spent the last seven years building. Is it worth that risk to you? You've got so much to lose and he . . ." He jutted his chin in the direction of the war room. "Has *everything* to gain.

Including a shiny new reputation to replace the one he ruined."

"Only if he's right. I don't want to take down Higgie if he's innocent. I just want to find out the truth."

"Culver isn't interested in the truth," Dan said. "He's a damn vigilante, and that's what cost him every job he's ever had."

She couldn't argue with that. "Dan, I spent hours in the middle of the night reading files, poring through trial transcripts, considering every angle, and looking at all possibilities, especially about those tattoos. I think he's on to something, and that's all that should be important to you."

"Alone?"

She frowned at him. "What?"

"Were you alone with your files?"

"*Yes,* I was alone. Come on, Dan. You're bigger than this. You're smarter than this. You're walking away from this case because of who brought it to us, not what it is."

He hesitated, then smiled that dear crooked smile that always got delivered with a gleam of green eyes. "I'm walking away because I see the writing on the wall, Juice. And it ain't my name up there."

She sighed. "That's what's at the heart of this, isn't it?"

"What's at the heart of this, my friend, is your choice to help a man who lied to you, put my life in jeopardy, and has proven that whatever skill he had as a cop and a Bullet Catcher was pickled with alcohol and tainted with self-loathing. A man who isn't qualified to shoot a bullet, let alone catch one."

"Dan, if Higgie is a murderer and enough of a manipulator to do what I think he's done, then I want to prove that. I don't care who brought the case to us. I have no intention of letting him work on it directly. He'll be entirely in the background."

Dan looked up at the second-floor library window. "He's not in the background now. As a matter of fact, he's in your office. Wonder how he got in there."

She followed Dan's gaze, and saw him. It was true. Jack always found ways into places he wasn't supposed to be. It was one of his secret weapons.

"Face it, Lucy. He'll work on this case because he knows every aspect of it, inside and out, and you're too smart to keep someone with that much knowledge off a complex job."

She turned back to Dan, ready to argue, but he just reached out and touched her hair, feathering the streak, quieting her fight. Was that for Jack's benefit . . . or hers?

He leaned a little closer and for a second she thought he was going to kiss her—something he'd never, ever done. But he liked the idea that the rest of the Bullet Catchers wondered about it.

"You want my advice, Juice?"

"Always."

"Be careful what you wish for."

She stepped back, narrowing her eyes at him. "All I wish for is to find the truth. To see the right person convicted of a crime. And most of all, to allow a woman who is imprisoned to go free and live her life the way it was meant to be lived."

He smiled. "I know. The question is, which woman? The one in that South Carolina jail or . . ." He tipped his head toward the estate. "The one in this one?" He chucked her under the chin. "Good luck, Juice."

He turned and went to his car, leaving her washed in the sunshine.

Even when he was mad and motivated by the worst of emotions, Dan Gallagher was light and whole and healed. And he was one of the closest friends she'd ever had.

She turned to the house, looking up to the leaded glass of her library windows, drawn to the shadow of a man who was none of those things.

CHAPTER
THREE

"No KISS GOOD-BYE?" Jack turned from the window when Lucy entered her library.

"And no secret Bullet Catcher handshake, either. What do you make of that?" She crossed the room, the only sound a whisper of silk trousers that moved with each elegant stride, her hair looking like a spill of black ink, glistening in the morning light as she reached for her BlackBerry.

Watching Lucy move was like knocking back the first deep gulp of single malt scotch—so good it hurt to swallow.

"Are you finished in there?" she asked, glancing toward the war room.

"All but the cleanup. Donovan Rush is going to dig deeper into Kristen Carpenter's death. Sage is going to comb through the Stafford trial files for any living members of the jury to interview, and I gave Roman the files on Vanessa's father's death. We're going to nail Higgins on one of these three murders."

Lucy looked up from the BlackBerry keypad. "What about the black market adoption operation? Finding a link to Higgie as the father of Eileen's babies will be critical to the case."

"I have a couple of ideas."

At his tone, she lowered the device and slid into her chair. "Hit me."

"We need DNA."

She nodded. "Absolutely. We'll have to be creative to get that."

He took the chair across from her. "Tell me something, Luce. What was it that got you in that file? The tattoos? The shitty trial? The sheer audacity of whoever is silencing witnesses and covering evidence? What got you to believe he's guilty?"

"I don't, yet. I want proof."

"Me too." He didn't need more than he had, but he knew she would.

"I want to know his motive," she said.

"He silenced two potentially detrimental women with one shot," Jack said. "How much more motive do you need?"

"To accuse a Supreme Court justice of murder, we need irrefutable proof."

"Establishing that he's the father of the girls will help," Jack said.

"But it's not enough. In fact, it could hurt us more than it helps. So the guy had an affair thirty years ago. If his wife forgives him, why shouldn't America?"

Jack stretched his legs and tunneled his fingers through his hair. "So, you left me and went right to work, eh?"

A smile pulled at her lips, which gleamed with cherry red gloss. "Yes, I did. Exactly like you knew I would, when you summoned me to play shooting games."

"I needed you on my team in that meeting." He tilted his chair back and grinned. "It worked."

"Don't be smug."

"It *did* work."

She shot him a look. "I meant about the team. It's mine, not yours." She waved the BlackBerry. "I'm calling the opposition right now."

The chair legs thudded to the floor. "You're calling Higgie?"

"The Court's in recess until October, but I have his cell. My guess is that he's at Willow Marsh," she said, thumbing the pad. "I have that number, too."

Of course she did.

"He's there," Jack confirmed. Higgie and his wife spent almost all of the summer recess at his estate on Kiawah Island, an upscale residential playground for the überwealthy. The place was secure, private, and utterly inaccessible.

Unless you had a resident's cell phone number programmed into your PDA.

"I'll tell you this," he said. "If the proof we want actually exists in some tangible form and Higgie has it, I'd bet we'd find it at Willow Marsh."

Lucy settled into her seat, one finger ready to hit call. "When I had dinner with him and Marilee last time I was in D.C., they invited me to spend a weekend there this summer. I think it's time I take them up on the offer."

"*We* take them up on the offer," he corrected.

Her look was deadly. "You need to stay as far away from him as possible."

"That's not the deal, Lucy."

She frowned. "*What* deal?"

"This is my case, and I'm using your resources."

"Jack, if he really is Wanda Sloane's killer, the father of those triplets, and the mastermind behind keeping Eileen Stafford in jail and silent for thirty years, then you know damn well he's been tracking every visitor she's ever had. He knows your name. *You* stay in the background."

There were plenty of ways around that. "You won't use that to keep me off this case."

"No. I'll use the fact that you are not legally allowed to fire a gun to keep you off the front lines. You can stay in the background, continue to be briefed, and certainly participate in the development of our strategy, but—"

"Fuck your strategy, Lucy. This is *my* case."

"You turned it over to the Bullet Catchers when you walked through my door, Jack. You are the client now, and if you recall from when you worked here, one of our driving principles is that the client is not always right—and is, in fact, rarely right because they have too much at stake. This case is a perfect example."

He could almost feel his blood bubbling, but merely stared her down. "This case is mine and I will not be in the background, briefed, or relegated to client status."

She held up one finger, smiling into the phone.

"Justice Higgins, I trust the recess is treating you well." The smile widened, along with a laugh that told Jack she didn't even need to identify herself. "Oh, yes, I am, thank you."

Jesus. She had the guy on the phone in twenty-two seconds. He stood, listening while he prowled the room. She might have the connections, but he had the knowledge. He'd lived and breathed this case for months and he wasn't about to sit in the backseat while she drove.

"Of course I heard about Justice Adler. A shame, really. Any news on his prognosis?"

She was quiet, her gaze on him while he paced, pausing at one original work of art after another. Typical Lucy decor: top-of-the-line everything and not a single photograph of a human in the place.

"Business is excellent; thank you for asking," she said. "As a matter of fact, that's why I'm calling. I wanted to let you know how much I appreciate the recommendation you gave to the partners of Gray Redding and Firestone. We're handling a number of investigations for them, as well as executive protection for several of their top clients. That's a terrific new account for us, and I owe you and Marilee another dinner. Are you planning to spend the rest of the recess at Willow Marsh?"

She listened, picking up a pen to scratch a note.

"Oh, really? Well, that'll be a bestseller. Have you chosen a ghostwriter yet?" She looked up, raising her eyebrows.

Higgie was starting to talk to a few people about

writing his autobiography. Jack had heard the buzz about it from one of his sources in Washington.

"I might have some suggestions, yes." She shifted in her chair, unfastening the single button on her jacket and leaning back as she talked. Her silk blouse showed the outline of what was undoubtedly some ridiculously expensive French lingerie. Even in the jungle of Malaysia, even underneath a torn, oversized men's T-shirt, she'd worn something lacy, sheer, and decorated with a hundred tear-drop-sized pearls that he'd popped off with his teeth.

The memory slammed him, sudden and vivid.

"And how is Marilee?"

The question pulled him back to reality.

"Ah, that's a shame," she said. "Chronic migraines are insufferable. I'm certain you have the best doctors for her."

Lucy turned on her laptop, still listening. "And has she tried acupuncture therapy? It's done miracles for my headaches."

She had headaches? There was so much about Lucy he didn't know. Except he did know about those pearls . . .

"Why don't I fly my personal acupuncturist down there, Justice?"

He dropped onto the sofa. She had a personal acupuncturist. Perfect.

"No, no—it's my gift to a good friend." She stabbed at the keyboard some more, then narrowed her eyes, scrolled down, then leaned back. "I'll come down with her so we can catch up."

She shook her head to communicate that she was getting a no. She clicked a few more keys, with enough speed to make him believe she had a purpose and was running out of time on the phone.

"I understand, and certainly wouldn't want to intrude when Marilee isn't feeling well." She scrolled rapidly, studying the screen. "By the way, I'm planning to attend the Habitat for Humanity fund-raiser in Charleston in a few weeks. I put it on my calendar months ago when I saw that you were keynoting, but with Justice Adler's announcement . . ." She let her voice trail and then brightened. "Oh, good. I'd love to see you then." The smile was only in her voice. Her expression was intense as she hit a few more keys and listened. "That would be perfect. A drink and a dance, then. I'm looking forward to seeing Marilee, too." She paused for a moment, listening. "Oh, she's not? That's a shame. Well, you give her my best and let her know my acupuncturist will call and set something up. I know she'll like the results. You take care. Good-bye."

She clicked off and stood, shedding the jacket and looking damn pleased with herself. "Mission accomplished."

"How? You didn't wrangle an invitation."

"True, but I will get someone in there with needles."

"Needles that will go into Marilee Higgins's skin, not her husband's."

She flicked the argument away. "I have the perfect person for the job, and when she leaves, she'll have his DNA, trust me."

"So other than that, you're going to see him at a party and have drinks." Jack shook his head. "I was hoping for more."

"There's plenty more. I'm going to take someone with me to that party—someone who will be set up as a premier ghostwriter who can help Higgie with his autobiography which will naturally involve a great deal of research into his past."

He propped his feet on the coffee table. "I like it. Especially since it could get me exactly where I want to be."

"Not you, Jack."

"Yes, me. If you're doctoring up a new identity, it'll be mine. I have to get behind his walls. I know what to look for."

"And you propose what? That we move into Willow Marsh for the rest of the summer and dig for the murder weapon?"

"Yes. That's precisely what I want to do." At her look, he added, "Come on, Luce, you're all buddy-buddy with the guy and you don't know about his famous vault?"

"I know he saves memorabilia, but anyone in his position would."

"He doesn't just save memorabilia; he's a pack rat with an ego the size of South Carolina. He's already funding a library to be built after his death and evidently has a massive safekeeping place that holds every document he's ever signed, every case he's ever presided over, everything he's ever touched. That's where we want to be. In the vault."

"You don't seriously think he's kept evidence of murder? What if he died? He'd never take that risk."

"Not overt, obvious evidence, no. But someone who knows every nuance of the case might be able to find something. Someone good at solving crimes and seeing patterns and knowing what to look for." He gave a hard, determined look. "He could be nominated to chief justice anytime, and everything would get pushed back for months or years. God only knows if Eileen will live that long."

"She considered that."

"And she should have the pleasure of walking out of prison and spitting in the face of the man who put her there," Jack said.

Lucy blew out a breath. "That's why you scare me."

"What? It's just an expression."

"No, it isn't. You don't want justice. You want to make the guy pay with pain and humiliation."

"Why shouldn't he?" he shot back. "He caused her enough pain and humiliation."

She leaned over the table, as if she wanted to throttle sense into him. "Our job is to investigate and discover evidence, then hand it over to the authorities."

Irritation burned. "So Higgie can be turned into a martyr?"

"I don't know," she admitted. "That's not my problem, and that's not why I'd take on this case. I would like to see Eileen free if she is innocent, and see the right person charged with the crime. I don't need to crucify him. But you do, and that's why having you on this case makes me nervous."

He shifted in his chair. "I just want clear and compelling evidence that he's guilty. How do we get that?"

She studied him doubtfully for a moment, then walked over to the window to think.

"What if he believed he had to start on that autobiography right away?" she asked. "It would force him to talk, to open this vault you say he has."

"How about we get him a publishing contract?"

She shook her head. "He could do that on his own. He's probably had a ton of offers." She narrowed her eyes, looking out at the hills. "I need to get that weekend invitation to work on him, and dig around."

"It could take longer than a weekend to get what we want."

"It could, but how else—" She turned to him, her eyes flashing. "What if we set up a full security detail on the estate?"

Bingo. "We'd have to convince him he needs a security detail. Something above and beyond the U.S. Marshals assigned to protect the Supreme Court justices."

"Those guys are good," she said. "I've hired a few."

"They're not Bullet Catchers."

She glanced over her shoulder, sending a stinger of a look at him. "You're doing it again."

"Doing what?"

"Playing me."

"I prefer to think of it as a sophisticated form of seduction. Getting you to a place where you can't say no."

She laughed softly. "Skip the foreplay, Jack. We're tight on time. What are you trying to get me to do?"

He stood, walking slowly toward her. "Get us a total access pass into Willow Marsh."

For a long moment, she stared at him so hard he could almost see the wheels turning. "We need to convince Higgie his life is in danger."

"A threat?"

"Bigger. Badder. More *instant*." She held up her finger as if she were pulling the trigger. "We shoot . . . and miss."

"An assassination attempt."

"That ought to do the trick," she said. "Especially if I'm the one who saves him. Then I can convince him that only Bullet Catcher security is enough. Will that work?"

"Like a charm. Where did you say that fund-raiser was going to be held?"

"The South Carolina Aquarium in Charleston."

"How's the security?"

"We could crack it. It will take a team of experts, some major planning, a few people to infiltrate the aquarium staff, a lot of research and background checks, a weapon stashed in the place, someone with perfect aim, and . . ." She backed up as she realized he was getting closer with each word. "Don't even think about it, Jack."

"What?"

"You won't be there. You have no part in this." She tried to step to the side, but he went the same way, stopping her. She lifted her chin, looked down her nose, and copped her badass boss look. "You are not able to be armed, you are not on my staff, you are not able to be objective, and you are not—"

"Going to let you do this without me."

"Let me?" She choked a laugh.

"I brought this to you, I know the case, I know the players, and I sure as shit can shoot better than you. I proved it last night."

"You will not fire a gun. If we did something this outrageous, I'd put a sharpshooter in place, a professional sniper. Wade could do it."

"Fine," he said. "I can compromise. But I'm there. I have to be there."

"No, you're too emotional about this case."

He was smart enough not to react to that. "Lucy, I can be as objective as the next guy."

She managed to sidestep him. "The record shows differently."

Forget smart. He grabbed her arm and yanked her back. "Fuck the record. That was an *accident.*"

She cut her gaze to where he held her, in a silent order to let go. Everything in him wanted to squeeze tighter, to show her who was in charge, to make his point, to . . .

Be precisely the person he hated most, and the one she would hate. He let go, and corralled his composure. "Lucy, you don't really think I fired at Gallagher on purpose that day, do you?"

"I told you why I let you go. You falsified records, you ignored orders, you took an unnecessary risk and—"

"I got under your skin." And *into* her skin. But he didn't need to say that. They both knew what happened in Malaysia. And they both knew that the shot that almost killed Gallagher happened ten days later. "That scares you, doesn't it, Lucy?"

"What scares me is when someone loses perspective. That's when they make mistakes. I cannot afford a mistake on something this big." He heard the tiniest note of relenting in her voice. She was considering the options, knowing what made sense. Trying to prove that their history didn't matter, that their attraction wasn't real. That she was stronger than that, than him.

He watched all those thoughts register in a millisecond of expression on her beautiful, exotic features.

And he knew he had her.

"You know you need me on this, Lucy. I know every player, every name, every nuance of this case."

"I need help and I need that information, but I do not need someone with a personal ax to grind. That's when you become a liability to me."

Time to concede. "I will not so much as touch a weapon. You have my word."

"Will you touch anything else you're not supposed to?"

"Only if you ask real nice."

She tried to hide a smile. "You're the worst, Culver."

"I'm the best," he corrected. "And I intend to prove it to you once and for all." He indicated for her to go ahead of him to the war room. "Let's go plan an assassination attempt, Ms. Sharpe."

He stayed a few steps behind to watch her walk, knowing that as long as he kept it playful and sexual, she'd never know the truth. Because if she did, she'd kick him out again—farther and faster than ever before.

Theo Carpenter made an imaginary lens out of his two hands and pressed them against the car window, visualizing the shot. The depressing haze of gray drapes the Blue Ridge Mountains in misery as the camera pans back to show the silver plaque on the stately brick wall.

Cedar Lawn Memorial.

Cue slow ballad, and cut to—

"Theo! Aren't you going to get out of the car?"

—to the grieving old bitch with a pickled expression of pure disappointment.

"Theo! I'm talking to you! Are you finally going to get yourself over to your sister's gravesite and pray or not?"

"Oh Jesus." He snorted. "There. I prayed."

Disappointment tumbled right into disgust, curling his mother's thin upper lip and narrowing her dull hazel eyes. "Fine. You just sit here and be that way. Kristen would be devastated that you won't honor her memory on the two-month anniversary of her death."

That would be taking hypocrisy and acting to a new and ridiculous level.

"Mom, Kristen isn't there. I don't think she gives a crap if I kneel down next to a pile of ashes that could be the remains of the cigar some dude in the funeral home was smoking, for all we know. Just leave me alone. I'm working on a new screenplay and I want to stay here and think."

"Why don't you think about getting your old job back?"

Oh, he couldn't have written that line better. Cutting and vicious and delivered with that lovely snarl. "Go pray, Mother dearest. I'm sure you have a direct line to God."

"I'm not talking to God," she said quietly. "I'm just trying to talk to my daughter."

"She isn't *technically* your daughter." He never missed an opportunity to remind her and everyone else that Kristen was adopted.

"Wasn't," his mother corrected, pain drawing her brows together. "And I miss her just the same."

She hoisted her hefty matronly ass out of the sedan and lumbered into the misty rain, disappearing behind the wall, laden with the mantle of grief.

How would she react if she knew the truth?

Hard to say. The misery over her daughter's death had become so much a part of her that she never even talked about anything else. It was almost as if it had given her something to live for, something to lord over people. No matter what they'd endured, it wasn't as bad as losing a child. It gave her celebrity status among her old-lady friends, special treatment at church, and, of course, the all-powerful and most important person in the universe had *come to their house* for the funeral. Roanoke would never be the same.

She should thank Theo.

She should be grateful that his actions gave her this gift. His brilliant plan had worked exactly as he'd imagined, and he felt no remorse. He'd only made the world a little bit better for a few people he loved. Really, really loved.

It was a shame, but it had been the right thing to do.

And, he thought smugly, it hadn't even hurt sweet little Kristen. She hadn't felt any pain at all. That was what was really important.

Now, with two months passed and all the i's dotted and t's crossed, he was certain it was all over. She was buried, the paperwork was complete, the investigation into the hit and run officially closed. Now, on to Phase Two. The next kill.

And this one *would* hurt.

Theo shifted in his seat with a frisson of excitement.

The Avenger. He was going to sell this screenplay, he had no doubt. What a movie it would make! Nothing like it had ever been done—he'd be lauded as a visionary writer and director. The next Quentin Tarantino. It would be bloody, too. Violent as hell. And no one would ever know it was taken from real life. They would just think he was brilliant.

He could see the reviews. *Former D.C. attorney hangs up his three-piece suit to follow his dream and wins the Oscar.*

So who would play the Avenger? He flipped down the visor to look at his face.

Matt Damon—Kristen loved that guy. And who could play her?

He closed his eyes and pictured her. Someone totally hot, but smart, too. Like . . . Keri Russell. Perfect. She even had the curly hair that Kristen was always trying to straighten. She would like that. He'd have to tell—

The driver's side door whipped open and his mother literally threw herself into the front seat with a wail.

Gallantly, he leaned forward and reached for his door handle. "I'll drive. You're in no condition." Good line, and well delivered.

She lifted her head and stared at him. "How can you not hurt? She was your sister."

"Adopted, Mom. Adopted sister who landed in my life and your doorstep when I was ten and she was five. It wasn't like she came out of the same womb I did. We didn't share a gene pool." It was important to remember that; it made it seem much less . . . evil. "I hurt . . . in my own way. But I'm a guy. We don't cry."

She took a shuddery breath and sat up. "I can drive."

In Theo's script, this would be the end of Act One. The cemetery diminishes in the distance as the clunky Buick pulls out. The actors' voices are heard over the music as the Avenger delivers the line that will change the course of the story.

"So tell me more about that fund-raiser in Charleston next week."

His mother shot him a look of surprise. "You want to go?"

"I'm thinking about it." Nonchalance was key.

"Well, I suppose I can arrange for you to go. But you . . . I thought you hated him."

"His Holy Higness?"

Kristen had made up the nickname years ago, and he couldn't resist using it.

"He's going to be chief justice of the Supreme Court, Theo," she said repressively.

"No, he's not," Theo replied quietly. "They'll never nominate him."

"Yes they will. He's a shoo-in."

"Whatever." He had to be careful. He knew His Holy Higness wasn't going to be around for the nomination, but only *he* knew that. "I haven't been down to Charleston in a while. It'll be kind of interesting to hear what the old coot has to say."

When I tell him the news. And then kill him.

"Okay," she said dubiously. "I don't think I can face the crowd, so you can have my ticket." Then she gave him a hard, warning look. "As long as you don't drink. You know how you get."

"I'll stay sober, ma'am. Sober as a *judge*." He grinned at his little joke, but she ignored it.

The Avenger was rolling into Act Two, and nothing and no one could stop him. If they tried . . . well, blood sold as well as sex in Hollywood. Maybe they'd have a little of that, too.

He closed his eyes and pictured Keri Russell instead of Kristen. A different face. A different name. But still, *his*.

CHAPTER
FOUR

SHE DREAMED OF Cilla.

Soft, sweet, helpless, crooning in a lavender-scented blanket, rooting for a taste of mother's milk. A newborn, not the toddler she'd been the last time Lucy rocked her to sleep. Only in the dream, she had blue eyes, not Lucy's brown ones with the tilt that spoke of her Micronesian blood.

His blue eyes. The eyes of the man who had killed her.

The wrongness of blue eyes in Cilla's tiny baby face punched Lucy awake with a searing black pain. She was instantly up, blinking in the dark, fighting to squash the image of her lost baby and erase the smell of lavender, seizing every brain cell she had to remember where she was.

Charleston.

The Vendue Inn.

The Higgie Project.

Alone.

She flung off the duvet and Egyptian cotton sheets that had been so welcoming a few hours earlier, letting the air chill her bare skin. Grabbing a bottle of water she'd already started, she chugged the rest, trying to fill the hole the dream had left deep in her belly.

But that hole could never be filled.

Once again, sleep was a lost cause.

Naked, she crossed the room to look out the window. At one on a Saturday morning, tourists and drinkers were still milling about, bar hopping around the waterfront.

None of her people was out there. They'd be sleeping, or reviewing plans that had been discussed to exacting detail, memorizing the routes they'd taken that afternoon when they'd all slipped in and out of the aquarium as tourists.

Her advance team would be preparing for the task at hand, studying their roles, testing their earpieces, practicing their identities, readying for their roles in the faux assassination that she and Jack had choreographed over the past two and a half weeks.

Fingering the edge of a velvet drape, Lucy looked at the wet pavement below. It wasn't raining now, but it had been while she slept. While she dreamed of her dear, dead baby.

She had to get out of this room. She had to forget.

Not allowing herself time to think about what she was doing, she seized her cell phone and hit a number.

"Insomniac Hotline. Culver here."

She smiled despite the ache in her heart. He pissed

her off at least once every twenty minutes, made her crazy from head to toe and a few choice places in between, but he never failed to pull a smile from her.

"I want you to take me somewhere I've never been before."

"I thought you'd never ask. You're in the monster suite on the third floor, right? Unlock the door and stay in bed."

"Meet me in the lobby," she said. "In ten minutes. Don't make me wait."

He was there, slouched in an overstuffed chair under a painting, as dark as the rest of the understated lobby in his black T-shirt, jeans, and dark chocolate hair that fell in careless layers to his collar. His jaw was shadowed with unshaved whiskers, his full lips slightly parted, and his smoky gaze heavy as it started on her face and meandered over her sweater and jeans, lingered on her boots, and took its sweet time on the way back up.

"I really don't want to go sightseeing, Luce. Can we just go to a bar and let me get drunk from inhaling you?"

She reached for his hand. "To the Philadelphia Alley, Culver. Now."

Instantly he sat up. "Yeah?"

"I want to see it the way Eileen did. And Wanda, the moment that she died there."

He put a hand on her back and headed toward the door. "We can walk. It's only a few blocks."

Autumn hadn't reached this far south yet. The day's humidity still hung over the city, mixed with the salt of the nearby sea, and a vague smell of fish and fresh rain. He guided her across East Bay Street and onto Queen, her stride easily keeping up with his longer one, despite the combination of brick pavement and boot heels.

They passed a small group of people surrounding a guide who spoke in a hushed whisper, pointing to the third floor of a brownstone.

"She was electrocuted, up on that balcony, during a horrible thunderstorm. They say whenever it rains, you can see . . ."

As they passed the ghost guide, Jack merely picked up the pace. "Let's beat them there."

"To the alley?"

"No doubt it's on the midnight ghost tour."

"Because of Wanda?" The possibility surprised her.

"Hell, no. Wanda Sloane's death barely made a blip in the local papers."

He slowed as they neared the entrance to the alley that ran between a sizable redbrick building and a ten-foot wall that enclosed a churchyard. Engulfing Lucy's fingers in his larger ones, Jack inched them deeper into the shadowy passageway, staying close to her.

The long, dark corridor of carefully laid bricks appeared empty, lit at the opposite end by a soft-toned street lamp. The only other way in or out of the alley was the gate ahead in the cemetery wall.

A fine mist had formed after the rain; their synchronized footsteps were the only sound. She curled her fingers deeper into Jack's hand, and tried to imagine that March night when Wanda Sloane was shot.

"Has Eileen ever told you why she came to this

alley at one in the morning? There doesn't seem to be any doubt that she was here, right?"

"She won't talk about anything that happened that night, but she's accidentally dropped hints and I suspect she received a message from Higgie telling her to meet him here. But according to the court transcripts, she was seen arguing with Wanda in the bathroom that day, and the prosecution's case was that Eileen knew Wanda lived near here and was known to walk late at night."

Lucy shook her head. "Hard to believe that flew in any court."

"Not when you think about the power Spessard Higgins had in this town, and in that courthouse."

Lucy looked around, taking in details. She saw one bag of neatly tied trash at the back door of a historic redbrick building, and a few puddles where the aged cobblestones had been chipped out, but overall, the city of Charleston treated this secluded strip like the rest of its historic, sacred ground.

"It is clean and quiet, and feels safe," she commented. "I suppose you could make an argument that a single woman would walk alone here at night."

"Not then. It was a different town in the seventies. Nearly bankrupt, and this alley was probably not part of any tours except some prostitute's route. Even the witness who claimed he saw Eileen running to her car, that way"—he pointed toward the opposite end of the alley—"was a confirmed heroin addict. That didn't make it into the transcripts, though. I dug that out on my own."

"You've dug a lot up on your own." She inhaled a sweet whiff of the jessamine flowers that bloomed all over Charleston. "Why?"

He looked at her. "To find the answers. Why else?"

"I mean why does this woman matter to you?"

"Because she's innocent."

"It's more personal than that."

He squeezed her fingers. "Everything's personal, Lucy. Why'd you call me?"

Speaking of personal. She stopped at the wrought iron gate. "Is this the spot? The files mention the graveyard entrance where they found her fingerprints, but there were no pictures."

"Yeah. Her prints were right here." He touched the handle, opening it. "They don't lock this at night, then or now. Did you notice from my sketches in the file that her fingerprints were facing this way?" He showed her the position.

"Confirming that she was inside when she touched the gate," Lucy said. "Let's go in."

They entered the graveyard, where the ground changed to soft grass, and hundred-year-old willows and massive oaks darkened everything. Marble markers, worn smooth with time, and a few moss-covered grave-stones covered almost every inch of root-gnarled ground. It smelled like earth and grass and rain. And death.

"Creepy," she whispered, automatically moving into the arm Jack offered around her shoulders.

"Creepy enough that you'd wonder why a very young woman waiting in an alley to meet her married lover would even step inside the gate."

"Unless Eileen was waiting to meet her married lover's new lover . . . and kill her, so she was hiding and waiting for her to walk by."

"Or she was waiting to meet the man who'd dumped her after he'd forced her to give up her babies, hoping he was going to change his mind, hoping he might offer her money or a chance to find out who adopted the babies, hoping he still cared for her."

His voice was rich with conviction, his arm tightening with every sentence.

"But she's never told you that, Jack."

"She's terrified to talk. But I know her; I know what matters to her." He guided her close to the wall and turned so she could see out the gate. "From this spot she couldn't have been seen, but she still had a straight view of anyone coming up the alley. See?"

They both looked that way, in time to see three young men approaching, laughing, pushing each other, a little drunk and loud.

Jack inched Lucy out of sight against the wall, using his whole body to cover her, taller than her by a good two inches since her boot heels were low.

"You don't have to protect me, Jack, I'm armed."

He looked down at her. "Who said anything about protecting you?"

The boys were past in a few seconds, but Jack didn't move.

The first smoky tendril of arousal curled low in her belly.

"You didn't answer my question." He tilted his head as if trying to decide which angle to kiss her from.

Any way would work. "What question?"

"Why did you summon me in the middle of the night, Ms. Sharpe?"

"To see the scene of the crime," she said.

"You're lying."

"I'm here, aren't I?"

"You want me to kiss you."

"That's quite an assumption." It just happened to be true.

He grinned, his teeth white against olive skin and black stubble, his eyes glinting dangerously. "But I notice that this time when I have you up against a wall there's been no threat to kick my balls from here to kingdom come." He inched closer. Warmer. Almost touching her from top to toe, exactly as she needed.

"The implied threat is always there."

He laughed softly. "You do want me to kiss you."

"What I want," she said with remarkable control, "is for you to show me the precise spot where Wanda's body was found, so I can figure out if it was even marginally possible to fire a gun from this angle and kill her."

He hesitated, still studying her mouth, still considering his move. "I already checked. It isn't, marginally or otherwise."

"Yes it is." She put her hands on his chest—rock hard and beating with the same accelerated heartbeat as hers—and pushed him back, turning. "A .25 caliber Raven Arms could easily hit her from here." She pointed to a spot directly across from the gate. "And it would look like the shot that killed her, especially to a jury predisposed to a guilty verdict."

"It could, *if* that's where her body was."

He took her hand and led her about ten steps to the other side of the gate, into an even darker corner of the graveyard. "That's where her body was found." He pointed into the alley to a spot fifteen feet away from the original. "But that wasn't in the official report submitted into evidence. Remember, evidence was tampered with by the real killer."

She considered that, lifting her finger to take aim, imagining the moment someone shot Wanda Sloane. "If that's really where she died, then someone inside this graveyard couldn't have fired the gun. But you can't see the whole alley. Someone else could have been out there."

"Someone named Higgins. Or did you forget what brought you to Charleston in the first place?"

She noted the edge in his voice, which reminded her of how personal this was to him.

"I'm just looking at the evidence, Jack. I haven't convicted our target yet."

Another bit of conversation floated over the wall that separated them from the alley, along with enough footsteps to tell them a much larger group was coming their way. He backed her into the wall and covered her, pressing his full body against hers.

"Where were we?" he said, tilting his head again. "Oh, yeah. Right about here."

The laughter and talk grew louder, but the sound took a backseat to the thrum of Lucy's heartbeat, and the devil who put his lips to her ear and whispered, "Stay real quiet now."

"In 1987, a local amateur photographer took a photo of that headstone right there . . ." The voice of the tour guide bounced off the alley behind them and footsteps grew louder.

Against her stomach, she could feel the bulge of Jack's arousal growing hard, and the pressure of his chest against hers. He took her face in his hands, brushing her lips with both thumbs.

"Kiss me now." He breathed the command on her lips, so close she could almost taste him.

Behind them, the tour guide droned, "In that photograph, the translucent image of a mother and her child appeared before that headstone on the anniversary of that child's death."

The words slammed her, drawing a slight gasp that he mistook for a yes. Instantly, his mouth met hers and he tunneled his fingers deeper into her hair, his lips open, hungry, hot, his tongue already taking ownership of hers.

Just forget. Let go.

She sucked on his tongue, drawing a low moan from him and a rock of his hips against hers, his rigid erection sending a wicked thrill between her legs.

He held her head in his large, warm hands as if she was precious and he adored her, as if the kiss mattered more than anything—and it was so perfect and sexy that Lucy completely let go.

She wrapped her arms around him, pulled his strong, lean body into hers, and kissed him back.

He ran his hands down her chest, his mouth following with a trail of kisses, his palms covering and closing over her breasts.

"Jack." She breathed his name.

"Shhhh," he murmured into the flesh of her neck and collarbone. "Don't let them hear us. They'll think we're ghosts."

He kneaded her gently, rolling his hard-on against her, pulling a moan of pleasure from deep inside her.

"But the most famous moment in Philadelphia Alley history was on a hot August night in 1771, when two local businessmen dueled on this very spot."

Behind them, more death talk. She arched and offered herself in response.

Jack kissed her again, cupping her backside with one hand and sliding under her sweater with the other.

"I have to touch you," he murmured. "*Have* to." His little exhale of desperation shot fire between her legs as he caressed the satin of her bra, her head singing with blood and arousal.

"No pearls," he mumbled. Nonsense. Blood-pounding, body-wrenching, juice-inducing nonsense. She matched his quickening rhythm against her, spurred by his hands and his hardness and how he made everything disappear. He curled his fingers over the peak, tweaking her into a nub, half-chuckling and half-groaning at her instant response. "One pearl."

She had no idea what he was talking about, but it didn't matter. Right now nothing mattered. She could come like this. She could absolutely lose it against this wall, hidden only by the wall and fog. She could—

"What about the other murder that took place here?"

The question sliced through Lucy's consciousness, jarring and strident. Jack's fingers froze. Her hips stilled. They both stopped breathing.

"The lady named Wanda who was shot here back in '78 in cold blood."

Jack lifted his head from Lucy's neck, his eyes black with arousal yet clear with interest.

"I'm sorry, there's no such ghost on our tour."

"Well, there should be." The female voice was moving away. "Because the killer got away with it."

Jack inched back, not taking his eyes off Lucy.

"What happened?" someone else asked.

"Who's the killer?" Another voice, more distant as they headed north.

"You'd be shocked to find out," the original voice said. "I can tell you this: it isn't the person in prison for the crime."

"Oh my God," Lucy whispered. "Someone else knows."

"Sorry, that's not on this tour. Let's move on to the next ghost, folks."

Jack broke away instantly. "We have to get that woman."

Frustration whipped through her, making Lucy want to scream and yank him back, but common sense quickly doused her arousal. She straightened her sweater. "Let's go."

He gave her a look mixed with appreciation and disappointment. "I'm not finished, you know."

They slipped out of the gate and hustled to catch up with the half dozen tourists, reaching them as the pack hit Cumberland, where the street was peppered with a few pedestrians.

"All right, stay together," the tour guide said, counting heads and stopping at Lucy. "I'm sorry, this is a private tour. We can't take add-ons at this point."

Lucy glanced around, checking out the four women in the group. "Understood. We were just walking behind you and heard someone mention a murder that took place here. Was that you?" she asked one of the women in the group.

"No," she answered. "It was . . ." She turned and looked around, frowning. "She's gone."

"Are you sure?" Jack said.

"Maybe she was a ghost," one of the men said, drawing laughter.

"You're welcome to book a slot tomorrow night," the guide said.

The group moved on, leaving Jack and Lucy standing on the street. He turned back to the alley. "Lucy, look."

A woman stood stone still right across from the gate, staring at the spot in the wall where the police report alleged Wanda's body had been. She looked fairly young, dressed in a shapeless jacket and jeans, honey blond curly hair in a soft halo around her head.

She leaned forward, close to the wall, and spat.

"What the—"

Lucy silenced him with a squeeze of her hand. "Let's just talk to her."

"Very carefully," he warned. "I don't want to scare her off. Make it real casual."

"Got it."

They started walking toward her, holding hands as if they were any couple strolling through the Charleston night.

As they approached she looked up, and Lucy caught a glimpse of pale skin, but her face was obscured by all that hair. In a flash, she flung open the gate and ran into the graveyard.

Lucy started in that direction, but Jack froze in midstep.

"Come on," she urged. "Let's—what's the matter?"

He let out a breath of disbelief. "She looked exactly like . . . Kristen Carpenter."

Lucy blinked at him. "She's dead."

"I know. But she looked so much like her. She looks exactly like Vanessa, couldn't you tell?"

"Let's get a better look." Lucy pulled him toward the gate.

"I got a good look," he said. "I've seen her picture and she's memorable."

Back in the graveyard, they moved silently, both squinting into the shadows, slipping around an angel statue, stepping over a marble stone. There was no path; every inch of space had been used to bury the dead.

Jack took her hand and kept her close.

"Don't worry," she whispered. "I'm not afraid of ghosts."

"That wasn't a ghost, Lucy. It was a woman who looked an awful lot like the one I've spent the last four months trying to find."

They heard a branch rustle and a footstep scuff.

"This way." He pulled her to the right, but another crack of a twig snapped to their left, then the echo of metal against metal, and footsteps.

"The other entrance," he said. "Over here."

When they reached it, the side street was empty.

He muttered a quiet curse, looking in both directions.

"Jack, it wasn't her."

"Maybe it wasn't," he conceded. "But whoever it was, she knew about the murder. And Eileen. And, she said, 'You'd be shocked to know the truth.' She knows a lot, and then she spat on the spot where Wanda's body was allegedly found."

All true, Lucy silently agreed. "But she didn't say his name. We might not have heard right. You don't even know for sure if the woman who spat on the ground was the one we heard."

He gave her a get-real look. "We heard fine. And I don't like it that somebody else knows."

"Neither do I. I don't like anything that makes our plan vulnerable."

"I don't want someone to get him before we do."

She glared at him. "It's not about *getting* him, Jack."

He took one more look around, then shook his head. "Come on. Let's go back to the hotel."

Inside the Vendue Inn, he walked her to the elevator and hit the call button. When the bell dinged, Lucy backed in and held up a hand to stop him from joining her.

"Good night," she said pointedly.

He gave her a half smile. "Got what you wanted, did you?"

"I wanted to see the alley."

The doors started to close. "'S all right, honey." Just as the rubber strips touched, he added, "Use me anytime."

The scary thing was, she might.

"Finish it off, now. Suck it hard. Fast." His words grew choked. "Harder!"

Delaynie looked up at the old rich guy, giving him her best eye twinkle as she traced the head of his dick with her tongue to delay the inevitable. She'd like more of these gigs, which the seriously high-end girls usually got, and Jarell had said this was a test. A test she intended to pass.

She swirled her tongue again, flicking underneath the head on that vein men dug having tickled so much. "You don't want me to rush it, do you, honey?"

He shoved himself toward her lips. "Finish it," he growled, one hand growing tighter on her tit and the other pulling her hair just a little too hard.

"Okay, take it easy." She pulled his dick deep into her mouth, sucked like a Hoover, and lifted her tits for him to squeeze. Who cared if she got a little bruised? He'd call Jarell and say she was good. Those upscale chicks got a thousand fucking dollars to do these old farts. She could do anything for a thousand dollars.

It took him a few thrusts to get going again, and she glanced up to gauge how much more her mouth would have to endure. Not too much. His jaw went slack and his eyes half closed and he called her a few hardcore names she'd heard a million times before. It didn't matter whether she sucked off a guy in a fancy condo South of Broad, or took it from behind in the hood. It was all too familiar.

And come to think of it, so was he. Even from down on her knees, the dude looked totally familiar.

He squeezed her again, pushing, grunting, and finally losing it. "Oh, fuck, here it comes!"

She braced herself for the finale, watching his face as it contorted in pleasure. He wasn't bad-looking, even with the white hair. He was—

Higgie! That's who he was. The famous judge! Holy shit, she'd just seen him on *Good Morning Charleston* today. Spessard Higgins, the big-time federal judge who was in town for some fund-raiser.

He gasped a little, groaned, and finally loosened his grip on her poor boob. Didn't he know that flesh was tender?

Right. If he did, he wouldn't need to pay prostitutes to get his rocks off.

She pulled back, wiped some jism from her lips, and smiled. "How'd you like it, Higgie?"

The slap came so hard and fast, it practically knocked her off her knees. Stunned, she couldn't even talk for a second as she covered her jaw and looked up at him.

"You aren't supposed to know my name." His voice was calm. Deadly, eerily calm.

"Sorry," she muttered, checking her lip for blood. "I saw you on TV today, and you're, like, the first famous fuck I ever did."

"That's why I got a street whore. So you wouldn't know me." Eyes like ice picks sliced her. "And we didn't fuck, little lady. If you tell anyone we did, you will be very, very sorry."

"No worries, mister. I'm a professional. I won't tell nobody."

He was looking at her like he didn't believe her, and chills broke out on her skin. She snagged her shirt, getting up on shaky legs.

He reached out, grabbed her hair, and pulled her up.

"What the hell?" she cried out, instantly looking for her bag. She'd left it ten feet away, never thinking she'd need a knife or mace with this old guy in this nice neighborhood.

"Let me ask you something, sugar." His voice was really nice all of a sudden, and the change kind of scared her. "Do you *want* to know what will happen to you if you ever tell anyone you met me?"

No, she didn't. "I *won't* tell anyone." She dropped the babydoll voice he seemed to like when she arrived, pulling her top on in a flash.

He took a step closer and she instinctively backed up. The dude was freaking her out. "I'll make sure your pimp takes care of you."

Great. There went her promotion. She copped a friendly smile. "No worries, big guy. I just want to take care of you." She held out her hand. "Two hundred bucks and I'm outta here with sealed lips."

He never took his eyes off her as he reached into his trousers pocket, his limp dick still hanging out of the tuxedo pants.

He pulled out two Benjies and she stuffed them into the pocket of her skirt.

He took a step forward, getting really close and making her back up. "You say my name to anyone, anywhere, and you'll be sorry."

She was already sorry she'd spent half her take on new clothes for this job, only to get slapped around. By a fucking judge, no less.

She couldn't get out the door fast enough. She started for the back entrance of the three-story building, the way she'd come in, like she'd been instructed. But she was so pissed, she stopped, changed her mind, and marched right out the front door just as a big-ass white limo pulled up. The driver got out, came around, and opened the door with a soft, "Mrs. Higgins."

Mrs. Higgins?

The woman who climbed out of the back was as rich and fine-looking as the limo that brought her there. She wore a black gown that probably cost a fortune, and a diamond the size of a walnut around her neck. She spoke softly into a tiny cell phone at her ear.

"I have a surprise for you, dear," she said, nodding to the driver as he closed the door. She covered the receiver and whispered, "Give us half an hour, Henry. Then we'll be leaving for the aquarium." Then back into the phone. "I decided I feel well enough to go after all. I've just arrived downstairs."

Holy crap. Talk about a close call.

Mrs. Higgie snapped her phone shut and looked up to the third floor with a devilish expression. She was probably in her sixties, but she had the creamy skin of a rich Southern matron and held herself like a younger woman, her dark hair not showing a single strand of gray.

Frozen with curiosity about the woman married to the asshole upstairs, Delaynie stayed on the steps, staring at her. The lady stopped, then raked Delaynie with a look of disgust.

What was up with that? She didn't look like . . . what had he called her? A street whore? This was a fifty dollar outfit from The Limited, for chrissakes. There was no reason to look at her like she'd been robbing the building.

What would Queenie think if she knew why Delaynie was there? The irony struck Delaynie hard, and she smiled and said, "Hi." She got speared with another withering look in return.

Hello? I've been sucking off your husband, lady.

The woman slowed, hesitating so Delaynie would move, her back stiff, her chin raised, her eyes shuttered just enough to communicate her distaste for the possibility that they might breathe the same air.

Man, if she hadn't looked at her that way, if she hadn't acted like her shit didn't stink, Delaynie probably would have let the whole thing go. Two hundred bucks was two hundred bucks.

But she *couldn't*. She been bitch slapped by the judge and sneered at by the wife.

Delaynie stepped aside. "He's got quite the loaded gun, your Higgie," she said, pulling a gasp from the other woman. She wiped her finger along her mouth, sore from the slap she'd taken. "Gets a little rough when he comes, though. Ever notice that?"

Soft brown eyes widened in horror, revulsion, and then a hint of hurt.

That made Delaynie feel like a total creep. What was wrong with her? So the bitch was loaded and stuck-up—it wasn't her fault she'd married a loser.

But the damage was done, so Delaynie walked away feeling like the piece of crap that she was.

CHAPTER
FIVE

LUCY WORE RED. Deep, fierce red, the color of blood.

"Expecting to get splattered?" Jack asked as she opened the door to her suite and let him in.

"Not when Wade Cordell is handling the weapon and his orders are to miss."

He resisted the urge to roll his eyes at the former sniper's legendary prowess.

"The color suits you," he said, drinking in the effect of long black hair spilled over bare shoulders and red silk.

"Thank you." She turned to a mirror in the entry-way and worked a diamond pin into the deepest point of a very low V at her cleavage.

He reached around her from behind, lowering his hands to hers. "Can I help?"

"Not from that angle."

He took a step closer, his hips touching her backside. "Better?"

She managed not to smile, though it took some

work. "This isn't a pin, Jack. It's my mike and it doesn't clip the standard way. I'll do it."

"Clever disguise," he said, not moving away but letting his knuckles graze the gentle rise of her breasts. "No one would ever look down there."

She locked on his gaze in the mirror. Her breasts were sweet velvet on his knuckles, and her backside curved right into the place where it belonged, but the look in her eyes was what stirred his cock.

The desire was clearly mutual.

He got close to her ear, his hand covering the mike. "We've got time."

She almost smiled. "And break with our carefully constructed plan?"

That wasn't a no, and she must feel his response as he pressed against her. The dress was skin tight, and his cock nestled right into the smooth line of her behind.

"It wouldn't take long," he said, his voice only half-teasing. "What do you have on under that dress?"

She slowly turned in his arms, her hips rolling against his rapidly rising erection, and looked up into his eyes. With the toe of her sandal, she grazed his ankle, then settled her very sharp, very high stiletto right on the most vulnerable spot on the top of his foot. One thrust and he'd be howling in pain.

"I have very dangerous shoes on under this dress," she whispered. "And absolutely . . ." She added a little pressure on his foot. "Nothing . . ." And more, bordering on pain. "Else."

With the flick of her finger, she touched the diamond pin. "We're on our way to the limo, Gabriel," she said softly, the echo of her voice loud in his minuscule earpiece.

Every word they exchanged would now be heard by the entire team.

Jack smiled. Did she think he couldn't take her without making a sound?

"I'll be checking later," he said, sliding his fingertips down her bare arms. "To make sure you were telling the truth about those shoes."

"I've never lied . . ." She stepped away to lift her wrap and a tiny clutch bag. She opened it, revealing her gun, then gave him a very pointed look. "To you."

A limo waited for them in front of the hotel and Lucy climbed in first, settling into the leather seat. Jack followed and sat right next to her.

"We're the only two in this car," she reminded him.

"Just the way I like it. Besides, it's part of the cover. I'm your escort. I'd be a fool to leave the side of a woman who looks like you."

"You'd *better* leave my side. Do not deviate from the plan, Jack. You want to go over it again?"

"Not particularly."

"I do. After the keynote, the second song is 'Endless Love.' I dance with Higgie; you take Vanessa to the Deep Ocean Gallery, away from the action and protected by a 385,000-gallon tank of fish water. Wade shoots, I jump into bodyguard mode and contact the seven Bullet Catchers who Justice Higgins doesn't even know are there, and all the exits are blocked. Owen lets Wade out the custodial stairway,

Marc stashes the weapon and gives him a janitor's uniform, Alex—"

He held up a hand. "I wrote the blueprints, remember? You want something cold to drink?"

"I'm in work mode, Jack."

"Well I'm in a limo with the sexiest woman on earth *mode,* the plans for the project are set in concrete and brilliant, I might add, and we've got twenty minutes with nothing to do but relax. And I was only suggesting mineral water."

She touched the pin, reactivating the microphone. "Jack and I are in the limo leaving the Vendue, Gabriel. I would like a full position report, please."

"Roger, Luce." The words came into Jack's ear through the invisible earpiece that everyone on the assignment wore. Only some of the team was miked, but they all could hear, and everything was controlled from a van parked half a mile from the aquarium. In it, Sage Valentine and Gabriel Walker monitored everything, including nine different images sent from tiny video cameras that Bullet Catcher Marc Russeau had installed shortly after he'd been hired as a part-time custodian at the aquarium ten days ago.

When Gabriel mentioned Vanessa's location, Jack turned to Lucy. "I'm still not in agreement with the decision to let her be here."

"It was important to her," Lucy replied. "She wants to see her biological father."

"Miranda doesn't."

"They may be sisters, but they're different. And I don't mind that she's here, as long as she's completely under protection. And she's *your* responsibility after the speech, when Wade is in position to take the shot. Don't forget that."

"In other words, don't break with plan."

"My cardinal rule."

"I know your rules, Luce." She needn't worry about him. He had no intention of screwing up a thing.

The limo, driven by another Bullet Catcher, took the circuitous route they'd mapped out, moving slowly with the Saturday evening traffic. It took almost a half hour before they pulled up to the massive glass and concrete structure hanging over the edge of Charleston Harbor, surrounded by patios that were already full with the black-tie set.

Jack picked up his tux jacket. "It's showtime, Ms. Sharpe."

"Yes, it is, Mr. *Fuller*." She lifted an eyebrow and checked him out as he leaned forward to slip into the jacket. "I'm sure you'll impress Higgie and get the job as his ghostwriter."

"I don't want to impress him."

"Jack." She squeezed his arm in warning. "Just follow the plan, stay in constant communication, and try not to let the guy know you're out to nail him to a wall and execute him."

"I'm not armed tonight." He lifted both arms and gave her an inviting look. "Strip searches are welcome."

But her gaze moved beyond his face to the window, and her expression became focused. He followed, squinting into the sunset across the street from the aquarium. "What is it?"

In his ear, one of the Bullet Catchers announced, "Seven has arrived," using the code name taken from Justice Higgins's position on the highest bench in the country, the seventh out of the current nine to be appointed.

A white stretch limo stopped in front of the main entrance, where security had cordoned off all traffic. But that wasn't the Supreme Court justice being assisted out of the back.

It was his wife.

"I thought Marilee wasn't coming," Jack said, a drop of worry sliding through him. "There goes the precious plan."

"Guess my acupuncturist did a good job on her migraines," Lucy said. "We can work around it—as long as Higgie's here and she's not a substitute speaker. That has happened before."

"Then we almost assassinate her."

She whipped around and glared at him.

"Just kidding. Maybe he's in the limo."

Marilee Higgins, wearing an elegant black dress and a glistening diamond necklace, waited as the limo driver draped her in a shawl.

Still no Higgie.

Another woman approached and they talked. The other woman nodded understandingly, called over yet another man, who could have been security or museum staff, and the three of them talked for a moment.

Still no Higgie.

Jack's gut tightened. After all this, if he didn't show . . .

"There he is," Lucy breathed softly as a shock of white hair finally appeared at the back door of the limo. She placed her cool, dry fingers over Jack's, opening up his fisted hands. "I thought you were so relaxed. No worries."

The big man climbed out, waved to a few people, and put an arm around his wife. Until that bastard paid for what he'd done to Eileen, Jack had plenty of worries.

"She was never on any guest list, even as a possibility," Lucy said. "But it doesn't change anything. In fact, when she sees how we work, she might be our biggest ally in getting us hired."

"Unless she refuses to let you dance with her husband. I've heard she's possessive."

Lucy shook her head. "Not at all. Anyway, it's not the first dance. She'll have that."

"You better hope 'Endless Love' isn't their song."

She smiled at him as the driver opened the door. "Their song is 'Moon River' and it plays first after the speech. Don't you think I'd cover a detail like that?"

The aquarium had made some effort at security; they'd set up a metal detector at the ramp to the second-floor entrance, which caused a backup of at least fifty people in an ill-formed line. The justice had already been swooped in through another entrance, as they knew he would be, and Lucy had already arranged to be precleared to carry a weapon in her handbag.

Still, security was light, and definitely not good enough. During the court recess, Higgie didn't even travel with any U.S. Marshals as bodyguards, although Jack still scanned every man he saw in case some were undercover. Not that it would hurt anything; they weren't really going to shoot the bastard.

When they reached the front of the line, Lucy had a quiet conversation with one of the guards, who made a call, then guided her around the machinery without drawing any attention. Jack walked through the detector, took her hand when they rejoined, and together they headed down to their position in the Great Hall.

Lucy curled through the pack of partyers like a bloodred ribbon, her long hair draped over her bare back, so shiny it picked up the bluish cast from the aquarium walls. When they had to move single file, Jack watched her narrow hips move under the silk of her dress, watched her tight, round backside sway with each stilettoed step.

"Look, Jack, a shark." He followed her gaze to a sand tiger careening through the two-story megatank that formed most of one wall.

"Not the one I want."

She glanced up at the second-floor balcony, where at least three of her men were stationed. "Be patient. Owen just followed him into the Salt Marsh. In the meantime, I'm thirsty."

He nodded and headed to the bar without asking what she wanted. They'd even planned that.

"Getting some mins, mate?" Fletch had pulled his

shoulder-length mane back into a tail for the occasion and traded his gold hoop for a tiny diamond.

"Thank God someone called the sobriety police," Jack said dryly.

Fletch grinned, dimples flashing. "I'm your best— and only—mate, so yeah. Just keepin' an eye on you."

"Don't worry about me." Jack turned to the bartender and ordered the waters.

"But I do," Fletch said as he leaned his muscular body against the bar and casually scanned the room.

He wasn't miked, like a few of the others, but could hear the same reports in his earpiece that Jack heard. "I'm damn glad Miranda didn't want to come tonight."

"I don't like it that Vanessa's here," Jack said. "But she was determined to see him, and I can't blame her for being curious about her biological father."

"She doesn't consider him a father." Fletch had been almost as deep into this case as Jack had been from the beginning, and was the reason the Bullet Catcher door had been opened to him in the first place.

"Have you seen him yet?" Fletch asked.

"Seven? At the limo."

"How's he look?"

"Alive, unfortunately."

Fletch narrowed amber eyes in warning. "It's smack talk like that Lucy hates, you know." His Tasmanian accent barely covered the harsh warning.

"I know what Lucy hates." And what she liked, too. But no one, even Fletch, who'd brought him into the company and was the only Bullet Catcher to remain his friend after Lucy fired him, knew about their history. "Can't help how I feel about the guy."

"Just keep that kind of stuff to yourself. You've got everything you've wanted from Lucy now, so don't screw it up."

Not everything. Jack accepted the waters with a nod to the bartender. "We're getting there."

"Seven is entering the Great Hall." The voice broke their conversation and Fletch nodded a quick good-bye.

"Off to my station, then. Good onya, mate."

Jack returned to where Lucy waited.

"I heard we have company," he said, handing her the water.

She never looked around, although the buzz in the crowd told them what the spotter in their ears had confirmed. The guest of honor had appeared.

Over Lucy's shoulder, Jack saw the crowd parting as if royalty were coming through, and got his first direct look at a man he'd grown to despise.

Higgie was even more imposing up close: the signature head of snow white hair, the arrogant jaw, the ever-present smile, the countenance of wisdom and insight and justice for all.

Lucy softly cleared her throat, her gaze on Jack. "If hatred had a face, I'd be looking at it."

Jack didn't attempt to change his expression as he stared at Higgie. "If despicable had a face, I'd be looking at that."

"Jack."

He sipped his water and ignored the warning in her tone, still locked on the justice.

"Seven approaching, Lucy," a voice in her ear warned. "At twenty feet, eleven o'clock."

Lucy gave a tiny nod. "And now, Mr. Fuller, the ghostwriter who is trying to get a very important job working for the man who is undoubtedly the next chief justice of the Supreme Court . . ." Her voice was soft despite its controlled edge. "It is *officially* show-time. Act, or lose the game."

Before he could respond, she turned to Higgie.

He held out both hands as he beamed at Lucy, charm rolling off him in waves, a smile so bright it blinded. "There she is!"

Lucy reached out for the hug, letting him embrace her, then lifted her cheek to give and take air kisses on both sides.

Jack kept his smile in place as Lucy introduced him and they shook hands, calling the older man "Mr. Justice" as was appropriate since they'd never met.

"This man is the writer you want, Justice. I'll send you copies of his books and references."

All produced, of course, by the Bullet Catcher machine.

Higgie looked hard at Jack, nodding. "Your recommendation is enough for me, Lucy. I want to start very soon." He leaned closer to the two of them, and added in a stage whisper, "I have a feeling my life could change at any minute."

Jack smiled. *Oh, yes, it could.*

"Any word on the nomination?" Lucy asked smoothly.

"I expect to hear something in a few days," he said, turning a bit to his left as though he were aware of someone over there. "And look who was able to make it tonight, Lucy. I guess I have you to thank."

Something in the insincere way he said that caught Jack's attention, but he covered quickly as Marilee Higgins joined their group, her dark-haired, soft Southern class a strong foil to her husband's big white-haired gruffness. They exchanged pleasantries and small talk for a minute, before Marilee tugged her husband's arm.

"There's the mayor, dear."

Higgie nodded. "Duty calls. Save me a dance, Lucy."

"After your speech," Lucy said. "You don't mind, do you, Marilee? After your first one, of course."

Marilee shrugged. "Of course, Lucy. He can step on your toes for a change."

Higgie feigned insult with wide eyes, then winked. "She's telling the truth, I'm afraid." Beaming, he turned to Jack for a handshake. "Mr. Fuller. We will talk."

"Thank you, sir. I'll look forward to that."

As they walked away, Lucy gave him a genuine smile. "Well done, Jack. Perfectly as we'd planned."

"Excuse me, Luce. I'll be right back."

She gave him a surprised look. "You're not supposed to leave my side until 'Endless Love.'"

He lifted the hand that had just shaken Higgie's. "I have to go wash the shark shit off."

He walked away, knowing that was exactly the smack talk Fletch had warned him about. But fuck that—sometimes a point had to be made.

Of course, he never clapped. Not even politely when Justice Higgins spoke of the accomplishments of Charleston's Habitat for Humanity leaders. He didn't laugh when the speaker shared inside jokes about the other justices and their secret habits. He didn't bow his head when Higgie called for a moment of prayerful silence for the health of Chief Justice David Adler who battled cancer.

Jack sat stone still during the whole keynote, which bothered Lucy more than if he'd tried to hold her hand, or sneak a feel of her leg, or whisper sexual innuendos in her ear. His loathing for the man was so tangible she could taste it in the air.

It worried her. That kind of hatred was all you needed to kill a man, and disregard anything like a plan, forgetting even the reason the plan had been made in the first place. When it got personal, it got dangerous.

No one knew that better than Lucy.

As Higgie cruised into his closing, quoting Benjamin Franklin about courage and justice and weaknesses in men, Lucy put her hand on Jack's thigh under the table, giving him a questioning look.

"I'm ready," he whispered.

That wasn't what she wanted to know, but she gave his leg an encouraging squeeze.

His eyes narrowed and she read the silent message. *That man has no right talking about courage and justice.*

"I know how you feel."

He gave her a surprised look. "I doubt you do."

Actually, she did. But this was no place to compare screwed up histories, so she just lifted her glass in the toast to the organizers, then joined five hundred devoted admirers who applauded him.

Now, it was time to almost assassinate him.

Each Bullet Catcher checked in, one at every possible exit.

Gabriel reported on activity recorded on every camera they'd hidden.

Vanessa stood at the next table, kissing Wade, for luck, no doubt, then inched to the position they'd arranged near Jack while Lucy danced with Higgie.

Roman Scott spoke quietly to the orchestra leader, quadruple checking the song list.

Higgie shook some hands, knocked back a slug of something golden in a tumbler, then put his arm around Marilee and took her to the dance floor as the strains of "Moon River" started.

Everything was going according to plan.

Until Marilee shook her head, leaned closer to Higgie and said something in his ear, then walked away, her head at a haughty angle, her shoulders squared.

Contingency Plan B. Lucy didn't want to dance with Higgie yet, so everyone knew that she would take a bathroom break for three and a half minutes to avoid that possibility.

"It's around the fish tank to the left," Jack said. "I'll be here."

"It's time for you to wander over to that table," she

said with a nod to Vanessa, "and start a casual conversation with her."

"I know," he said, his voice impatient and tense.

She picked up her clutch and casually touched the diamond on her chest, giving Jack a hard look of warning, while she alerted the team to her move. "I'm going to the ladies' room, Jack. Excuse me."

She was almost in the bathroom when Marilee Higgins barreled toward her like a missile, and Lucy had no choice but to stop and face a woman whose sharp-eyed glare always belied her smooth Southern style.

"I need to talk to you, Lucy."

It wasn't a suggestion; it was a command.

"Of course, Marilee. Is something the matter?"

"Not here," she said quickly, taking Lucy's arm.

Yes, here, Lucy thought, aware that she was in the line of one of the cameras hidden above the archway that led to the bathrooms. If they moved, her team could lose a visual of her at an extremely critical time.

"There's a table where we can talk," Lucy said, easing her off to the side, slightly out of camera range, but a quick glance up to the second level reassured her that Owen Rogers was right in his designated spot, watching.

Marilee gave the hall the same cursory glance, including a look to the upper level to follow Lucy's gaze, then gently indicated for Lucy to join her at the table. Her demeanor was as casual as if they were sitting down for tea, but Lucy could feel her underlying tension.

Something was definitely wrong.

Touching her mike to be sure it was on, Lucy took the seat next to Marilee and gave her a concerned look, searching her face for a clue. "Is it one of your migraines?"

"My only migraine is Spessard Higgins."

Lucy drew back, so surprised that she thought Marilee was making a joke. But the look on her face said she wasn't.

"Tell me what's the matter," Lucy said, slowly and with interest, despite the fact that the orchestra was starting the second verse of "Moon River."

Every minute mattered if they were to stay on plan; moving to contingency always increased risk.

"Higgie's cheating on me."

Lucy didn't react. "Are you sure?"

"Relatively. That's why I need your help. I can't trust anyone else to do what I know you can do. I need confirmation." Her gray eyes narrowed to silver slits. "I want you to investigate him."

Lucy managed not to react, even at the low whistle of surprise she heard in her earpiece. "Marilee, that's a tall order. You are asking me to investigate a member of the Supreme Court for infidelity."

"I can't trust anyone else, Lucy. A leak to the media and this nomination would be history. His entire career could be ruined, and we've both worked much too hard to let that happen."

Lucy never took on cases of marital infidelity; it wasn't what the Bullet Catchers did, and, frankly, it wouldn't change anything in a forty-some-year-old marriage.

But, Marilee was handing her the very thing that she had come here to get, without the risk of a single shot being fired.

"I think it would be unspeakably difficult for us to watch him that closely," she said, choosing every word with the utmost care.

In her ear, Gabriel spoke softly. "Prepare positions for possible Contingency Plan C."

That was to wait four songs and try again. Lucy would have to pull out her handkerchief from her clutch to initiate that plan. Above her, she knew Owen watched carefully.

"Has something happened, Marilee, that makes you think he's involved with someone?"

Marilee sighed, smiled at a couple passing by, and waited as the orchestra began the last verse of "Moon River."

"I strongly suspect he has various liaisons. Not all of them are . . ." Marilee looked down for a moment, straightened the huge canary diamond ring on her finger. "Relationships. More like . . ." Her cheeks darkened. "Ladies of the evening."

"Higgie does hookers." She recognized Fletch's voice and heard the others chuckle in her ear.

What a total waste of resources that investigation would be. But Marilee was opening a door that they'd otherwise planned to shoot their way through in about five minutes.

This was eminently easier and safer.

"If you want me to, I'll do what I can," Lucy said.

"But only if you're sure you want to know. What will you do with the information?"

"That's my business," Marilee said, raising her chin. "But whatever I do, it won't hurt his chances of becoming chief justice. This is a lifelong dream, and men of power have been known to stumble due to certain human weaknesses. I won't let that happen to Spessard."

"Marilee, I obviously can't put a tail on a Supreme Court justice. The U.S. Marshals would be all over me in five minutes."

"We don't have to use them as security," Marilee said quickly. "When we do have protection, we use them since they are provided by the government."

Lucy nodded. "I know that."

"But it's perfectly reasonable for us to have private security. Many of the justices do."

"You would like us to protect him and investigate him?"

"What I'd like to do, Lucy, is surround him with prying eyes so that for the next few weeks, the man has no opportunity to give in to any weaknesses. Once he's chief justice, I hope he'll realize that . . ."

"Yes," Lucy said. "This could work."

Marilee nodded enthusiastically. "I've thought about this ever since you were kind enough to send your acupuncturist to me. I knew you were the perfect person to help me. We normally only hire bodyguards following controversial rulings, but I've talked about it recently, and he knows I feel vulnerable out there in the marsh on Kiawah Island. I can convince him we need security."

"I could put a crew on your estate to watch the compound around the clock, as bodyguards. He'll have less freedom, and if he still . . . strays . . . you'll have the information you want."

Marilee's mouth tightened in a satisfied smile. "Perfect. You are the only person on earth who can do this."

"That's not true," Lucy said.

"The only person I *trust* who can do this," Marilee corrected. "I know you won't leak anything to the media." She reached out and closed her diamond-laden hand over Lucy's. "Thank you."

Her years in the CIA enabled her to look Marilee straight in the eye and respond with genuine warmth. "It's an honor to have your trust, Marilee."

The first few notes of "Endless Love" filled the hall, just as Higgie's baritone voice called across to them.

"There are the two most beautiful women at the party." He strode over, a highball in one hand, his other outstretched. "Which of you gorgeous women is going to dance with me?"

Lucy stood to decline. She had a minute to give the signal to call off the shot. If she didn't have a chance to say it into the mike, she had to get into the middle of the Great Hall, in front of the right camera, and in sight of her men on the floor above. *Now.*

"He's all yours, Lucy," Marilee said with her most gracious smile. "I'm going to socialize with the many people here who we like to think of as influencers.

With the nomination coming up, I think my husband needs all the influence he can get."

"Peeshaw on influence!" he proclaimed, raising his glass higher. "I'm relaxin' tonight. Lucy?" He held out his arm to escort her. "I believe they are playing our song."

"I believe they are, Justice."

She had to steer him into the direct shot of the camera she knew was hidden on the sixth window pane from the center in the three-story-high glass wall to her left.

"If you'll just give me a moment, Justice." She paused right under the giant balcony where Fletch, Roman, Owen, and, most important, Wade with his weapon, were stationed. "I'm getting warm."

Deliberately, she opened her clutch.

"Lucy's delivering a message," Gabriel announced.

She pulled out a large rhinestone clip and snapped it into her hair. "Now," she said with a confident smile, "I can dance."

"Mission is dead," Gabriel said. "Cancel the shot. Mission is dead. Repeat: Cancel the shot. Mission is over."

She massaged her neck as though it hurt, looking straight up into Wade Cordell's blue eyes. He nodded once.

There would be no attempted assassination to foil tonight.

Of course Jack had heard the entire conversation, and no doubt he'd have plenty to say about Higgie's indiscretions. He'd also give her grief about breaking with plan, but this was obviously an instance where that was called for.

As Higgie turned her into his arms, her gaze landed on Vanessa, standing exactly where she was supposed to at her table.

Then her heart dropped. Where the hell was Jack? Killing the shot did not mean leaving his assignment, which was to stay with Vanessa.

As Higgie danced her deeper into the floor, she placed her hand on his shoulder and followed his smooth steps, hoping to help guide him around so she could see the spot where Jack was supposed to be standing.

"So what did you think of my speech, Lucy?"

"Brilliant." *Damn him. Damn that man.*

"You've heard it before."

She forced herself to smile up at her six-foot-five dance partner and think about the conversation she'd had with Marilee, not the one she was going to have with Jack.

"Just once, when you spoke in Chicago last year. It's still inspiring. I especially love the Franklin quote."

"Thank you. And thank you so much for the acupuncturist. Not only did she help with Marilee's headaches, but she got rid of my acid reflux."

And got your DNA. "She's very good," Lucy said.

"Marilee seems much better, much happier, don't you think?"

Could he be that clueless? "I think she's very excited about the possibility of your nomination to chief justice."

He gave her a wry look. "We both are."

"As you should—"

"Oh!" His face and body crumpled, just as a gunshot flashed in Lucy's peripheral vision. Higgie folded to the ground with a thud, sending an instant gasp throughout the crowd.

"Justice!" Lucy dropped to her knees, instinctively covering him in case of another shot.

"My leg!" he growled. "Christ, I've been shot."

Blood oozed over the parquet floor as Lucy squeezed the microphone on her chest.

Who didn't get the signal?

"Close every exit. No one leaves or enters." She kneeled next to the judge. "I have security here. We'll help you."

She barked orders into the microphone, pulling out her gun and holding it in position as a warning and protection.

"I am close protection security," she announced to the gathering crowd. "Make room for my team."

"I'm a doctor!" a man shouted, muscling his way forward.

Lucy nodded, and spoke into the mike again. "Box formation. Now!"

Four Bullet Catchers appeared exactly as planned and formed a safety net around the fallen judge.

Except *nothing* was like they'd planned. He wasn't supposed to be hit. She was supposed to throw him down after a bullet hit the ground, not his leg.

In her ear, each Bullet Catcher reported from an exit. Riverside Terrace. Locked and checked. East

Wing. Locked and checked. Gift shop. Locked and checked. Discovery Lab. Locked and checked. Ocean Gallery. Locked and checked.

"Where's Jack?"

Nothing. No answer. God *damn* that man.

Over the heads of the curious and terrified, Lucy caught Vanessa's stunned gaze as she stared at the man on the floor.

"Where's Marilee?" someone hollered.

"No shot was fired," Wade's soft Southern accent drawled in her ear.

"A shot was definitely fired," she replied. The question was, by whom?

"Lucy . . ." Higgie gasped from the floor and she leaned next to his face.

"It's all right, Justice," she assured him. "An ambulance is on the way and I have men here on security. We've locked it down. We'll find the person who shot you."

He nodded, closing a weak hand over her wrist. "Thank God you're here. Find . . . get . . . Marilee."

"We will. And we'll keep you safe. And her."

"Yes . . ." He closed his eyes and moaned in pain. "Make sure . . . she's safe."

"All the Bullet Catchers are stationed at their exits," Gabriel said in her ear. "Wade is now leaving for the custodial entrance."

Lucy took advantage of the noise and mayhem to ask the question again. "Where's Jack?" she demanded in a quiet but gruff voice.

"He left through the Discovery Lab door," Fletch reported. "Right before we knew there'd been a shot." She heard a subtle note of apology in his voice.

"Why?"

"I believe there was a lady involved."

A *woman*? At a time like this?

Lucy looked down at the blood oozing, Higgie's white face, then around at the circle of concerned guests, Bullet Catchers, and two U.S. Marshals.

Already, sirens screamed.

No, this was definitely nothing like they'd planned. But when Jack Culver was involved, it was exactly what she should have expected.

CHAPTER
SIX

IF HE'D HAD a gun, Jack would have taken a shot. Just to stop her. Just to make her turn around, take off the damn wig, glasses, and some of the layers that made her look fat, and prove to him he wasn't imagining this.

Kristen Carpenter was not dead.

But he was unarmed, so he just bolted in the same direction she'd run, outside to the wide open patio where she'd expertly threaded through packs of guests, moving too fast for him to catch up without knocking someone over.

The shocking announcement in his earpiece stunned him into stopping his chase.

Seven was down. Shot in the leg.

What the hell? Lucy just canceled the shot less than a minute ago! He wouldn't have run after *anyone* if she hadn't, even Kristen Carpenter.

No Bullet Catcher fired the gun. Was that why this woman was running? He'd been watching her closely enough to know she hadn't taken a shot, but maybe she'd known it was going to happen.

He saw her zipping past the line of parked limos, darting into traffic without much caution. Kind of the way Kristen Carpenter had been killed two months ago. He'd seen the ME's report himself.

So who the hell was he chasing?

In his ear, hell broke loose. Lucy barked orders, Bullet Catchers checked in from every corner of the damn fish tank, and Higgie moaned loudly enough to be picked up on Lucy's microphone.

The second time Lucy demanded to know where he was, Jack pulled the piece out of his ear and stuffed it into his pocket. He had no mike, and he wasn't about to stop and phone in to tell her to chill out because he was chasing a suspect.

He spotted her just as she made it across the street and headed into the wooded park, almost immediately disappearing into the darkest shadows a good five hundred feet away from him.

Who was this woman? And why did she have the very face he'd committed to memory since he'd finally identified the last of the Stafford triplets?

He never would have picked her out of the crowd, a plain woman with short black curls and rosy colored glasses and a frumpy figure. Until she walked past Vanessa, did a classic double take, and visibly paled.

That's when she'd landed right on his radar—not because he suspected her of being Kristen, but because she'd eyed the woman he was protecting.

Then she'd disappeared, until he and Vanessa had walked to the bar and he saw her again, deep in conversation on a cell phone. He got a good look at her then and quickly realized she wore a wig. When she looked up and stared across the Great Hall at Higgie, he saw her eyes were exactly like Vanessa's. Very much like Higgie's. And her face had the same sharp cheekbones as her sisters. The kicker was the mole right above her lip. She'd tried to cover it with makeup, but when she moved the phone, it had wiped away enough for him to see it.

He crossed the street, certain he'd seen her go to the right, away from any people. Already the limo drivers were getting out of their cars, cell phones were ringing, and sirens wailed through the warm Charleston night.

Up the street, the lights of the restaurants and a theater spilled into the outer edges of the park but didn't provide enough illumination for him to find her.

He went on gut.

Which hadn't been the most reliable navigation system for the past few months.

As he got nearer to a cluster of trees, he saw movement, something dark falling to the ground. A figure rushed forward, stripping out of the jacket she wore.

For an instant, she ran through some light and Jack could see her silhouette—a much thinner silhouette than the one she had when she ran out of the aquarium.

It didn't even matter if she was Kristen or not; this woman was involved in the shooting. He jogged closer, watched her flip the curly wig onto the ground and shake out a mane of wavy golden blond hair.

Kristen's hair.

He slowed his jog, wanting to observe everything before he moved in. He wasn't armed, and she could be. Even from this far away, he could hear the digital beep of her cell phone. She reached into a pocket and answered, just as she tossed her glasses away and started toward the street.

She was *not* getting away. If he had to tackle her to the ground and eat a bullet, he didn't care. She was not getting away from him.

Jack moved stealthily, close enough now to catch the tone of her voice if not the actual conversation. And her tone was rich with fury.

"Why did you do that?" He caught the demand clearly, since she was yelling into the phone. She reached the edge of the park, where a side street ran along the northern perimeter. A few cars were parked, and none was moving.

He'd get her when she got to her car, when she stopped to find her keys, rooting through her purse. He'd quietly slip right up behind her and say her name. She'd turn and he'd know.

A car turned the corner in front of the park and headed down the darkened side street, high beams bathing his target like a spotlight. Long and slender— like her sisters—she moved gracefully across the street.

The car slowed. Shit! It was picking her up.

As it stopped, she ran right in front of the car, just

as Jack reached the sidewalk, forcing him to make an impulsive decision. He'd just throw himself on the hood when she climbed in and—

"Stop right there, Jack." The growl in his ear was accompanied by a ferocious grasp of his elbow, yanking him back. The nose of a gun smashed into his kidney. "You're wanted by the boss."

Jack jerked his arm with all the might and anger that rocked through him, practically spitting in Owen Rogers's smug face. In his peripheral vision he could see her open the passenger door to climb in.

He could be throwing himself on the windshield right this minute, apprehending a suspect and solving a crime, but for this *goon* Lucy had sent to find him.

"Let's go, Culver."

"All right, dickhead!" Jack jerked again, freeing his arm, but Owen stabbed the gun harder, in a true Bullet Catcher power display.

The exclamation got the woman's attention. For one frozen millisecond, she looked across the roof of a little blue Saturn. Her hair lifted in the breeze and her eyes—those Stafford-Higgins eyes he knew so well—peered into the park.

He had to do it. He *had* to know.

"Kristen!" he called.

Her expression changed to flat-out horror as she dove into the car, slammed the door, and it shot off into the night.

"Lucy wants you in the limo. Right now, Culver."

Jack just stared at the car in total, abject disbelief. He'd found her, and he'd lost her.

All because Lucy had to have control over every man on her roster, and even those who were not.

"I have him," Owen reported into a tiny mike. "I'll have him in the limo when you're ready, Luce."

Jack was so mad he couldn't speak.

He didn't care what Lucy said, did, ordered, bought, paid for, arranged, or believed to be true. He would find Kristen Carpenter, and he would drag her sorry ass to that prison to meet her mother.

And then he'd turn her over for the assassination attempt she was obviously involved in.

But first, he was going to teach Lucy Sharpe a lesson about control.

Lucy practically threw herself into the limo, fire shooting down to her toes at the sight of Jack lounging along the backseat bench, his tie loose, his hair tousled, a drink in his hands.

Owen Rogers sat bolt-straight across from him, glaring at his prisoner, his hands resting on a Glock on his lap.

Jack held up his glass. "Need a drink, Luce?"

She ignored the question and looked at Owen. "Thank you. You can meet us back at the hotel for the postevent briefing. There's quite a bit of work for us to do, but I have to go to the hospital to meet Mariliee first."

Owen nodded, giving Jack a dirty look. Holstering his gun, he climbed out of the limo, closing the door hard enough for her to know he didn't like being called away from the good stuff to babysit.

Corralling everything she needed to remain perfectly calm, Lucy smoothed her gown and settled into the seat facing Jack. The limo pulled into traffic and she simply stared, waiting for an explanation.

He pointed at a spot on her skirt. "So, a little bit splattered after all."

"As if you didn't know."

His mouth quirked up. "The first accusation flies in under fifteen seconds. We have a record, team. Are they listening?"

She snapped the diamond pin, which had been turned off since she arrived at the car, and tossed it into the drink well next to her. "You'd better have a damn good explanation."

"No, Luce—*you'd* better have a damn good explanation. I was chasing a suspect through the park when Conan the Barbarian decided it was time to bring me home for dinner."

She blinked at him. "You had a suspect?"

"Kristen Carpenter."

She blew out a breath of exasperation. "You have got to be kidding me. You went running after a phantom again?"

He shot forward, so furious the drink splashed on his hand, and he slammed it down on the plastic bar next to him.

"She *isn't* a phantom. She was there, and she ran, seconds before the shot was taken. She bolted into the park, stripped out of her disguise, and got picked up by someone who squealed away. Moments after an assassination attempt, which she was undoubtedly *part of.*"

They stared at each other, anger bouncing between them like lightning bolts.

His jaw clenched to hold back what she imagined was a very dark curse. His eyes were locked on hers, and he was furious.

"Don't you want to know what happened?" she asked.

"Since you already assume I do, why bother? And I heard your conversation with Mrs. Higgins. Nice to have the keys to the kingdom handed to us by a woman scorned. Let's get in there and start investigating and protecting."

"That's right, Jack. There really *was* an attempt on his life, and now my company is on the line to protect a public figure whom we are secretly investigating for a thirty-year-old murder."

"Maybe we'll get him on solicitation of a prostitute instead."

She rolled her eyes. "I don't even take infidelity investigations."

"Yeah, leave those for the starving PIs."

"So now I'm damned if I do, and damned if I don't," she continued, leaning back as adrenaline slowly dissipated through her system, leaving her wiped out. "If I find out he's guilty of murder, how is that protecting the man who just begged me to keep him safe?"

Jack hissed a breath of revulsion. "He's safe. He hasn't spent the last thirty years in jail for a crime he committed. Eileen has."

She studied him, leaning forward to secretly sniff. What was he drinking? Had he been drinking before he went running off after some woman who his over-active imagination told him was someone who was dead, autopsied, and buried?

He grabbed the glass. "You're not fooling me, baby. Taste it."

"No need."

"Taste it," he said again, a little forcefully.

She shook her head, but he was up in a flash, kneeling in front of her, one hand taking her face, the other raising the glass. "C'mon, Luce. You want to know. You're wondering if it's rum or scotch or whiskey in here. You're thinking I was already on a tear when I started seeing things at the party, breaking with plan, and running through the park after an apparition."

"Let me go." Her words were muffled in his squeezed hand.

He stuck the glass under her nose. "It's straight Coca-Cola, but I see the doubt in your eyes. Taste it."

"No."

He threw back a huge gulp, tossed the empty glass on the floor, and pulled her face to his. Crushing her mouth, he squeezed his fingers to force her lips to part and spewed the drink into her mouth.

Coke. Pure and sugary and not mixed with anything but his hot, wet tongue.

They did not close their eyes. It wasn't a kiss. It was a statement.

She pulled back, swallowing the syrupy liquid without choking. He stayed right in her face, inches away. "Do I pass the sobriety test?"

When he released her, she wiped her mouth and narrowed her eyes at him. "I believed you."

"You never believe me."

"I believed it was Coke."

"Do you believe it was Kristen?"

She didn't answer but reached for her clutch when her cell phone vibrated inside it. She flipped it open while Jack returned to his seat.

"A nine-millimeter Browning was found under a table," Roman said as she answered. "They've taken it for prints."

"Which table?"

"Sixty-three, to the north side of the dance floor. We might be able to pick something up on the camera. Gabe is already running the tapes. Why did you go dark on the comm line?"

"I'm on my way to the hospital," she said, dodging the question as she glanced at Jack. He still hadn't taken his eyes off her. "Anything else?"

"The marshals are in charge and they're calling in the FBI, and the Charleston PD is swarming, so we're low on the hierarchy at the moment."

"We don't officially have the job," she said. "I'm going to the hospital to finalize it. Even so, we'll be providing protection and security; we won't get to investigate this shooting. Not officially, anyway."

"I know that," he agreed. "But we have some friends already. And I just picked up something from a local cop."

"What's that?"

"When they did a fan out, two officers found something interesting in the park across the street."

"Yes?"

"A black wig, glasses, and some pillows that might be a fat suit. Someone wanted to change the way they looked on the entryway cameras."

Why couldn't she have just believed Jack? "Keep me informed, Roman, and when you're done there, return to the Vendue. We'll debrief when I'm back from the hospital."

"What about Jack?"

She looked hard at the man across the car. "What about him?"

"Is he still on the team?"

Jack knew what question had been asked; she could tell by the look of challenge that slightly narrowed his eyes.

"Of course he's on the team. He's the only one who saw the suspect in the park. His ID of those tapes will be critical."

She flipped the phone shut and wet her lips, the pressure of his mouth still lingering on her lips.

The limo slowed in front of the MUSC trauma center, the lights of an ambulance illuminating the inside of the limo in red as she opened the door without waiting for the driver.

"I'll be right back," she told Jack.

"I'll be here," he replied. "Unless I see someone I need to talk to."

In other words, he'd do whatever the hell he wanted

to do, regardless of what she said. "Fine. I'm going to close some new business."

"You're just freaking out, K. Relax. There was no way you heard him right, over all those sirens."

"Theo, listen to me. He called me Kristen! I heard it as clear as a bell. Two guys standing in the park, staring at me, and one of them called me Kristen." She stabbed her fingers into her hair, scratching where the stupid wig had irritated her scalp. "Why did you leave me waiting for so long? What were you doing?"

"Circling around looking for you. Did you get rid of the whole disguise?"

"Yes, just like you told me to. If we get pulled over now, I won't look like anyone who was at that party." She narrowed her eyes at him. "Did you do it?"

"I missed."

She let out a breath of total despair, dropping her head back on the seat. "Damn. He's going to figure it out soon."

"No way. At least you got out okay, and I just pulled every string I ever had and some I didn't know I owned. And as long as nobody saw you leave, we're fine."

"Fine?" She practically popped out of her seat. "Some guy knows I'm alive! He just called out my name."

"You just need to lay low now, K. And I . . ." He swiped his hand through his hair. "Have to think of another way to get rid of that man and make sure you're safe. That's all that matters in the whole world."

The tender tone in her brother's voice pulled at her. He'd risked everything to keep her alive, and every day his schemes got bigger and wilder. And more dangerous.

But she had no one left to trust. Once anyone found out who she was, they'd go right to the man who wanted her dead. Even her mother couldn't be trusted.

"We should just leave, go out west. You can pursue that film career in LA you've always wanted."

"We need money, K. Anyway, I thought you wanted to live in Montana," he added quickly.

"It just seems remote and safe." She crossed her arms and swallowed the misery that had engulfed her ever since she'd decided to confront Spessard Higgins with the truth . . . and then got jumped by someone with a knife two hours later.

Thank God her brother had driven up at that very moment. He'd turned his life upside down in the past two months to keep her safe.

"Anyway, I'm not out of ideas. I thought of something huge today at the apartment. It's the perfect plan."

"Uh-oh." She smiled. "Those words are starting to terrify me."

"I'm serious. I know how to get the money we need, and while we're waiting for it . . ." His eyes widened and she could practically see the wheels spinning. "A way to keep an eye on that son of a bitch so he can't get near you." He pulled into the parking lot of the Red Roof Inn.

"Theo, if you do anything to make him realize it's you, then he's going to link it right to me, and he's going to figure out I'm not really dead. He knows what you do for a living."

"Did."

He shouldn't have quit his job, but she let it go. "The man is powerful. He can pay for things to be done—hasn't he proved that already?"

"But he's in a weakened state now."

She studied her brother's face in the dashboard lights. "I still think we're better off running than trying to kill him."

He turned, a dark look in his eyes. "I can't spend the rest of my life worrying about you every single second of every single day. He wants you dead."

She swallowed and looked out the window. She *was* dead. The reality of it always hit her hard.

"Don't worry, princess," he said, patting her leg.

She moved away, hating the patronizing tone, touch, and nickname. "Stop it, Theo. Use my new name. I'm Jennifer Miller." She closed her eyes and leaned her head back. "Kristen Jeanne Carpenter is dead."

"Thanks to me."

"Yes," she agreed. "Thanks to you."

Theo had called in every favor with all his old contacts from the DOJ and Social Security to save her life by ending it. He had loads of experience helping clients in the Witness Protection Program, and after the second time someone tried to kill her in two days, his solution had seemed brilliant.

Now she wasn't so sure.

"Aren't you glad I made you go tonight?" he asked.

"No."

"Come on, you can go out in public and not be recognized now! This was a huge breakthrough, and I'm really glad you were there." He smiled at her. "Really glad."

"The most bizarre thing happened," she said. "I saw this woman. She looked so much like me, it was weird."

"See?" he said smugly. "Lots of people look like lots of people. That's why you shouldn't freak when someone calls you Kristen. Just look them straight in the eye and say, 'You must have me confused with someone else. I'm Jennifer Miller.'"

"But her face, it was . . . I don't know. It just gave me chills, I don't know why. It was like . . . I knew her."

"You're scared and vulnerable right now," he said, parking the car in front of her room. "You sure you're going to be okay? Maybe I should stay with you."

"I'm fine." She opened the door.

"You could stay at the apartment tonight, K. No one will see you."

"I can't take that chance. Too many people know me there. Are you going to call Mom and tell her what happened tonight? It would be kind of weird if you didn't."

"I hate to talk to her. She just bawls about you."

Her heart actually dropped inside her chest. Poor Mama. She hadn't done anything to deserve this grief. "Theo, I really think if we tell her, it would be okay."

"Don't even think about it, Kristen." There was no arguing with that voice. "You know full well who she'd tell. Hell, she'd tell the whole world, because she can't keep her mouth shut. But she'd especially tell *him*."

"Not if she knew he tried to kill me."

He shook his head. "She'd never believe you, Kristen. She thinks he's God on wheels."

Sadly, she agreed. She blew him a kiss, climbed out, and walked to the door, knowing he'd watch until she went inside and locked the door. When she saw his car pull away, she slipped back out to the car she'd rented with cash the day before, and drove away.

CHAPTER
SEVEN

SHE STILL HADN'T taken off the dress. Or the shoes. In fact, Lucy hadn't done a single thing to get comfortable as they gathered in her sprawling three-room suite, while reports drifted in from the aquarium, and Sage accessed the impressive Bullet Catcher databases on her laptop to cross-check every person on the guest list.

Jack rolled up his sleeves and prowled around the dining table they'd transformed into a conference center, leaning over long-haired, ponytailed Gabriel Walker to soak up every frame of video they had.

No Kristen Carpenter, and only one shot of a woman he thought he'd seen. But it was grainy and at an angle that denied him a chance to see her whole face.

All the while, Lucy calmly managed, questioned and considered, decided, weighed, theorized, researched, and prodded everyone around her to do the same. She spoke on the phone with Marilee every hour, finalizing arrangements for the Bullet Catcher team to arrive at Willow Marsh tomorrow, though Higgie was still in surgery and would be in the hospital a few more days.

When they found the footage that showed a dark-haired woman running out the door, followed by Jack, seconds before the shot was fired, Lucy gave him a barely perceptible nod. For her, that was an apology.

It was almost 3:00 a.m. when everyone else left. Owen was the last to go, his husky shoulders still straight in his tuxedo jacket, his focus still on Jack as if they were lifelong enemies. He didn't say a word, but his body language screamed, *Do you want me to take the shithead who broke with plan out of your room, Madame the Boss?*

Jack was not only allowed to live another night, but also to stay on in the suite. Rumors would definitely fly.

He dropped into a club chair in the living room, plopped his feet on a hassock, and hunkered down to watch her move around in her long, bloody dress and bad-girl heels.

"I suppose you want a proper apology." She straightened papers on the table without looking at him, a thick lock of black hair falling forward and covering half her face.

When he didn't answer, she continued organizing things into neat Lucy-like piles. "I didn't see her face, and I still think you're imagining who she is. But I do agree that this woman must be involved or she wouldn't have left like that. So you were somewhat

justified in breaking plan and leaving the premises."
She finally looked up. "Is that what you're waiting to
hear?"

"No."

"Then what?"

"The first shoe to fall."

She walked across the room toward him, taking the
chair directly opposite. "I think it fell when someone
shot Higgie. The other shoe will fall when the next assassination attempt occurs."

"I was being literal." He moved to the hassock in
front of her, then cupped her heel. "This shoe. I want
to see it fall. On the floor."

She tried to move her foot out of his grip, but he
held tight.

"I'll undress when I'm alone."

"Taking your shoes off isn't undressing. It's called
relaxing." He indicated his open collar and rolled-up
sleeves. "See? Let the day end. And free those little
painted toes from the torturous high heels."

"They're very comfortable, but thanks for your
concern."

"I'm not concerned." He settled her foot on his lap,
curling his fingers around her slender ankle to find the
buckle. "I have a weakness for you in bare feet."

"I don't allow weaknesses on my team."

He looked up at the smile in her tone, catching the
teasing twinkle in her eye.

"Since I'm not officially on your team, we don't
have to worry. How about a foot massage?"

She hesitated, then put her fingertips to her temples. "The ache is in my head, to be honest."

"Then we'll start here"—he unbuckled the shoe—"and move up."

She sighed in surrender as she let her head drop back. "I hope I'm making the right decision about the tapes."

"You are," he assured her. "There's not a single image of the shot being fired, so you're not withholding evidence."

"But there are pictures of almost every person there."

"Not every person." He slid the shoe off her foot. "You heard Roman: security did let a few people out. And they have pictures of everyone who went past or through the metal detector. Even the seven or eight people who were Higgie's guests and not on the list."

She nodded. "Maybe your mystery woman was one of those."

"Maybe. But if you come clean with our tapes, Higgie will want to know why you planted video cameras." He closed his palm over the delicate, high arch of her foot. "He'll have enough questions about why you travel with a full security team. Jesus Christ, you have sexy feet."

She just laughed softly. "That feels good."

Her flesh was creamy, tight, smooth. Everywhere, he remembered. Every single inch of her body was like milk and honey. No wonder she made him hungry. He rubbed the ball, then thumbed the tight muscle along the bottom of her foot.

She let out a soft groan of satisfaction and lifted her left foot. "Here. Let the other shoe drop."

Smiling, he unbuckled the strap and let the shoe thud to the floor, then put both of her bare feet on his lap. A few more inches and she'd know exactly how hard this was making him.

Her eyes were closed; her head was back. Her shoulders finally dropped as he massaged, moving up to her ankle, then a slow swirl over the silky curve of her calf.

She opened one eye. "There you go again. Dipping into places you don't belong."

"I belong wherever I am. Relax and hush."

Amazingly, she did.

Then she said, "We have a problem, Jack."

"We have many," he said dryly. "Like how much I'm enjoying this." He skimmed his finger along the bottom of her foot and watched the toes curl involuntarily. "As are you."

"I'm serious."

"So am I. Serious as hell." His jaw ached from how much he wanted to slide any one of those beautiful, shapely toes between his lips. He slipped a finger under her baby toe, marveling that anything could be that tender. "Which of the many challenges that lie ahead is a problem, Ms. Sharpe?"

"This whole plan went out of our control tonight. None of the aftermath of a shooting was in our strategy. That bothers me."

"Yet we still go to Willow Marsh in a security capacity. And after your conversation with Marilee in the hospital, we don't have to do hooker investigations."

Lucy opened her eyes just to roll them to the ceiling. "Nothing like a brush with death to make you forgive the one who done you wrong. She already had a private nurse lined up, and a team of ten more."

"We need to check out every one," he interjected.

"We will. But Jack, she was so focused on saving him. And protecting him. She wants an army of Bullet Catchers, armed and stationed at every corner of her estate. This is a big job now."

His fingers stilled. "We're still *investigating* him, Lucy. Our goal hasn't changed, just our entrée into the compound. I'm still the ghostwriter he needs to hire." He stroked her calf again, inching her skirt higher so he could look at her legs. Next, he'd work it up to her thigh.

"What if he has no interest in spilling his guts to a ghostwriter now?" Lucy asked.

"After this, he'll want to even more than before. Don't underestimate that man's ego." He eyed her, his interest torn between the struggle on her face and the soft, sweet flesh in his hands. "For one thing, he'll be convalescing with nothing to do but talk to me. Plus his mobility will be severely limited, which means we can get around him easier. And during my interviews, I can get what he needs from his so-called vault." He squeezed her foot.

She wiggled her toes. "Don't stop."

"I love it when you beg." He massaged behind her knee now, moving the dress higher. At the sight of her taut thigh and the shadow between her legs, hunger gnawed.

"I hate coincidences, Jack. The fact that he was shot by someone in the aquarium in the same five-minute time frame that we'd planned to do it makes me crazy. There's a piece of the puzzle we're not seeing."

"*You're* not seeing it. I am. And her name is Kristen."

She lifted her head to look at him. "Jack, how is that possible?"

"Maybe she faked her own death. Maybe someone is impersonating her. I don't know how, who, or what yet. But I will."

"I'll help," she said softly.

He smiled and walked his fingers way up to her thigh. "Give the girl a foot rub and she'll give you the world."

"What do you need?"

"The usual. Access, information, maybe someone inside the morgue who's willing to talk for money."

"Whatever I can spare. But I still think you're crazy."

"I am. For these feet." He squeezed again.

She lifted her legs and gently escaped his grasp. "Thank you."

"The pleasure was mine."

She acknowledged the compliment with that look that she always gave him when he flirted with her. Like she tolerated it because, deep inside, she loved it.

He stood and headed to the bar to grab a water for each of them. He wanted to touch, to kiss, to get under that dress—but until she agreed, he'd settle for talking and solving problems with her.

"How you gonna tackle this one, Luce?" He opened a bottle and took it to her. "You know you want to find the shooter before the marshals or FBI, just on principle."

"You know me so well."

"Not that well. Are you a list maker? Cause and effect diagrams? Risk analysis?" He twisted the cap off his water and lifted it to his lips. "Drill problems down to bite size? What's the first thing you do when you're facing an insoluble puzzle?"

"I call Dan."

He managed to swallow. *Talk about a fucking mood killer.*

"So call him. In fact . . ." Jack glanced around for her phone. "What's his speed dial? One? I'm sure he has all the answers and can solve all your problems."

"Stop it, will you?" She didn't move from the chair but followed him with narrowed eyes.

"I'm serious. Dan's your sounding board. He's your main squeeze. Give him a jingle and see if he can figure out what the hell happened tonight. I mean, he wasn't there, but he's brilliant. Where is he?" He knew how it sounded, but, shit, he couldn't stop.

"He's working for a client in New York. Very busy."

"I'm sure he's not too busy to take a call from his boss at three in the morning. Wouldn't be the first time, right?" He just couldn't stop.

Lucy looked at him calmly. "This is why there were rumors that you were jealous of Dan when you—when he was shot."

Jack rested a hip on his chair, looking down at her. "Let's just discuss this one last time, Ms. Sharpe. We were on an assignment together. Shit got messy. Someone tried to attack the principal. I shot the assailant to stop him at the moment Dan moved out of formation, a fact he fully acknowledges. My bullet hit his back. I did not misfire to take down the competition."

She stared up at him, silent for a full ten seconds. "He's not your competition," she finally whispered.

"He's half in love with you." He realized, instantly, what that said about what he considered competition.

"He is not," Lucy said, but the words sounded hollow.

"You're right. He's all the way gone."

"He's not. We're friends. Very, very good friends." She set the bottle on the end table and gave him an icy look. "Frankly, it's none of your damn business. We're finished tonight."

He stood. "You can't dismiss me."

She stood as well, no longer eye-to-eye now that she was barefoot. "I just did."

"Too bad, 'cause I'm not ready to leave." He dropped his gaze to her low, low neckline. "I still don't know if you were telling the truth before."

Her breasts rose and fell, her nipples straining the flimsy silk.

"Not tonight, Jack."

"No? Why's that, Luce? Because whatever black and nasty misery made you call for relief last night isn't bothering you now?"

Her arm twitched as though she actually considered slapping him. Then she raised her chin and met his gaze with one that was near-black. "I have different problems. Work problems."

"Oh, I see. So you want Dan."

"I don't *want* anyone." She sidestepped him, reaching to snag his jacket from the back of a chair, and held it out. "All I want is for you to leave."

"I'll leave when I'm ready."

"Oh, don't go all alpha on me, Jack." She dropped the jacket and walked away, her dress swishing.

The dress that had nothing underneath.

"It's three in the morning. Go to sleep." Her voice was totally professional and she picked up a piece of paper from the table.

He slapped it out of her hands, his blood pumping hard again, but not from lust.

"Sleep? I don't do that much better than you do." He put his hands on her shoulders and pulled her closer to him. "You want to know why?"

She just looked at him.

"Because I just roll around all night thinking about you, thinking about that night." He pulled her an inch closer. "I just sweat and ache and *remember*."

"Lucky you, having such nice memories to keep you awake."

"What the fuck does that mean? They aren't nice for you?"

"Other things keep me awake, Jack."

"Like what?" Dan?

She closed her eyes. "Go."

"Like *what*, Lucy?"

She wrested out of his grip. "Go to bed, Jack. Roll around and remember. That's all I can offer you tonight."

He worked hard, damn hard, to keep from yanking her into him and devouring her. "Do you want to know what I remember?"

"The sex, I imagine."

He touched her chin with his index finger, seeing the tiny blue vein in her throat jump. "What I remember," he whispered, "is how you cried."

"That's enough." Her voice was low and rough.

"You cried, and not because you had the fuck of a lifetime. Not because you came six, seven, nine times all over me like thunderclaps."

"Stop it, Jack." She mouthed the words, but he refused.

"You cried from raw, real, heart-wrenching pain. Secret pain. Some dark place that you fall into sometimes and have a really hard time climbing out of."

She was pale.

"You cried because you hurt so bad, and the only thing that could keep you from sinking into that abyss . . . was me."

"Are you finished yet?"

He leaned closer, inches from her face. "You don't want Dan Gallagher when you hurt like that. You want me."

She lifted her chin, and almost met his lips. "And when you hurt, you want a bottle of booze. We all have our crutches."

"I don't want to be a crutch."

Her exotic, tilted eyes were so black he could see his reflection. "Too bad. That's what you were that night."

The words hurt as if she had slapped him.

He pulled her straight into his chest and kissed her fiercely, holding her so closely he could feel every bone and muscle and, God, curve of her body.

She went limp, infuriating him by not responding.

He delved his tongue into her mouth and she let him, but still didn't kiss him back. She was motionless. Ice. Stone.

It was much worse than if she'd squirmed and yelled at him to stop.

He let go as quickly as he'd started.

"Have you had enough?" she asked.

"Enough?" He slid his hands around her neck, surprised to find it damp, considering her determination not to feel anything. "Not even close."

Her halter top unhooked in one easy move, and he had it down so fast she barely had time to gasp. It fell to her waist, revealing her firm, sweet, rose-tipped breasts. He could have sworn she arched a little, just to jut those peaks right at him.

"The fact is, Lucy, I could eat you up, swallow you whole, suck the sweat off your skin . . ."

Her nipples hardened and a flush rose on that skin.

"Then I could tie myself up in your hair . . ." He took two handfuls and dragged his fingers through it, grazing the sides of her breasts. "And then I could bury myself all the way inside you until I was good and lost . . ."

He pushed the slippery fabric the rest of the way down her body. It fell in a pool, leaving every inch of her exposed. Still, she didn't move.

"And it wouldn't even be *close* to enough."

He stepped back, drank in every curve and angle, every shimmery shade of ivory and cream and one strip of sleek ebony pointing straight to the only place in the world he wanted to be.

This time, the hunger slammed him stupid.

He put his finger on his lips, then transferred it to hers. "Good night, Ms. Sharpe. Nice to see you were telling the truth, too."

He scooped up his jacket and walked slowly to the door.

"Jack."

He turned the knob and left without a word.

One of them, at least, had gotten a lesson in control.

Chapter
EIGHT

WILLOW MARSH WAS a huge compound, made up of a sprawling three-story main house, a four-bedroom guesthouse, a boathouse and dock, a formal garden with a gazebo and tool shed, and a small cottage referred to as "the office."

That was the one place the Bullet Catchers were not able to secure. Only Higgie had a key to the sacrosanct three-room structure, so Marilee asked that they wait until the justice got home from the hospital to discuss how best to secure his private rooms.

Naturally, that made Lucy want to get in even more, knowing that Jack's "vault" was undoubtedly somewhere inside.

Still, in the four days since she'd moved her security specialists into the compound tucked into the eastern outskirts of a marshy haven on Kiawah Island, they had accomplished a lot. They'd installed perimeter barriers, intrusion detectors, security lights, closed-circuit television cameras, monitoring systems, and watch stations to block the outside world.

The morning Higgie was due to come home, Lucy headed over to the gray clapboard cottage, blueprints and a proposed security plan in hand, planning to circle the buildings to find vulnerabilities. When Higgie got home, she'd tour the inside.

A wall of French doors with closed blinds lined the deck, but every one was locked. The other three walls of the building had only a few windows; there was no front entrance.

Lucy cruised the wide-planked deck, peering through narrow openings to what appeared to be a darkened office, and checking the angle of the roofline. With her hand over her eyes against the bright sunlight, she squinted above the last set of double doors when a movement inside caught her attention.

Approaching slowly, so whoever was in there didn't realize she'd seen them, she made her way closer, still shading her eyes and looking up as if she were studying the roofline, adjusting her position to find an opening in the blinds.

Again she picked up movement, sudden and swift.

Someone was definitely in the cottage. She rounded the building, peeking in windows, but each was closed with wide plantation shutters that denied any view inside.

Lucy knocked hard on one of the French doors, but no one answered. Only the last door had an outside lock. It wouldn't be impossible to break in, although if she waited, whoever was in the cottage had to come out eventually.

She gave it five minutes, checking the sides of the building again, but never losing view of the deck. Certain no one had left, she returned to the door that had a lock and pulled out her key ring with the elegantly designed lock pick that all Bullet Catchers carried. She slipped the slender needle into the lock, shimmied it a few times, and heard the click that told her she'd opened it.

An argument for increased security if she ever had one.

The door opened to an office, silent, dark, and crammed full of furniture and *stuff*. A gargantuan desk took up a whole corner, with cushy guest chairs and a chunky credenza behind it. A sitting area with a fireplace filled the opposite side of the room, and two walls had floor-to-ceiling bookshelves.

Every single inch of shelf space contained memorabilia, photographs, plaques, certificates, and formal documents set in glass, with the pens that signed each on display. She counted four presidents in photos with Higgie, half a dozen senators and congressmen, two A-list movie stars, and Mickey Mouse with the former president of Disney flanking the justice in full robes.

Could more crap be stashed away somewhere, or was this actually the vault that Jack wanted to find?

She crossed the gleaming mahogany floor to a set of double doors that opened to a wide, dark hallway. An Oriental runner covered the floor and masked her footsteps as she passed a galley kitchen with a small eating area on her left and a spacious master bath, sauna, and a small exercise area on her right.

Both were empty. At the end of the hall there was another door, and she knew from the blueprints that it was a private living area. Who was back there, and why? Owen just told her that Marilee had gone to the hospital to pick up her husband, and no one was allowed in the cottage.

Maybe someone had come to clean it. But why wouldn't they answer her knock?

As she approached, she automatically rested a light hand on her weapon. Whoever was in this house, they didn't belong and didn't expect her.

She opened the door with a quick push.

It was a sparsely decorated bedroom, and it was empty.

Had she imagined the movement? Except for a small loveseat under the window, the entire room consisted of a huge sleigh bed and a night table with one lamp. The only art was a hanging pewter sculpture of a long-beaked tropical bird, and, at the foot of the bed, a Persian rug with the distinctive red dye of a Tabriz covered wide-planked wooden floors.

She looked under the bed and found nothing; the closet was empty but for a pair of men's pajamas, a cotton robe, and slippers. She walked across the room, stymied. Dropping onto the bed, she looked at the single item on the nightstand, a Bible.

She picked it up and let it fall open. When it did, she saw a thin newspaper clipping tucked deep into the spine.

Curious, she lifted it out and unfolded it four times, sucking in a soft, surprised breath at the black-

and-white picture in the middle of a carefully cropped death notice, the name jumping out at her.

Kristen Jeanne Carpenter.

A thousand chills rolled down her spine.

So he knew her, or of her—exactly as Jack had said. She glanced down at the open page, the type tiny in four narrow columns.

Under the obit, a passage had been underlined.

As is the mother, so is the daughter.

She folded the obit exactly as she'd found it, slipped it back into place, and closed the book.

Just as the distinctive sound of a pistol being racked cracked right behind her. She didn't move, cursing herself for sitting with the door behind her.

"No one is supposed to be in here."

Higgie. Slowly, she turned. "Justice?"

She met the steely gaze of a man in a wheelchair, a sturdy-looking pistol aimed right at her.

"You're lucky I didn't shoot first, Lucy. How did you get in here?"

"I picked the lock, and so could anyone else with basic skills. This cottage needs better security, Justice. I hope this proves that to you."

He lowered the gun, his look hard on her face, with no indication that he was concerned she'd found something in his Bible. "A man's got to have a place where there are no cameras," he said softly.

"I understand, and we want to ensure privacy that won't compromise—"

"Don't give me that load of crap, Lucy. You'd stick a closed circuit TV and one of your men in my toilet if you thought it would keep me alive longer." There was a glimmer of humor in his eye.

"We will do whatever it takes, Justice." She moved away from the bed, coming around to greet him. "I was supposed to be notified when you arrived so I could greet you."

He lifted a shoulder. "Maybe there's a flaw in your system. Just like in my door locks."

Reacting to the tease, she reached down to greet him with a quick hug. "You look terrific for a man who took a bullet on the dance floor."

He maneuvered the chair around skillfully, indicating for her to lead the way back to the office. "I look like a truck ran over me hard, then backed up to make sure I was dead," he drawled in that famous South Carolina baritone.

"Well, you're not dead," she said matter-of-factly. "And I'm here to make sure you stay that way."

"Thank Jesus for that, ma'am. I admit I don't remember very much, but Marilee tells me your team was exemplary at the aquarium." He positioned his chair near the desk and gave her a firm nod. "I can't thank you enough, Lucy."

"That's why I travel with a full security contingent in public situations. And you already thanked me with the vote of confidence, Justice. I realize you have the option to have a free team of U.S. Marshals here, and you've chosen us instead. I appreciate it."

"Marilee chose you, but you'll get no argument from me. It's a small price to pay for peace of mind."

His mouth quirked up in another smile. "Well, not so small if I recall your fees."

"Before you worry about the bill, let me tell you how we've set up the security."

She got a waved hand in response. "Whatever. I trust you, Lucy. Just no cameras past this room." He pointed to the double doors. "When I go back to that area, I want to know I have privacy."

"That's a deal," she agreed.

"All I care about is the investigation. Tell me everything. What have you found out by digging around my house and private quarters?"

The investigation? "The Bullet Catchers are here on a security detail, Justice; the FBI is handling the shooting."

"Come on, Lucy, I've known you a long time. You've got your pretty red fingertips into everything. And I know you've got close connections all over the FBI, but they won't tell me anything. What have they found out?"

"They haven't shared anything," she said. "Although I know that they are looking for individuals who might have particular grievances with the Court."

He shook his head. "That list is long, if you start to count right-wing evangelists who don't like my rulings on abortion and left-wing nutcases who don't like my rulings on capital punishment. And don't forget politicos with agendas for the next chief justice nomination, and conspiracy theorists who think I'm in cahoots with the president. I may even have pissed off a few lawyers in my day." He swatted some imaginary flies as if they were annoying him. "All a complete waste of tax dollars, if that's who they're investigating."

She frowned, not understanding. "Trying to find who shot you isn't a waste of tax dollars."

He eyed her with the expectant look of a professor who thought his top student ought to know the answer. "Let me ask you, my dear. If you were in charge of the investigation, where would you start?"

"With everyone who attended the fund-raiser."

"Of course," he replied. "And you may not know this, but they should: I have never, in all the years I've been on the bench at the circuit, state, and federal level, had a death threat."

"Never?" She found that impossible to believe.

"I am an expert at making people like me, haven't you noticed?"

"I have," she admitted with a smile. "Your popularity is off the charts, Justice. But the very nature of what you do has to leave one side disappointed, mad, or feeling like they've been sold short. Every ruling you've ever made has angered someone. So I think the FBI is doing exactly what they should be doing."

He slammed his hand on the armrests of the wheelchair, the *thwack* surprising her with its force. "They're not looking close enough to home."

"Specifically?"

"My office, my staff, my very small world. I knew hundreds of people on a personal level at that fundraiser. It was a Charleston reunion for me. Lots of people from my past."

He *wanted* them to look into that? Not the hope of a man with a murder in his past and a very broad-based coverup.

"You think the would-be assassin is someone with a grudge from the past?"

"It could be. Considering the venue they chose."

"Is there anyone in your past, in Charleston in particular, who might feel you'd wronged them enough to want you dead?"

"Possibly."

Inside her jacket pocket, her cell phone vibrated with the 911 rhythm from Avery.

"Then we should look into every one of them." She stood as though the thought made her want to pace, walking to one of the bookshelves to peruse the awards and pictures, turning from him to surreptitiously slide out the phone and read the front panel.

DNA results back. SH is the father of the ES triplets.

She turned back to him. "If you like, Justice, the Bullet Catchers can initiate a very private investigation of your immediate circle. And of anyone in Charleston you might share a history with."

He nodded slowly, considering that.

"As I say, it would be utterly confidential and secret. That assumes, however, that you'd be willing to be completely open with me about your past. I'd need private information."

"There is . . . was . . . someone," he said, his words halting. "But she's . . ." He shook his head. "It would be impossible for her to get to me."

"She?"

She fingered the phone she still held in her pocket. Was he referring to Eileen? Certainly not a direction he would send her to investigate if he were guilty of the crime that put Eileen in prison.

His smile was wicked. "A few ladies have liked me."

"I bet they have." She took a seat to ensure they were on the same level, to build his trust and open him up. "Let me reiterate, Justice. No one but a few people very, very close to me need ever know. I would handle this personally."

His elbow on the armrest of the wheelchair, he thumbed his chin. "The thing is . . ." he said softly. "The nomination is right around the corner, and I don't want anything to derail it."

"Or anyone," she added. "It's up to you. All you need to do is give me names, dates, occupations if you remember them. We'll find out where these people are now, and if they were anywhere near the vicinity of the aquarium or had connections to people who were there."

He held up a hand. "I need to think about it. Some people's feelings need to be considered."

Like his wife's, no doubt. "Of course. But no one in your family or close circle need ever know of this investigation until we find a suspect."

He nodded, still thinking.

"When can I get on your calendar to help you compile some names?"

He choked a laugh. "My overcrowded calendar? Please. I have no work to do, and with this . . ." He gestured to his injured leg. "My recess plans are ruined. All I had in mind was to work on my memoir. Where is that ghostwriter you brought to the fundraiser?"

Waiting for permission to enter the compound. "Ready, willing, and able to take the job."

"I imagine that young man will do anything to be near you."

She gave him a surprised look.

He chuckled, pleased with himself. "I'm quite adept at sniffing out the true character and motivation of people. Don't forget what I've spent my life doing."

"I won't, and please, if you prefer to work with another ghostwriter, it won't make any difference to me. Feel free to interview others."

He pointed at her, a real smile in his eyes for the first time. "Call your young man and get him here for dinner. I'll bore him with some war stories, then I'll work up a list, and you can start your investigation right away."

"He'll be delighted." So, so delighted.

After the bone marrow transplant, Eileen never returned to the infirmary. They kept her in a quiet wing of Richland, as they called the hospital, isolated from everyone but some nurses and doctors, since she was highly susceptible to infections.

And that was fine. It wasn't freedom, but it wasn't prison. During those early days, she'd been so horribly weak and miserable that she couldn't enjoy her taste of freedom anyway. The only thing that kept her hanging on to life was the hope that when she was strong enough, they'd let her see her daughters again. Their earlier visits were only a blur.

But Jack had promised her she could. He'd promised her so many things, and he had mostly delivered.

Now today, her daughters were coming and she was awake, lucid, and almost giddy with anticipation. Her girls. Elizabeth, Anna, and Christina.

She'd never told anyone that she'd named them. Not even Jack. But that night in July thirty-one years ago, she'd handed over nameless babies to a nurse at Sapphire Trail. But, in her heart, she'd given them the three prettiest, classiest names she'd ever heard.

One, she was almost certain, really had been named Christina. Or something close. For some reason, that thrilled her.

She was the one who'd visited most recently. Just a couple of days ago. Or was it weeks? Hard to say. There was no window in this room, and most of the time Eileen didn't know if it was day or night, let alone what week.

She did remember one thing about her visit with Christina. The girl had said *his* name outright. Eileen just looked at her. Though . . . she may have nodded.

She shouldn't have taken that chance, but the drugs had made everything sort of hazy.

But today she was clearheaded. She wouldn't make that mistake again, no matter what her girls told her.

When she heard footsteps and voices in the hall, she tried to take a deep, calming breath, because it couldn't be good for her to have such a jittery heart. But how could she not be excited?

Someone laughed softly, and a man's voice carried through the hall.

"Hello?" A soft tap on the door of her tiny room was followed by the face of a young woman, haloed with dark curls, her deep blue eyes the same color as the set that used to meet Eileen in the mirror every morning. "Oh, you're awake."

It took everything Eileen had not to cry. She managed a croak of "Hello," and tried to clear her throat, suddenly dizzy at the sight of the delicate beauty in the door.

"Eileen . . ." She took a few steps closer, her dark blue eyes misting over. "I'm Miranda Lang."

Anna. Eileen decided instantly that this one was Anna. As a lump lodged in her throat, she drank in the lovely angles of her face and the intelligence in her eyes. She tried to sit up, to get closer to Anna.

"Don't strain yourself," she said, moving quickly to Eileen's bedside. "You're not supposed to push like that."

Eileen stared at her, unable to speak. "Anna," she murmured, lifting her hand.

"No, it's Miranda," the young lady corrected, closing warm fingers over Eileen's cold ones. She glanced over her shoulder at the door as a man appeared, tall and burly-looking with long hair and golden eyes. "And this is Adrien Fletcher, my fiancé."

"Ms. Stafford." He sounded like he had an English accent, one Eileen could have sworn she'd heard before. Maybe when she was in a coma.

"How do you feel?" Miranda asked. "You look wonderful."

"So do you." Eileen felt a smile pull at her lips, an equally warm one returned by Miranda.

Eileen glanced at the door. "Is there . . . are there others?"

"Vanessa is outside," Miranda said. "She thought we might want a few minutes alone first."

"I want you together," Eileen said. "All three of you. Please."

An unreadable expression flitted over the pretty girl's face as she glanced at the man. "Can you get them, Adrien?"

Them. Thank God. They are all three here. Joy bubbled through her, so powerful she could feel it in her veins.

"This is a very happy moment for me," she said.

"I know. For us, too." Miranda's brows knit. "I mean Vanessa and me. She's here with Wade, who found her for you."

"Vanessa." Eileen rolled the name over her mouth. Nope. Too fancy, that name. She would be Elizabeth.

"It was Vanessa who was able to donate her bone marrow to you," Miranda told her.

And the daughter of the man who'd once, long ago, come to visit her. She'd told him some things that she shouldn't have, and he never came back. That scared her back into silence. Even with Jack, she'd never tell the truth anymore.

A woman stepped into the room and Eileen sucked in a quiet breath at the sight of her. Pale blond hair exactly like her own used to be, with a spark in her eyes that reminded Eileen of herself. It was like looking in a mirror thirty years ago, except her eyes were a paler blue. *Like his.*

"Hello, Eileen," she said, approaching the bed with a confident stride.

"I owe you my life," Eileen whispered as the woman came closer, flanked by the man named Adrien and another just as big, but with short-cropped hair and a handsome face.

"I think it's the other way around." She even sounded like Eileen, this Vanessa.

"I called you Elizabeth," Eileen told her. "In my secret fantasies, I . . ." She looked from one to the other, then pointed to Miranda. "I named you Anna." She smiled, not caring that a tear rolled down her cheek. "And now where is Christina?"

"What did you call her?" Vanessa asked.

Miranda paled. "Her name . . ."

"That's quite a coincidence," Adrien said, slipping his arm around Miranda. "Your other daughter's name is Kristen."

"I know." Despite orders, Eileen sat up, thrilled. "She told me."

Both girls drew back in unison. "You *met* her?" Vanessa asked.

"She was here, and she told me her name was Kristen. So it's very close to Christina." She looked toward the door. "Is she out there, too?"

No one answered, but they all exchanged looks of dismay and disbelief.

Something was wrong.

The temperature in the room dropped . . . or maybe just Eileen's blood had run cold.

"Is she here, too?" she asked.

"No, she isn't." Vanessa closed her fingers around the railing of the hospital bed.

"What's the matter?" Eileen asked, looking from one to the other. "What is it?"

Neither answered. And then she knew exactly what was the matter.

"Oh." The sound escaped her lips like a soft mew. "No."

Each of the girls took a hand, closing their young, strong fingers around Eileen's hands.

"She was killed in an accident," Miranda said.

Pain punched. Not like the pain of sickness and near death. A different pain. A wicked, hot, brutal, razor sharp slice of pain that took her breath away.

"An accident?" she managed to say, squeezing their hands with the pathetic amount of strength she had. *Please, God, no. Don't let it have happened. Don't let him have done this to her.*

All she'd done was nod when Christina said his name. She didn't tell her! *Oh, God.* He was the devil. Worse.

"It was no accident." Vanessa's voice had a hard, bitter edge. "We all know it was no accident."

The words rose in Eileen's throat like bile. "He can do anything."

"Do you mean Justice Higgins?" Vanessa asked.

Eileen froze. She'd told Christina, and now she was dead. She'd never make that mistake again.

She closed her lips to keep a word from coming out.

"You don't have to worry about what you tell us," Vanessa said. "We're safe."

Wade stepped closer to the bed, his gaze sharp even though his voice was softened with a slow Southern accent. "We're professional security specialists. Nothing will happen to them. No one can do anything, Miz Stafford."

Someone could. But the man's determined voice and his military stance did give her some comfort. These two were safe.

But . . . Christina. Her dear Christina.

Grief rolled through her. And anger. And hate.

"It's my fault," she said, choking on a sob. "I shouldn't have told her when she came here."

"When?" The girls spoke in unison again.

Miranda's boyfriend moved closer. "She's been gone for two months."

Had she dreamed it? Had it just been a fantasy?

No. She'd been here, in this very room. With pretty blond waves and smiling blue eyes.

But they all looked as if they thought she was crazy. Only one man would believe her.

"Where's Jack?" she asked.

"He's working," Adrien said.

He hadn't been here for so long. "Is he okay?" Because the devil could get him, too, just to spite her.

"He's fine. He's busy," Vanessa said. She looked up at her sister, and all four of them exchanged more looks, the men nodding as though giving her permission to go on. "He's investigating a murder.

Murders," she corrected. "Since there are more than one."

Oh God, if he got too close to that monster . . .

He'd spent more time with her than any other human being in thirty years. He'd talked to her, listened, and cared. She loved Jack almost as much as she loved these two girls.

"He has to be very careful."

"He is," Adrien said. "He's surrounded by the best security in the world."

"How did he know . . . who to investigate?"

Miranda took Eileen's hand and led it to her nape. "You marked us."

Eileen shuddered. "Yes."

"So he's right," Vanessa said. "Spessard Higgins is our father."

"Shhhh." Eileen hissed the warning. "He could have people anywhere."

"And he killed Wanda Sloane, didn't he?" Vanessa insisted in a hushed whisper. "That's what you told my dad, isn't it? Did you tell that to Howard Porter?"

"Did he tell you that?" Eileen asked, dodging the question.

Vanessa's eyes narrowed. "He never had the chance."

Oh, God. How many deaths would be on her conscience? She shook her head and tried to release her hands. "I don't know. I don't know . . . anything."

"Yes, you do," Vanessa said. "You know *everything*."

She did. And it didn't matter how big and strong the men who protected her daughters were, or what kind of security surrounded Jack. No one was safe when that man was involved.

"Please, Eileen," Miranda implored. "It isn't easy to go after a man that powerful, but Jack and Lucy can do it."

"Lucy?" Jack had mentioned her. Many times, he'd talked about Lucy, and Eileen knew, even though he'd tried to hide it, that he loved this Lucy lady.

"She runs a security and investigative firm where Wade and I work," Adrien explained. "She's heading up the investigation."

"If she gets too close to the truth he'll kill her, too," Eileen warned.

The other man smiled. "Not too likely, but anything you can tell us, any piece of evidence you know that would incriminate him, will help."

"No one can get to him."

Vanessa lifted a brow. "You don't know Lucy. She's living at his house right now. She has total access."

"Tell her to be careful, too."

"Please," Vanessa urged, squeezing her hand. "Help us get you out of here. Tell us what happened that night."

"You don't have to spend the rest of your life in prison, Eileen," Miranda added. "We're protected. And we want to see justice served."

Eileen closed her eyes and shook her head. Justice would never be served. He'd come here and kill her with his bare hands. Then he'd go after her girls.

"I'm tired now," she announced.

Miranda gripped the bed railing. "Eileen, please. Don't you want to be free? Don't you want to see him pay for what he did to you—to us?"

"I gave you away before . . . the murder."

"But if you weren't in prison," Vanessa said, "I would have met you fifteen years ago."

"He stole your life and put you in here," Miranda added.

Eileen said nothing.

"Didn't he?" Vanessa urged.

"I killed Wanda Sloane," Eileen said quietly. "You're wasting your time. I'm tired now, girls. I need to sleep."

Vanessa released her hand with a soft curse, and Miranda sighed.

"Let's go," Wade said. "Let her rest."

He led them out, but the man named Adrien stayed behind. Eileen kept her eyes closed, pretending to be asleep, waiting for him to give up.

After a moment, he leaned very close. "Jack's my best mate," he said softly. "I know him better than anyone in the world."

She opened her eyes and met his amber ones. Yes, the Australian friend. Jack had talked about him, too.

"He's a fine young man," she said. "And I don't want anything to happen to him."

He nodded, stroking a tuft of hair under his lip, holding her gaze. "No, me neither. But you know, Eileen, he's had quite a time of it the past year. Made some bad mistakes, lost his job, had a few run-ins with the bottle, if you know what I mean."

She did; Jack had even told her that. "He's smart and strong. And I want him to stay alive."

"If he could solve this case," the big man said, "not only would you be out of prison and your two daughters able to live without twenty-four-hour security, but Jack would be happier."

She curled her fingers around the blanket. Jack had done so, so much for her, and now she could help him.

"If I say anything . . . he could be killed."

"If you don't, he might anyway. Please help him, Eileen."

She lay very still, thinking of what she might tell this man. Remembering the night she'd witnessed Wanda get shot. She'd hidden behind the cemetery wall, saw Higgie's back and the face of the woman he was kissing against the wall.

Heard the shot, saw her fall, listened to Higgie run.

She'd witnessed the entire thing.

Then she'd run away, driving like a fool through the streets of Charleston, making it almost to the West Ashley bridge before that son-of-a-bitch cop pulled her over and shone a light on the murder weapon in her front seat.

He'd known she'd be there. He'd known she never locked her car. He'd put a gun on that seat . . .

"Maybe," she whispered, "he should look for the real gun—because the one in my car didn't shoot her."

The gun was probably in the bottom of Shem Creek, but she wanted to help Jack somehow.

The man surprised her with a kiss on the forehead, his little beard tickling her skin. "Good onya, Ms. Stafford. We'll be back soon, I promise."

"You take care of . . . my daughter."

"I plan on it. Forever." He winked at her. "No worries, mum."

But she had worries aplenty.

She closed her eyes and pictured her girls, including the face of the one daughter she'd never see again.

Maybe it was just her imagination that Christina had been here.

So many deaths pressed on her conscience. She hadn't pulled the trigger that killed Wanda, but so many people died because of her, she should give up her fantasies and stay where she belonged. In prison.

CHAPTER NINE

"IF YOU'RE DRUNK and passed out in there, Culver, I'm going to finish the job with my bare hands." Lucy pounded the hotel room door.

The lock turned and she braced herself for the worst. Red eyes, three days of beard, sunken cheeks. She knew he'd talked to Fletch last night, so he must have heard that Eileen had learned of her daughter's death.

That was just the kind of thing that could send Jack to the—

The door opened and every inch of visible space was filled with wet skin, wet hair, wet man.

Shower.

"O ye of little faith." He grinned, playful and evil as he opened the door wider in invitation, the remnants of shaving cream like a beard along his jaw. "But if there's a job you want to finish with your bare hands, step right in."

Water-slickened black hair dripped down to his

broad shoulders, and droplets slid down the planes of his chest.

As he tucked the corner of a white towel at his waist, a trail of water followed the line of soft, dark hair that pointed due south.

He was one flick of the wrist away from full exposure.

She tucked her hands into her pants pockets and forced her gaze up, but his wet lashes made his eyes smokier and sexier.

"Showering at ten in the morning?" she asked, as if it was a sin. She breezed by him, the scent of soap and shampoo and man assaulting her.

"I hit the gym at eight and showered at ten. Are you not getting my hourly agenda updates?"

"It's a good idea to check in once in a while, since you're on assignment."

"I'm in a holding pattern while you set up shop at Higgie's house," he corrected, closing the door. "Am I in?"

"You are." She picked up a pair of jeans balled on a chair and dropped them on the floor before sitting. "You're expected for dinner with the justice and his wife tonight. Assuming you pass his test, you can start the interview process tomorrow morning."

He went into the bathroom, his back fully visible as he bent to the sink.

"Excellent." He splashed his face, then grabbed another towel and swiped himself dry, dropping it on the floor as he returned to the bedroom. "Have you found anything? Like his legendary vault?"

"I've been in his office, which is really a library and the closest thing to a vault he has. Sorry, the murder weapon wasn't on display."

He dropped onto the unmade bed and faced her, his legs spread just enough to reveal the darkness under the towel, a wry smile on his face. "All this time apart and all I get is accusations and sarcasm?"

"The mission . . . is changing."

The smile evaporated. "I don't like the sound of that."

"I don't think he's guilty of that murder."

"What?" He shot forward.

"Just wait," she said, holding up her hand. "He's asked me to conduct a confidential investigation into the people in Charleston from his past. He's convinced that someone in his inner circle fired that gun, and thinks the FBI is wasting their time looking for lunatics with political agendas."

"Fuck." He blew out the word softly, pushing himself off the bed. "You've gone to the dark side."

"Oh, Jack, come on. Why would a man guilty of murder practically hand me a ticket to go dig into his past? And invite a ghostwriter in for in-depth interviews about it? Wouldn't he be more secretive—especially about his associations when he lived in Charleston? That would be a direct link back to Wanda Sloane and Eileen Stafford."

"Why? Because his ego has no bounds. Because he's paid off anyone who knows or would reveal the truth. Because he's an abusive son of a bitch."

She frowned at him. "Unfaithful, corrupt, and egotistical, maybe. He *might* even have had something to do with Wanda's murder. But abusive?"

"Something to do with it?" His dark eyes flashed. "Jesus, Lucy, what kind of power does that guy have over you? A week ago you set up a massive operation to get 24/7 access so you can prove he committed this crime, and now you've let him off the hook and are probably going to ask me to go easy on him in interviews."

He bent over to grab his jeans off the floor, then marched back into the bathroom—and dropped his towel without closing the door.

She stared at his sculpted backside, taut and carved like the rest of him, the muscles tightening as he stepped into his jeans, zipped, snapped, and turned to glare at her. She didn't pretend she wasn't staring.

"So is that it? You came to tell me you've changed plans and, what, you want me to back off?"

"I wondered how you were doing," she said honestly. "And I thought you'd be interested in something I found tucked into the Bible next to his bed."

He snorted softly as he stuck his bare feet into Docksiders. "The perfect nighttime reading for a killer. What was it?"

"Kristen Carpenter's obituary."

That got his attention.

"And he'd underlined Ezekiel 16:44."

"As hard as this is to believe, I don't have my Bible verses memorized. What does Ezekiel sixteen have to say?"

"The whole verse, if I remember correctly, is: 'Behold, every one that uses proverbs shall use this proverb against thee, saying, as is the mother, so is her daughter.'"

He processed that for a second. "And her obit was there? Well, that tells you that he knew Kristen, and knew she was his. More evidence."

"True, but not evidence that he killed her."

"He didn't."

She blinked at his turnaround. "You changed your mind?"

He threw a duffel bag on the bed and rooted through it. "I don't think he killed her, because I don't think she's dead."

This again. "Her obit would say differently."

"She went to see Eileen."

Lucy leaned forward. "How do you know that? When?"

"Fletch told me that Eileen said the third daughter had been to visit her, and even had her name right. Sort of." He pulled a dark T-shirt over his head and shook the last of the water out of his long hair.

Lucy sighed. "Have you found out anything else about her?"

"Just that she worked in a museum and lived alone. I'd like to go to D.C. and dig around, but I thought I should stay here in case I got the call to Willow Marsh. I did get something last night from a friend who works at the *Post and Courier* and has gotten me some addresses in the past. Lots of Carpenters in Charleston."

"You think she spent time here?"

"She's around here," he replied, doggedly sticking to that present tense. "And sometimes people go where they have relatives. So I've driven around to many of them; talked to a few. I left the downtown addresses for today." He took a look at the heels she had on under her trousers. "You could have come with me, but Charleston's all bricks and you'll twist an ankle in those things."

She lifted her feet, showing the bright red soles of new Louboutins. "I can walk to the moon in these. I'll go with you."

He smiled and reached for her hand. "Why, 'cause you missed me?"

She let him pull her up, only a little surprised when he used enough force to bring her body against his. She looked him in the eye, only about an inch shorter in her heels. "Of course I didn't miss you."

He smiled and moved closer. "Liar." His lips were inches from hers, his face so close she could see the last few droplets of water on his lashes and brows. He held her gaze one heartbeat too long, then stepped away to the bed, flipped a pillow, and picked up a Ruger.

He gave her a daring look, and she shrugged. "It's your ass if you get caught carrying without a license."

"So it is." He grinned. "But you like my ass. I saw you looking."

Lucy walked to the door while he grabbed the key, a wallet, and sunglasses and tugged a baseball cap low over his eyes.

The look was hip and sexy, but that probably wasn't why he wore the hat.

"Trying to blend in with the crowd?"

"As if that's possible next to you." He held the door open, and as she passed him, he pushed a long lock of her hair over her shoulder and let his finger graze her neck. "You just stand out with your shocking hair and silky white suits."

"I'm not trying to hide," she said, her nape tingling from the contact.

"Admit it. You missed me." He curled a strand of her hair around his finger and leaned closer.

"You're delusional, Culver."

"You're transparent, Sharpe." He tugged the lock of hair. "Tell the truth. You've been rolling around in sweaty sheets thinking about me."

"As I recall, you've already admitted it's the other way around."

"Hell, yeah." He reached behind her and hung a Do Not Disturb sign on the knob and tucked it into the jamb. "And at least I'm honest about it."

The first address was a dead lead, but since the walk took them along the seawall known as the Battery, and through a park shaded with ancient live oaks and easy paths, on a sunny autumn day next to the most gorgeous woman on earth, Jack opted to focus on the positive.

The sun danced over the Atlantic, and across the water, the flags of Fort Sumter snapped in the wind. Tourists, locals, and a few cadets from the Citadel peppered Charleston's famous walkway that lined the southernmost tip of the city, and holding Lucy's hand to weave their way through the crowds was the most natural thing in the world.

Definitely a positive.

She didn't let go when they were alone, either. Nothing Lucy Sharpe did was arbitrary, even something as casual as holding someone's hand.

"Let's take Water Street," he suggested, guiding her toward a row of candy-colored three-story mansions, each bearing its own hyphenated name and rich history.

Going on gut in the direction of King Street, he cut through a narrow alley that opened up less than a block from the address for a B. Carpenter, 5 King Street.

The gray three-story apartment building was nestled on a beautiful, picturesque corner of the residential street, the front of the property loaded with trees, benches, and a water fountain.

"Pretty pricy real estate," Lucy noted.

Still holding her hand, he walked up to the front door, waiting until a young mother came out with a baby carriage. He held the door for the carriage, and they walked right into the locked lobby.

A row of brass mailboxes confirmed that 318 belonged to B. Carpenter, and they took a hushed elevator to the third floor.

"I think we intimidated the last couple," Lucy said, referring to the lead they'd started with that morning.

He smiled. "You're the intimidating one, Luce. That was the first time I had a door slammed in my face in three days."

She shrugged. "Then you handle this. I'll stay in the background."

He raked her from head to toe, enjoying every inch along the way. "Yeah, like that's possible."

When the elevator door opened, they found 318 at the end of the hall. Lucy stepped around the corner, where the trash chute was tucked away.

"I'll be back here," she said. "You do the talking."

He rang a bell and stood in the center of the doorway, letting his face be seen by the person he heard walking to the door.

"Can I help you?" a young man's voice called.

"I'm looking for Kristen." The use of the first name always made it sound personal, and not like he was a cop or PI. That usually worked to get the door opened and be told no one by that name lived there.

This time, it was met by silence.

"Is she here?"

He heard the deadbolt slide and watched the knob jiggle and the door slowly inch open. Through a crack about three inches wide, a young man with thin black hair and beady eyes looked back at him.

"Who do you want?" he asked.

"Kristen. Is she here?"

Another inch, revealing an undershirt and worn blue sleep pants. "Who are you?"

Every cell in his cop-instinct-honed body said he'd

hit the jackpot. Simply because the answer wasn't what it always was: Get lost, no Kristen here.

"My name's Jack Fuller." He used the alias Lucy had given him, half out of habit and half because he sensed he didn't want to come totally clean with this guy. "I'm a friend of hers."

The close-set eyes narrowed even more. "Then you would know she's dead."

Jack feigned shock. "No. Seriously? What happened?"

"When's the last time you talked to her?" he asked, looking Jack up and down. "And what did you say your name was again?"

"Jack Fuller. And I haven't seen her in, oh, two or three months."

"When she was here in May?"

"Yeah, last spring. I've been out of the country on business and this is the only address I had for her."

The guy opened the door just wide enough for Jack to see he was tall and wiry, probably stronger than he looked.

"Well, she's dead."

"I'm really sorry to hear that. And . . . you are . . . ?"

"I'm her brother, Theo." He looked a little perturbed. "Didn't she ever mention me?"

"Theo? Yeah, of course. You, uh, live here, right?"

"When I'm in town. My mother owns this apartment."

Jack put his hands in his pockets and shook his head. "Well, I'm really sorry to hear about Kristen. What happened?"

"Did you sleep with her?"

Jack actually drew back at the question. "Uh, no. I didn't." He studied the guy again. "I only met her once."

"Well, she's dead."

Every instinct in Jack screamed with certainty that something wasn't right with this guy. Guilt, instability . . . whatever, he knew where Kristen was.

"Do you mind telling me what happened?" Jack asked. "I really thought she was a great girl."

"She was hit by a car. Hit and run. Up in D.C., where she lived."

"God, what a shame. I'm . . . wow. I'm really sorry, man."

"Yeah, thanks." Theo shook the door a little to indicate he was about to close it. "Sorry to be the bearer of bad news."

"You know," Jack said, easing his foot closer to the opening. "You don't seem so upset about it."

He looked down at Jack's foot, then back up, his eyes blazing. "Back off, mister. She's dead and you can leave now. How upset I am is none of your business"

He slammed the door hard and snapped the deadbolt into place. Jack stood there for a second, staring at the lock, then turned to see Lucy inching out from behind the wall.

She lifted one eyebrow.

He motioned toward the stairwell behind her, and they both headed to it, not speaking until they were on the other side of a steel door.

"He's lying," Jack said.

"He's hiding something," she agreed.

"We have to get into that apartment." As he gazed through the chicken wire window of the fire door, a stunner of a thought occurred to him. "She could be in there."

They looked at each other for a moment, both zipping through various scenarios, when the sound of the door in the hall got their attention. Jack immediately moved them out of the line of vision through the window, seeing Theo leaving his apartment, a cell phone to his ear, a baseball cap pulled low over his eyes.

"Let's go in now."

"One of us should talk to him," Lucy said. "He has more information—a lot more. You've met him. You go surprise him downstairs and I'll go inside and look around."

"Do you know what you're looking for?"

"Kristen?"

He grabbed her chin and gave her a quick kiss. "That's my girl." Then he turned and jogged down the steps to meet up with Theo in the lobby.

Theo hadn't used the deadbolt, which made Lucy think he was in a huge hurry. Her pick got her into the apartment in less than two minutes.

Without making a sound and holding her breath for an alarm that didn't ring, Lucy stepped into a tiny vestibule that opened up into a living area and kitchen. Sunlight streamed through blinds along one wall, warming a hardwood floor and highlighting the light coat of dust on everything.

Whoever owned the place either wasn't around often or didn't clean. The furniture was nice but not expensive, the rooms decorated without too much imagination.

Her fingertips grazing her Glock, she scanned the area for any sign of who might live there and found plenty of it. Above the sofa, on bookshelves, over the TV, and on every end table were pictures. Family pictures, she surmised, and if the guy talking to Jack was thin, pale, and dark-haired, then he was really Kristen's brother, because he was in most of the pictures alongside a blond girl who was a carbon copy of Vanessa Porter.

Blonder as she got older, and perhaps a little heavier than Vanessa, but the face was so similar that there was no doubt they were related.

A heavyset woman had her arms around a graduate in one picture and was seated in a family portrait in another.

And right in the middle of it all was the motherlode of suprising clues: a signed eight by ten picture of Spessard B. Higgins. She squinted at the writing, making out the words.

"All the best to one of the best . . ." with a flourish of a signature. Not seriously personal, but not a mail-order autographed picture of a Supreme Court member, either.

Lucy moved through the rooms quickly. A master bedroom with a neatly made bed, a dresser with more pictures of Kristen and, she presumed, Theo.

The next room was cool and unoccupied. A single

bed. An empty dresser, no clothes in the closet. At the end of the hall was one more room, but that door was locked.

Lucy knocked lightly. Listened. She knocked again, pressing her ear against the door. Was Jack right? Was Kristen in there?

She tried the knob again; it was a flimsy residential lock. With one solid *thwack* of her hip against the door, it broke, and Lucy entered. This bedroom was very dark, with drawn blinds shutting out as much light as possible. A mattress on the floor was partially exposed with the fitted sheet twisted out of place, and the other sheets were balled at the bottom of the bed. Men's clothes were everywhere, and the room smelled damp and musty. Like . . . sex.

She sniffed again. Sweat and semen. She took a few steps into the room, noticing an industrial-strength padlock on an armoire.

Whatever Theo Carpenter was hiding, she'd bet it was in there. She tried to open it, but couldn't. Drawing her gun, she shot the lock off, then opened the doors. She blinked at the sight, her stomach rolling just a little.

Kristen Carpenter's image took up the whole back panel. She was naked, hair dripping, getting out of a shower. The picture was grainy, clearly taken from a hidden closed-circuit camera. The bottom shelf was filled with pages from the Internet.

Pages about poison. Knife wounds. Gun shots. Suffocation. Strangulation. Broken necks. Fatal accidents.

A mountain of instructions on how to kill someone.

Something slammed hard in her back, shocking a breath from her and knocking the gun from her hand.

"Wrong place, wrong time, lady," the voice in her ear growled. "Party's over for you."

Chapter
TEN

JACK BEAT THE elevator by about three seconds, pulling his hat low and pretending to check a mailbox as the doors rolled open.

The skinny prick wasn't on it.

Shit.

The elevator closed and went back up to the third floor, stopped and headed back down. Jack waited again, certain Theo would be there this time. But it was just an older woman carrying a toy poodle. As he was about to get in and ride it up, he glanced toward the back exit and saw the little blue Saturn roll by, driven by a blonde.

The hair color and the Saturn told him who it was. Kristen.

He jogged straight to the back, trotting down the three steps and throwing the glass door open to see the back end of the car turning right on a side street that connected to the back alley.

Was she parking? Coming home? Visiting her brother?

He *knew* it was her. The way she held her head, the wave in her hair, and it was the same car he'd seen her climb into in the park. He ran down the alley as fast as he could, leaping over some trash, maneuvering around parked cars.

He reached the corner, looked right, and caught a glimpse of the car heading south down one-way King Street. She must be looking for a place to park.

Rather than follow her in circles, he backtracked to the alley entrance of the building, swearing softly when he realized the door was locked. If she got inside and went upstairs, she'd run smack into Lucy.

He pulled out his phone to call her, but on the fourth ring he saw the blue Saturn turning into the alley again, driving right toward him. Great! He could get her when she walked up these stairs and . . . suddenly, the car stopped, screeched into reverse, and accelerated like crazy down Tradd Street.

There was too much traffic for her to get too far. And goddammit, he wasn't going to lose her this time.

He ran at full speed, knowing he shouldn't abandon Lucy in case Theo came home, but he had to get Kristen. And Lucy, of all people, could handle herself.

"Take the phone out!"

Lucy had no choice. The nose of a gun was slammed against her back, hard enough for her to know the guy had no compunction about pulling the trigger. Even if she kicked, whipped around, and took him down by hand, she'd be shot.

It was better to wait for a more intelligent way out of the situation—wait for him to make a sloppy move, to give her the right instant to act.

She slowly reached into her pocket and pulled out her cell phone, holding it up.

He seized it and she heard it clatter across the room.

"I don't know who the fuck you are, lady, and you know what? I don't care." He shoved her to the right. "Get in the closet. Now."

He jammed her into a dark closet so tiny that Lucy could barely move. His hard push made her lose her balance, and in the millisecond it took to get it back he slammed the door.

She reached for the door handle and jerked, but he'd locked it already.

She flattened herself against the wood, realizing that the door, like the tiny closet, was solid wood, and she had no chance of breaking it like the one that led into the room.

At least he hadn't shot her. She inched away from the door, deeper inside the closet, letting a thick wool coat fall over her. If he did decide to take a shot, it might offer some protection.

She stood still, listening for footsteps or an indication of where he was.

Theo Carpenter had a very sick thing for his sister, if she was indeed his sister. And he had enough information on how to kill her that Lucy would bet good money he had.

She heard movement, footsteps, some kind of distant repeated clicking, and tried to imagine what he was doing. Since he hadn't gone down to where Jack was waiting, Jack would be back up here shortly.

If Theo didn't answer the door, he'd break in. She closed her eyes for a second, grateful that he carried, whether it was legal or not.

If Theo *did* answer the door, would Jack figure out she was being held in here? After she didn't answer her phone? Probably. Then what would he do?

Knowing Jack, shoot the guy and come in and get her.

There was something to be said for that vigilante streak of his.

It had grown quiet outside and she put her hand on the doorknob, ready to use her lock-picking tool, but it was smooth, with no inside lock.

An inch of light came in through the bottom and she crouched down, peering underneath to look for Theo's feet.

Only to smell something bitter and horrific and powerful.

Rotten eggs? Sulfur? *Oh God*. Gas.

The distinct odor of mercaptan, added to natural gas so it could be detected in case of a leak. But would it be, in this quiet apartment building midmorning? Would anyone call the fire department?

More important, would they do it fast enough? Because if he'd turned on all the burners on the stove, it would only take one spark to start a fire.

And she would be locked in the closet.

She backed up and threw herself against the door,

attacked the handle, kicked, pounded, and screamed as loudly as she could.

She immediately blew all the air out of her lungs and forced her body into a stand, willing herself not to give in to the inevitable sleep that exposure to the gas would cause.

She closed her eyes and remembered the Internet research in Theo's armoire. Death by asphyxiation from exposure to gas. Low levels couldn't kill her. But being trapped in a closet when the building was on fire certainly could.

Where is Jack?

"Damn it!" She cursed herself for not having a phone or gun.

The gas fumes grew stronger as Lucy fought with the door, forcing herself to take shallow breaths.

Ten minutes passed. Fifteen.

Where in God's name was Jack Culver?

She started to slide down, too dizzy to stand. Crouched on the floor, she stuck her face between her knees and her chest, taking advantage of the little pocket of air.

Then she smelled smoke and heard the pop as something caught fire. Help would come now. And maybe they'd find her, she thought sleepily, her brain slower with every passing second.

She opened her mouth to scream again but didn't have the strength.

Her head felt as if it was no longer attached, her ears ringing and her nose starting to sting from the first tendrils of smoke that curled under the door.

She managed to get out of her jacket and put it over her face, praying for a smoke alarm. For a solution. For Jack.

Her head cleared for a second; then the fumes hit her brain. Her eyes rolled back in her head just as a window exploded with a loud pop, and the sound of glass crashing reverberated everywhere.

At the edges of her vision, darkness closed in. Lucy dug deep into her training, taking shallow breaths, the jacket still over her face. She threw herself against the door again, but it was too much.

She rolled into a ball, facedown, giving into the gas, knowing the flames would burn through the door any minute. But she didn't have the strength to fight them.

Her last thought was of Cilla, and why she'd never told Jack the truth.

Jack pulled out his phone, hating himself for losing the car again. He looked up at the building and saw smoke. On the third floor. In the apartment at the end.

Before he could even process that, the window he was staring at blasted open, the explosion literally rocking the ground underneath him.

Lucy!

He ran at full speed, barreling to the front entrance and yanking the door from the hand of someone running out screaming, "Gas leak! Fire!"

He tore up the stairs, dodging panicked residents running down. The fire door was open as people streamed through it, far too freaked out to notice that he shot the door to apartment 318 open.

"Lucy!" He took in the kitchen, engulfed in flames, and the burning blinds along the living room windows. "Are you here? Lucy!"

She hadn't answered her phone, and he'd called four times. His gut burning, he dropped to his knees and headed in, not sure if it was the most heroic or most stupid thing he'd ever done.

She *had* to have gotten out of here. She was the most resourceful woman in the world.

"Lucy!"

But what if she hadn't? The place reeked of gas—enough to slow down anyone, including Lucy. He might die trying, but he wouldn't leave her.

He crouched down, eyes tearing, as he headed toward a hallway, looking in empty rooms, screaming her name as he got to the last. The roar of the fire was loud, but not loud enough to drown out a thump. A voice. A cry for help.

God almighty, she was in the closet.

"Get away from the lock!" he hollered. "I'm going to shoot it off."

He did, yanking open the door as she spilled out. He scooped up her nearly unconscious body and ran from the bedroom, staying low.

The hallway was total chaos with people screaming, alarms blaring, and smoke rolling through in black clouds. In the stairwell he placed her on her feet, holding onto her.

"Lucy." He shook her and her eyelids fluttered, her head lolling. "Look at me."

She was alive. That was all that mattered. He threw his arms around her and squeezed her, dragging her toward the steps.

"Kristen . . ." she muttered.

Yeah, Kristen. He'd been so determined to find that woman he almost let this one die. Sick with the thought, he pulled her down the steps. "Come on, Luce. You need fresh air. Let's get out of here."

Sirens howled and the shouts of firefighters rose up the stairs. But Lucy wouldn't move. "Jack, there's . . . stuff . . . Kristen's pictures."

"Move, Lucy!"

A firefighter in full gear came barreling up the stairs. "She need help?"

"No," Jack said. "I'll get her down there."

He half-lifted her and headed down the stairs. She gave up the fight and let him hold her up, but by the time they were at the bottom, her head seemed much clearer and her eyes were focused again.

"Let's get out of here," he said, pulling her to the street. "We don't want to get caught in this."

He plowed through the gawkers and firefighters, walking briskly against the crowd, the madness the only reason no one even gave them two looks.

He hailed a cab and saw the fight cross her face, then the surrender. He gave her a nudge into the back of the taxi, then slid in next to her.

"Vendue Inn," he told the driver. Then he turned to Lucy, who was still pale, still gulping air.

"Oh my Go—"

He didn't let her finish. He pulled her into his arms and smothered her face with a kiss, breathing his air into her mouth, his life into her body.

And his love, his useless, unwanted, unrequited, undeniable love, into the soul of the only woman who mattered.

She managed to pull away, looking at him like he'd lost his mind.

He had. He'd almost lost her. And even though he'd never have her, he couldn't live if she weren't somewhere on the face of this earth.

"Why are you kissing me?" she demanded.

He tried to smile. Tried to play the sex card that he always used to cover his real feelings.

Because I love you.

He crushed the words and kissed her again. "What? You never heard of Rescue Sex?"

She almost laughed. "You're out of your mind, you know that?"

"Yeah." He'd known it for a long time. But she never would.

"Where were you?" she asked.

"I saw Kristen."

Closing her eyes, she shook her head. "I really think she's dead, Jack. And you'll never guess whose picture is—or was—hanging on the living room wall of that apartment. Higgie's."

CHAPTER ELEVEN

"I NEED TO be alone, Diane."

"I'm sorry, Justice Higgins, I can't allow that." The nurse quietly closed her novel and looked across the office. "Doctor's orders are clear. I assure you, I don't mind sitting here while you go through your paperwork." She smiled benevolently. "I can call the male nurse if you wish to visit the men's room."

"I wish to be alone in my office." He gave her a matching phony smile, pulling out his mental file on everything he'd picked up about Diane since she'd arrived with the other nurses for round-the-clock babysitting.

She was about forty-two, maybe a little older. She had a teenager whom he'd heard her fight with on the phone when she thought he was out of earshot. She was single. She was probably killing herself to make ends meet, and worried about the boy at home while she was on this assignment.

So she either wanted to get back to her son, or make more money.

Whatever her weak link was, Higgie would find it. And exploit it. That's how he got everyone to do what he wanted.

"Diane, I would very much like you to remain in this room while I go to the back, alone, for thirty minutes."

"I'm sorry, Justice. I will arrange for a different nurse to stay with you or call your wife, but I am not leaving you alone. Those are the doctor's orders."

His wife was the last person he wanted with him.

"How much money do you make, Diane?"

Her smile was tight, probably the same I-know-what-you're-up-to look she gave her teenager. "Not enough, and I will not accept anything to leave you alone, Justice."

He feigned insult. "I was merely going to offer you a letter of recommendation. A letter written and signed by me about your extraordinary performance in difficult circumstances. A letter that would live in your file and ensure job security or perhaps a new position, should you seek one."

"I know what you're doing, Justice Higgins."

He leaned forward and gave her a piercing look. "Or I could write a letter that said just the opposite. That would probably get you sent back home quickly, back to . . . what's your son's name again?"

"Tyler." She eyed him with surprise, then disappointment. God, he hated that look. That instant when someone realized he wasn't a saint. But for every person who glimpsed his darker side, ten million didn't. A few had to be sacrificed.

He opened his drawer and drew out a single sheet of creamy parchment paper and reached for the Montblanc he'd been given by the last president. "Which letter should I write?"

Slowly, she stood. "I guess this is a no-win situation for me."

He nodded. "That is the essence of being a judge. Now, if we can strike a deal here, my dear, you could have a fruitful and comfortable stay at Willow Marsh, with a much stronger position at your professional bargaining table next time you sit there. Or . . ." He held up his hands. "Home to Tyler."

She exhaled in resignation and defeat. "Would you like me to wheel you into the back bedroom, sir?"

"That won't be necessary. I can operate this thing."

"You can?"

Of course that surprised her; he'd let nurses push him for the last few days. No need for them to know he was already working on his own mobility.

"Don't leave this room," he warned, knowing that some security camera would pick up her image the moment she stepped into the hall, and one of Lucy's ubiquitous men would be up there in a flash.

"Open that door." He nodded to the exit that led to his private rooms. "And wait for me."

She did, holding one of the two doors for him as he powered himself through to the other side. As he passed, he gave her a look. "I'll know if you leave. Or call for assistance."

She just nodded and closed the door behind him. He locked it and glided the high-end chair past the bathroom and weight room to the bedroom he used when he worked late. Or didn't want to be near Marilee.

The trick was going to be moving the rug.

But he had to know that while he was in the hospital, no one had disturbed the space.

He maneuvered the chair to the bottom of the bed and tried to kick the carpet away. Cursing the excruciating pain in his leg, he looked around the room for some kind of tool, his gaze landing on the long metal sculpture of an ibis hanging over the bed. It would work, if he could get it down.

He motored over and reached to knock one side off its hook, the metal hitting the headboard with a loud clunk.

"Justice Higgins!" Diana called, a note of panic in her voice. "Are you all right?"

"I'm fine," he said, clenching his jaw to work the metal sculpture down. It landed on the bed with a soft thud.

He lifted one corner of the throw rug but it flopped back into place. Biting back a frustrated grunt, he hooked the long, pointed beak on some fringe, then pressed the lever of the wheelchair to use its power to pull back the rug.

It worked, revealing nothing but wide planks of dark hardwood. To the naked eye, nothing at all.

To him, the ultimate security. Once Marilee had invested hundreds of thousands into an underground heating, cooling, and irrigation system for her precious garden, adding on to it for his private purposes wasn't difficult and since he'd done the work while she was spending a summer in Europe, no one but the builder knew it existed.

Making it the perfect hiding place, the ultimate safe room, and an escape route without his ever being seen.

The dial was going to be tricky, but he gripped the body of the metal bird and worked the tip of its beak carefully, pressing the numbers that opened the door. He couldn't go down until he could walk again; but he just wanted to be sure no one had found this. And he would know—instantly.

The floor silently slid back on metal rails, revealing a dark black hole and a curved metal staircase leading down. He peered over the edge into the darkness, at the sixth step where a feather was . . .

Not visible from the damn chair. He *had* to be sure everything was untouched. Using the steel bird for leverage, he leaned as far over the edge as he could, but still couldn't see.

Was the feather still in its place? He risked another inch and one front wheel suddenly slipped over the edge, tipping the chair precariously. Instinct made him stab the metal beak into the floor, just in time to keep the whole chair from rolling into the hole and sending him plummeting.

He waited, frozen, knowing that one wrong move could cost him his life. Should he call for the nurse? Someone could break down the door, but then his secret would be out.

He could *do* this, damn it.

With a low growl, he pushed the metal beak harder into the floor, using all his strength to right the chair. If he could just get that one wheel back up . . .

Sweat stung his neck and trickled down his back. He bit his lip so hard he drew blood. He stabbed the beak harder into the floor, actually bending the metal from the weight. His arms started shaking and he opened his mouth to call Diane, just as the wheel lifted back over the edge. The jolt of it knocked the whole sculpted bird from his quivering hands and it fell into the stairwell, clunking all the way down until it thudded to the bottom.

Where he would have been, if the damn thing hadn't saved his life.

Air escaped his lungs with a whoosh of relief.

He'd left gouges in the floor, but they'd be covered by the rug. The next time Marilee traveled, he'd have them fixed. Using one shaking finger, he motored away from the hole, closed the door, and flipped the carpet back in place.

If anyone ever found out about his secret place, he'd do whatever needed to be done to silence them. He could do anything.

Hadn't he just defied death one more time?

Lucy didn't decompress after her brush with death. She didn't even shower. For the next few hours, she sat cross-legged and barefoot on Jack's unmade bed, making calls on his phone until Avery could get a new one delivered, dispensing orders, digging through databases, and firing questions at Jack.

By late afternoon, she had the Bullet Catcher machine in full force searching for every morsel of information about Theo Carpenter, working fast so they could get back to Willow Marsh for dinner.

Until Marilee called and canceled, saying that the justice wasn't feeling well.

"Fine with me," Lucy said when she told Jack why Marilee had called. "More time to work on this."

"Or make a little side trip." He stood, grabbing the soot-covered jacket she'd flung on a chair. "Come on, let's go."

"Where?" she asked, starting to push herself off the bed

"Columbia. It's a little over two hours, and if we hurry, we'll catch Eileen after dinner and before she sleeps."

"I don't want to go."

"You don't? All this work you've done, and you don't even want to meet the woman? Why not?"

Ten different reasons echoed in her head. "We have too much work to do."

"Make calls in the car."

"We might have to go back to Willow Marsh at any time."

"You have a team of experts there. You can be gone a few more hours."

She blew out a breath. "She's in mourning, Jack. She just found out her daughter is dead. She wants to be alone."

This last one got her an incredulous look. "She's been alone for thirty years."

When she didn't move, he tossed the jacket onto the bed. "Stay if you want, Luce. I need to talk to Eileen about when Kristen came to see her."

So he hadn't given up on that. "Jack, I told you—"

"Plus, they moved her back to the prison infirmary yesterday, and when I called, I found out the head nurse has quit. If I don't get over there and tell those imbeciles she's allergic to strawberries, she'll be covered in hives by next week."

Lucy's mouth fell open a little. "You really care about her."

"Imagine that. A human heart beating in my hairy chest." He gathered his stuff and headed to the door, pausing to look at her. "Will you be here when I get back?"

She hesitated just one second, then changed her mind, something she rarely did. "I'll go with you. But on the way over, you have to tell me why."

"Why what?"

"Why this particular woman matters so much to you."

He smiled. "All right, Luce. Let's go."

He didn't tell her that, or anything, for more than an hour. While he drove the straight, boring highway across the state, she watched the sun setting behind the hills on the horizon, and nearly slept.

She must have actually dozed off, because he woke her when he put his hand over hers and said, "You know about Fletch?"

She opened her eyes and looked at him. "What about Fletch?"

"About his childhood."

"Some. I know his father was rough on him, and that he left home as a teenager and lived in the bush with Aborigines. Why?"

"That's our common ground. When I met Fletch on that job in Sydney, before I brought him into the Bullet Catchers, we got loaded one night and swapped similar stories."

"Why are you telling me this?"

"Because I want you to know that what I'm about to share with you is not something I tell people . . . sober."

She curled her fingers into his, waiting.

"And I like to keep it short," he added.

"All right." Meaning no big emotional revelations, she supposed.

"I watched my father beat my mother."

"Oh—"

"To death."

"Oh." She squeezed his hand. "Jack."

He stared straight ahead, the only sign of emotion a slight pulsing of a vein in his neck.

"How old were you?"

"Ten. Old enough to ache to stop him, young enough to be terrified to try. And he got off on a technicality." He snorted softly. "Our marvelous legal system at work."

"So Eileen is, what? Your chance to make things right?"

He sliced her with a look. "Yeah, maybe. And I want to see the son of a bitch rot in jail and fry in the chair for what he did. I want justice."

"You want retribution."

"Semantics, sweetheart." He took his hand away and turned the wheel.

The hills around Camille Griffin Graham Correctional Institute, as it had been called for many years since it was changed from a state penitentiary, looked far too beautiful and peaceful to be the outskirts of a prison.

Jack had arranged for a quick security check, and he walked through the place like a regular, even on a first-name basis with a few people.

A nurse and a stocky female security guard manned the infirmary desk, a stark reminder that it was a prison.

"I heard Risa flew the coop," he said to the nurse.

"That's right," she said. "Quit suddenly a few weeks ago."

"Really? I thought they'd have to carry the old battle-ax out of here in a box."

She looked up at him, her smile tight. "Well, I'm the new battle-ax, honey, and I'm not the pushover she was." She checked something on a form and handed it to the guard, then gave a cold look to Jack. "Inmate 604353 is the third door to the left. You have fifteen minutes."

"I wonder if—"

"Starting now."

Jack closed his mouth and nodded, guiding Lucy away. "Risa was at least human," he said.

"Meaning she flirted with you."

"No, meaning she was kind to the patients. This is why I want Eileen out of this place."

"Jack, they're inmates first and patients second."

Inside, one bed was empty, but in the other, a tiny, bald woman lay sleeping, her skin yellow in the fluorescent light of the windowless room. Jack walked around to the other side of the bed and studied her for a minute before leaning closer.

"Hey, pretty lady," he whispered. "I brought a friend to meet you."

Who would ever have thought Jack Culver had such a tender streak? Lucy pulled her gaze from his face to study the woman who somehow brought out a side of him that she would've sworn didn't exist.

Eyelashless lids fluttered and a breath of a smile pulled at Eileen's dry lips. Though she was only fifty-six, a lifetime of pain and heartache had obviously aged her as much as the battle with cancer.

"Is that my angel Jack?"

Lucy looked across the bed and Jack winked at her, not the least bit embarrassed by the comment. "In the flesh."

"Who's that with you?" Eileen inched her head to the right to focus on Lucy, then her eyes widened with recognition. "Oh, I've heard about you. You're Lucy."

For the third time in less than a minute, Lucy was stunned. "Yes, I am," she said. "And I've heard about you, too, Eileen."

"You helped find my daughters," she said. "Thank you."

Lucy put her hand on Eileen's. "Any help you received from my company is because of Jack, and because Miranda and Vanessa have fallen in love with two of the men who work for me. So they're like family now."

Despite the pain on her face, she managed a warm smile. "Aren't they pretty girls?"

"Very pretty," Lucy agreed. "Smart and resourceful, too."

"How do you feel, Eileen?" Jack asked. "Was the trip back from the hospital okay?"

"Fine. But Risa's gone."

"I heard."

"I don't like the new one," she said in a whisper. "She's a bitch."

"I know," he whispered back.

Something passed between them, a silent communication that spoke volumes about their relationship. Something so strong that Lucy couldn't help but wonder: since their bond was so powerful, why hadn't Eileen told him the whole truth yet? Was he being fooled by her?

"Hey, I heard you met my buddy, Fletch," Jack said, pulling a chair over to sit by her, and indicating that Lucy do the same on the other side.

"The one with the accent."

"Yep." Jack inched closer. "He told me you had a very special visitor."

Eileen just tightened her lips and shook her head quickly.

"She was here, wasn't she, Eileen? Did you tell her something that you haven't even told me?"

If it was possible for Eileen's thin skin to go whiter, it did. Her eyes closed and she tried to swallow.

"Jack," Lucy said softly. "Don't." He had no idea what dark hole this poor woman had fallen into. There was no way to describe it.

Just thinking about it, Lucy's own dark hole opened up, her stomach churning with familiar grief.

Eileen gave her a grateful look. "I can't talk about her yet," she whispered.

"I know," Lucy said, reaching for her hand. Only a woman who'd lost a child could understand the depths of that misery. Even a child a woman never knew.

"You can," Jack insisted. "You don't have to be scared anymore. And, Eileen . . . she's—"

"Jack!" Lucy glared at him. "Please. For one minute, come talk to me outside."

He looked at her, ready to argue, but he must have seen something dead serious in her eyes, so he stood and followed her into the hall.

"Lucy, I have to find out who she was with and when she was here—"

"Don't you dare give that woman false hope," Lucy hissed. "When the truth comes out, she'll have to grieve all over again. Don't you understand that? It could kill her."

"What if I'm right, Lucy? I know that you find it impossible to believe that anyone could know more than you do, but what if I'm right?"

"Then you can tell her when you know for sure— without making her die inside all over again."

He surveyed her face long and hard as he considered that. Blowing out a breath, he said, "Okay, fine.

I'm going to talk to the nurse, and to the guard to check her visitor list from when she was in the hospital. You talk to her for a minute."

She watched him walk down the hall, then went back into the room, her heartbeat fast.

She hated this subject. This pain. This reliving.

"Jack went to talk to the new nurse," Lucy said.

"When I was first in prison," Eileen replied, turning her head to look at Lucy, "I used to have fantasies. Now I have Jack."

Lucy laughed softly. "He's pretty good fuel for a woman's fantasies, I'll give you that."

"Not those kind," Eileen said. "Different fantasies. About . . . being free."

"Eileen." She closed her fingers around the aluminum bed rail and took a breath. "I'm sorry about Kristen."

Eileen flinched.

"When you lose a child," Lucy continued softly, "you lose a limb."

"It's more like an organ," the other woman replied. "A heart ripped out and . . . and . . ."

"A hole is left behind."

Eileen surveyed Lucy's face, a deep crease forming between her missing eyebrows. "You know."

Lucy nodded, swallowing hard. "There's nothing you can do about the hole."

"And the pain? Does it go away? Does it ever become . . . bearable?"

"No," Lucy said. "But you learn to live with it."

"Oh God." Eileen's voice cracked. "I can't. It didn't

hurt this much when I . . . when I went to prison. Or when I gave them up for adoption."

"Because you had hope," Lucy said. "You had your fantasies and dreams. Now they've been stolen forever."

"By him," she stated. "By . . ."

"Justice Higgins?"

"Yes." Eileen reached out for Lucy, her touch desperate. "I'm scared. The girls . . . and Jack. If he knows, he'll kill them. I worry so much, I think it could kill me."

"You should use your strength to heal, Eileen. Miranda and Vanessa are safe and protected, and Jack is smart and capable."

"He needs lots of protection," Eileen said. "He's got a tender heart and it's been broken."

It had? Another side of Jack she didn't know. "He's very fond of you."

"And you."

The slight vehemence in the statement surprised Lucy, but she leaned forward, determined to get the conversation back to Eileen's secrets. Maybe, since they shared grief, Eileen would tell Lucy what she'd refused to tell anyone else.

"What happened the night Wanda was killed?" Lucy asked.

She looked away, at the ceiling. "What happened to your child?"

Lucy swallowed. "Did you see him pull the trigger?"

"Was it a girl, too? A baby? It must have been, you're so young yourself."

"Did he wait for her to die, or run away from the crime the instant he shot her?"

"Did you ever get to hold your baby?" Eileen reached for Lucy's hand again. "I think that might even be worse, having held her."

Oh, yes. Much worse. "If the gun was in your car and he ran in the other direction, do you think it's possible he had an accomplice?"

"Did your baby die of natural causes?"

They stared at each other, the standoff hanging in the air. Lucy closed her eyes and dug for strength.

"No. She didn't. And the only moment of true peace I've ever had since that day was when the man who killed her died."

"He did? How?"

Lucy stood and looked down at Eileen. "I shot a hole in his heart to match the one in mine."

Eileen didn't flinch. She didn't even blink.

"I'm scared," she finally admitted. "He can do anything."

"So can I."

Eileen nodded slowly. "I guess you can. No wonder Jack loves you."

She's given to fantasies, Lucy reminded herself. "What happened that night, Eileen? Did he invite you to meet him in that alley? Did he set you up?"

"He called me. I remember so clearly, because I had just gotten one of those expensive phone machines and it was the very first message I ever got."

"Did you see him shoot Wanda Sloane?"

"I was hiding behind the wall, and they stopped.

He was kissing her, his back was to me . . . then . . ." She bit her lip. "You really shot the man who murdered your baby? Yourself?"

"Yes, I did."

Two strong hands landed on her shoulders, making Lucy jump and whip around to come face-to-face with Jack, whose gaze was firmly on Eileen.

"Did you see Spessard Higgins kill Wanda Sloane, Eileen?" he demanded.

How much had he heard?

Eileen just looked at him, her eyes swimming with unshed tears.

"Did he, Eileen?" Jack's hands tightened on Lucy's shoulders as his voice grew insistent.

"Yes."

He inched Lucy to the side so he could get closer to the bed. "Can I prove that?"

"He was having an affair with her. She wrote him letters. I saw them."

"That doesn't prove murder," Lucy said.

"But it might prove motive," Jack replied. "Or be enough to blackmail his ass."

"Or you can just let her shoot him!" Eileen pointed to Lucy. "For me."

Jack cut his gaze to Lucy, a curious and bemused look on his face. "That's not usually her style, but maybe we can work something out. For you."

Eileen blinked, sending a tear down her cheek. "I always thought my guardian angel would be a lady," she told Lucy. "So when Jack showed up, I didn't believe in him. But you're the one I've been waiting for. You are."

Lucy took the woman's hand. "We just want to see justice done."

"No," Eileen said. "You kill him for me."

Lucy bit back a smile. "Maybe we can just make sure the right person is in jail for this murder."

"That's not enough." Her nails dug into Lucy's skin. "You know that's not enough."

Lucy lifted Eileen's hand and kissed her knuckle. "It will feel just as good." That was a lie, but she had to say it. "Now I'll let you say good-bye to Jack."

As she walked into the hall, she heard Eileen say, "Oh, Jack. No wonder you love her."

She didn't wait to hear his smart-ass retort; she couldn't take it right now. She moved away from the door and leaned against the cool wall, closed her eyes, and tried to breathe.

"I had no idea you had a hidden vigilante streak, Ms. Sharpe."

"I don't." She stood straighter and squared her shoulders. "And I had no idea you loved me."

She expected a matching "I don't," but he just shrugged and smiled.

"Guess we were bound to find out each other's secrets sooner or later."

CHAPTER TWELVE

MILE AFTER MONOTONOUS mile, the darkness almost as suffocating as the silence in the rented SUV, Lucy visualized sturdy cement blocks that she could line up and pile high into an impenetrable wall around her.

But Jack would just tear it down. He was a master at timing . . . and of getting into places where he didn't belong. Like her bed. And now, her soul.

Any minute, the barrage would begin.

You had a baby? You lost a child? You shot the killer? You survived that, Lucy? Is that what turned your hair white? Is that why you need to control everything right down to the last molecule? Is that why you devoted your life to security and investigations? Is that why—

"Are you cold?"

She'd lifted her legs and had both arms wrapped around them in a classic fetal position. "No." Not on the outside, anyway.

He just stared ahead, letting the pressured silence build back up again.

So no discussion of the murder, the victim, the truth. Of the crime that took them to Columbia, or the one she'd confessed to Eileen.

Seeing her agony mirrored on Eileen Stafford's face had cut her to the core, and made her remember that all the success and money in the world could not erase what she had endured.

"You hungry?" he asked when they passed a sign for an exit with fast food and gas.

"Not really, but you can get something."

He got a sandwich at a gas station, eating and sipping a soda while he drove. She didn't even open the water he brought her.

Finally, they pulled into the parking garage at the Vendue Inn. She stopped at the front desk to pick up the clothes she'd had Avery order from Saks for her, not even looking in the bag. With every step, she coiled tighter, ready to unravel. Somehow she held it together until they got to the room.

The privacy sign was still tucked into the jamb. In the room, the giant bed remained unmade and the desk was exactly as they'd left it.

Still, Jack gave the room a thorough check while she dropped her handbag on a chair and shed her weapon.

"I'm taking a bath," she announced, closing the bathroom door with a solid thud.

Without turning on a light, she moved robotically to the oversize tub surrounded by marble. She grabbed something that looked like bath gel, opened it, and sniffed coconut.

Fine. Anything but lavender.

She dumped it into the water and undressed. A haze of steam lifted from the water, and when she climbed into the tub, she sucked in a breath at the burn.

But that's what she wanted. Physical pain to fight the emotional.

She lay back and closed her eyes.

She wanted to be coddled and carried away to another world, where people didn't kill and mothers didn't drown in sorrow. She wanted to hold Cilla. She wanted to take Eileen's pain away.

It seemed like hours in the bath, but the water was still hot when the door opened and a stream of light preceded Jack's entrance, then darkness descended as he closed it behind him.

"I brought you some chocolate," he said, approaching the bath, even though it had to be pitch black to his unadjusted eyes.

"I don't eat chocolate."

"I know that, but . . ." He crouched down on the floor to face her. "The only other option in the minibar was alcohol, and I didn't think I could take booze and you naked in the same room. And I thought it might make you feel better."

He unwrapped a large foil-covered candy bar, and it made her think of when he'd undressed her.

He took a bite of the corner and she watched the chocolate slide between his lips. Would she taste it when she kissed him?

"Look at you," he said, meeting her gaze. "I believe I see a hint of a smile behind the bubbles."

"An optical illusion. Did it ever occur to you that I want to be alone?"

"Then you should have locked the door."

He took another bite, and the faintest hint of bittersweet chocolate mixed with coconut in the air, the aroma almost as enticing as the way he watched her from under his lashes.

"You sure?" He held the candy out. "It's damn good. Sweet and rich and decadent."

She lifted a bubble-filled hand. "Let me smell it."

He slipped the foil covering into her hand. "That'll make you want it even more."

She inhaled, closing her eyes, letting the delicious scent shoot straight to the pleasure zone in her brain and wipe away some pain.

That's what she needed. Pleasure. She sniffed again. "Wow. That smells good. Is it good?"

He laughed softly at the little tone of desperation in her voice. "Yeah, it's good. Why don't you eat it?"

"No." She handed it back. "Chocolate gives me migraines."

"Really." He helped himself to a healthy bite, sitting on the floor. "I didn't know that about you."

She laid her head back and closed her eyes so she didn't have to watch the deadly combination of Jack and chocolate. "There's a lot you don't know about me."

He was silent for a few seconds. "Evidently there is."

Ah, here we go.

A few bubbles popped. Lucy exhaled. He snapped off another piece of chocolate. She should just tell him the whole story, unemotionally. Get it out, get it over with.

She lifted a leg from the water, setting it on the edge of the tub so foam and water dribbled down over the marble ledge, the air instantly chilling her skin. His gaze moved to her calf, then her toes, with a look that probably matched the one she'd given the chocolate.

Her pleasure zone tingled.

"All right," she finally said.

"You ready now?"

"Yeah. Give me a bite. A small one."

Smiling, he broke off a corner of chocolate and scooted closer. "Let me feed it to you so you don't get bubbles all over it and ruin the taste."

"Okay."

First, he waved the bar under her nose. "Did you know that the sense of smell is the most powerful one you have?"

Her eyelids fluttered as she inhaled it, her mouth already watering. "Yes, I know that. Memories are triggered by scents."

Like lavender.

She bit it right out of his hand, her teeth scraping his skin.

"Ouch! You're vicious when you give in to temptation, aren't you?"

She just stayed very still, letting heaven ooze over her tongue, her eyes closed, her sudsy hand closing over Jack's arm unconsciously.

His chuckle brought her out of the taste trance.

"Oh, that's divine," she said as she swallowed, getting the last little bits of sin and deliciousness mixed in her mouth.

"So are you."

She opened her eyes to see him studying her breasts, exposed as the bubbles dripped away when she had sat up to take her bite. A totally different kind of pleasure pulled low in her belly.

She didn't move.

Neither did he. "So is the headache a guarantee after one bite, or can you escape punishment for your bad deeds?"

"It depends on which bad deeds."

"Eating chocolate. Letting me see you naked. Killing for revenge. I guess the list of bad deeds is pretty long."

She knew he'd get there eventually. "I don't always get a headache," she said, scooping up a handful of bubbles and letting them fold through her fingers. "I've learned to manage the pain."

"Have you?"

She refused to look at him, knowing the sympathy and friendship and, God, something even deeper she'd see in his eyes would break her.

"Go ahead," he whispered. "Tell me."

"I can't, Jack. I just can't talk about it."

"You don't have to," he said, finding her hand and kissing her knuckles. "But if you want to, I'll listen. And I won't pass judgment."

"I'm not afraid of judgment. If I'm in trouble for what I did, then I can burn in hell and I don't care."

"Then what are you afraid of, Lucy?"

What *was* she afraid of? The pain? The exposure?

The very memory of what she had and lost? The guilt over the horrific ramifications of her actions?

He set her hand on the marble and ran his fingers up her arm, over her shoulder, to the white streak of hair that ran down the left side of her part.

"Did you get this when she died?" His voice was low and gentle.

She shook her head. "Later."

She didn't want to do this. She didn't want to cry and talk and dredge up the past. She wanted comfort and peace, and this sure as hell wasn't the way to get it.

She shot up, standing so fast that water splashed him. "I'm done now."

He stood more slowly, running a finger along the suds on her stomach on his way up. His fingertip stopped just below her breast, and their eyes met.

"What are you afraid of?" he repeated.

The burn of his finger made her want it to move higher, to touch every inch of her, to make her forget. "I'm not afraid of anything," she whispered, arching just enough to send a subtle message.

Touch me. Make me forget.

"I think you are," he replied, moving closer. "I think you're afraid of ever being vulnerable. And pain makes you vulnerable. Wanting something you can't have makes you vulnerable." He stroked the bottom of her breast. "Welcome to my world."

"What do you want that you can't have?"

He caressed her skin, gliding over the wet flesh, making her nipple bud in his palm. "What do you think?"

She sighed, a soft and ragged release. "You know you can have me. Right now, right here. On the floor, in the dark."

"That's not what I want this time." His voice was gruff, his look so intense, it made her dizzy.

She cupped the massive erection that bulged against his jeans. "I don't believe you."

"A boner?" He let out a dry laugh. "Yeah, that's what you do to me, Luce. Every time I'm near you. But that isn't the only thing I want."

She couldn't let go. She curled her fist against the outline of him, instantly remembering his size and power and stamina, and the way he'd filled her up on that hut floor on the other side of the world. He'd made her forget. He'd made her insane and sweaty and wild with climaxes that healed her. Not completely, but they'd helped.

"I want you, Jack," she said. "Now. Tonight."

She felt his erection stiffen even more, and he winced. "Last time didn't turn out so good, as I recall."

"Is that a no?"

He laughed. "Hell, no. It's a warning that you might be biting into one big piece of chocolate, baby. And you might like the way it tastes tonight, but you're gonna have a motherfucker of a headache when you wake up in the morning."

"That assumes I'm going to sleep." She tightened her fingers, her throat dry with how much she wanted to open his fly and touch him. She wetted her lips and looked up in invitation. When he didn't move, she took one step closer and let her wet and hardened nipples graze his T-shirt.

Why wouldn't he kiss her?

"You want permission?" She took his lower lip between her teeth and sucked it in, tasting chocolate and mint. "Here it is. Do what you want. To me." He still didn't kiss her back, but his hard-on felt like it could come out of his jeans. "Right here, Jack. Just like last time."

He gripped her waist and lifted her from the tub in one easy move.

"Not the floor." He scooped her into his arms, going to the door and flipping it open with one hand while holding her steady in his arms. "And not anything like last time."

He dropped her onto the sheets he must have smoothed while she bathed, locking her in place with his knees as he unsnapped his jeans and lowered his zipper, letting himself spring free.

"I liked last time," she admitted, the sight of his engorged erection twisting her desire so tight.

"Last time I just wanted to fuck you blind, stupid, and sorry, Lucy."

The words stunned her, forcing her up on her elbows. "And this time?"

One side of his mouth quirked up into that insolent smile she hated and loved, and he lowered his head, breathed softly on her mouth, then denied her the kiss she wanted. He skimmed right over her breasts and stomach without making contact.

Wordlessly, he lifted her knees, spread her legs, and dropped his head.

And licked her. Once. Swift and hard and furious.

She bucked and gasped.

Then again—slower.

She balled the sheets in her fists at the sensation of his hot tongue on the tight knot of arousal.

The third time was slowest of all, making her crazy, making her heart wallop against her ribs, and her thighs want to squeeze his head as she groaned.

His teeth closed over her in a gentle bite; then he sucked, swirled, and slipped his tongue so many times, she wanted to scream at the insane jolts of pleasure punching through her whole body.

His fingers gripped her thighs, then slid up over her stomach and found her breasts just long enough to tweak her nipples and earn another moan. Then he returned to her hips, lifted her a few inches off the bed, and flattened his tongue to taste her in one more endless, sinful stroke.

With the tip of his tongue, he circled her clitoris, maddeningly slow to start, then faster and faster, until she dug her fingers into his thick hair, fighting the urge to jam herself into his mouth.

He tucked his hands between her thighs and opened her gently with his thumbs, breathing fire on her moist flesh, whispering her name, moaning softly in appreciation of what he tasted and smelled and saw, taking more and more of her until he covered her whole mound with his open mouth.

Then he entered her, delving his tongue impossibly

deep, his broad, wide hands holding her hips firm as she arched and writhed and lost every last little bit of power over her own body, climaxing with exquisite, brutal, sweet pleasure against Jack's mouth.

She forgot everything, forgot the need for control. That's what Jack did to her. No one else ever managed that but him.

He kissed her quivering thighs, licked his way up her stomach, kneeling up to loom over her again, his hard, beautiful cock throbbing as though he'd enjoyed that as much as she did.

"Take your shirt off," she said.

He smiled, wiping his mouth with the back of his hand. "That's all you can say? 'Take your shirt off?' "

"Take your shirt off, please?"

He laughed and whipped it over his head in one easy move.

"Come close to me," she whispered, beckoning him to her face with her hand. "Come here. To me."

He lowered himself on top of her but still didn't kiss her mouth, instead tasting one breast, then the other, holding her like she was precious and using his magic tongue to make her back bow and her body hum again.

"I want to kiss you, Jack."

"You just want to taste chocolate."

She pulled him up, bringing his face to hers. "I *need* to kiss you."

He nuzzled into her neck, placing tiny kisses on her throat and under her ear, caressing her breast as she explored the planes of his muscles, the coarse hair, his own hard nipples.

"Hey." She took his chin and tugged him to her. "Why won't you kiss me? You kissed me plenty that night we went on a wild goose chase in Kuala Lumpur and ended up in the rain forest. You kissed me up against a mud wall, remember? And went exploring up my shirt."

"And found pearls."

She frowned. "Pearls?"

"Little tiny delicate pearls all along your bra."

"You remember that?" Such a funny thing for a guy to remember.

"I remember everything." He slid over her, bracing his hands on her shoulders, his swollen erection firm against her stomach. She rolled a little to ride it, already heavy with need to have him inside her.

"Kiss me," she demanded.

"I am kissing you. I'm kissing every inch of you, in case you hadn't noticed."

"Kiss my mouth."

His lips curved in a killer smile. He had an amazing mouth. Generous, wide lips with perfect teeth and that ingenious, talented tongue. She lifted her head off the bed to get to his mouth, but he inched back.

So she just opened her legs, riding the length of him, staring at this man who had some gift, some hold over her. "I want you to kiss me."

"Is that an order?"

She nodded.

"My, my." He raked her with another sensuous look. "Pretty, pretty Lucinda Sharpe, all wet from her bath and begging for kisses."

He was teasing, but there was something in his voice that pulled at her. Like maybe he was trying to lose himself with sex, too.

She tunneled her fingers into his hair. "So who broke your heart?"

The smile disappeared. "What are you talking about?"

"Eileen told me someone broke your heart. Who was she?"

His look was pure incredulity. "Are you serious?"

For a wild and insane second, she thought he was going to say it was her. But it had always just been sex between them, nothing more. He'd made that perfectly clear with every tease, every playful innuendo. And she certainly hadn't broken his heart when she let him go from the Bullet Catchers. His spirit, maybe, but not his heart.

"The only thing ever broken on me was this." He held up his index finger. "And it's fixed."

"So Eileen was having fantasies again?"

"Now let me ask you something." He rolled his erection against her again, a dead sexy move that didn't match the serious look in his eyes.

Not now, Jack. Don't ask about it now. "What?"

"Why are we talking instead of what we're supposed to be doing?"

She smiled and ran her hands down past his washboard abs and closed over his erection. He let out a soft, husky grunt, thrusting into her hands once, then again, slowly.

"Back on safe ground," he whispered, reaching across to the nightstand for a condom.

"Safe is a relative term," she said.

He kneeled back and rolled the condom on, his eyes dark with arousal. "Safe enough."

He bent down a little, sucked her nipple again, then kissed her other breast as he maneuvered between her legs.

She spread for him, holding her breath as the tip of him touched her opening. He slowly eased in deeper, and she closed her eyes to revel in the sensation.

Then he plunged right into her, shocking her with the impact and a crushing kiss. His lips were wet and warm, and his body was hot and hard, and neither was enough without the other. He took her mouth and took her body and wouldn't let go. She worked his lips, curled around his sweet tongue, and rode him with relentless, mindless strokes until she exploded again, turned inside out by the raw pleasure.

She ached and rolled, he pushed and thrust. She clung to him, kissing, needing, filling herself with Jack until she felt him stiffen with the one last bit of restraint . . . then he finally, finally broke the kiss to moan her name over and over as he rocked helplessly with release.

He slumped onto her, spent, barely able to breathe, his heart hammering against her chest. She held his arms, his shoulders, burying her mouth in his neck, kissing his jaw, tasting salt and skin and the roughness of his whiskers.

He shifted his weight, sliding off to lie next to her, gliding his hand over from her hipbone to her breast, and then under her hair.

Turning to him, she outlined the edge of his lips. "So you held back that kiss just to make it even better?"

"I wanted to kiss you at the same time I got inside you. I wanted both."

She turned on her side to face him. "How was this different from last time?"

"Last time," he said, threading her hair as it fell over her shoulder, fluttering it like it was silk in his fingertips, "I let you call the shots. And when it was over, you got rid of me."

"I didn't—"

"Yes, you did."

"I had to let you go after what happened, Jack."

"Whatever. You kicked me out of your life."

She tried to think of something to defend herself. "I know that the two events sort of coincided, but I never . . . I didn't want . . ." She blew out a breath. She just had to tell him outright. "It wasn't that I kicked you out of my life. It was that I won't let anyone in."

"You just let me in."

She shook her head. "This was Rescue Sex just like you said. Band-Aid sex. Feel-better sex. Make-the-unhappiness-go-away sex."

He closed his hand over her waist and pulled her into him. "I hate to break it to you, Luce, but this wasn't any of those things. This wasn't even sex."

"Then what would you call it?"

He just smiled. "Different from last time."

"I realize this is a big switcheroo, Officer Kuhns." Delaynie crossed her arms and gave the policeman a smug look that matched the one he was giving her. "I realize that not too many, uh, ladies like me pop into your police station at midnight without wearing handcuffs. But I'm a citizen, too. And I know who started that fire down on King Street today."

The detective all but rolled his eyes. "And you know there's a big fat reward for information. But it's for real information, Miss Duvall. Not something made up by a prostitute who took the night off and watched the news."

The arson investigator named Plunkett leaned across the table and gave her a slightly friendlier look. "Go ahead. We're listening."

"The guy's name is Higgins. He's a judge. And it was either him or his wife."

Kuhns spewed his coffee and Plunkett's eyes popped.

"Spessard Higgins, the justice of the U.S. Supreme Court?"

"I know he's some kind of big deal judge," she assured them. But he was also an SOB who'd slapped her around, and she wanted to crush him.

The reward would be nice, but that guy had to *pay* for what he did. "I'm one hundred percent absolutely certain that was the building, and I visited that very apartment with the window blown out, the one on the left side of the third floor. And he lived there."

"We know who owns the apartment, ma'am. We've been in touch with the owner, who wasn't home."

She looked from one to the other. "He lives there. I saw his family. I saw his freaking picture on the wall."

The two cops looked at each other as if they

couldn't believe what they were hearing. *What assholes!* She'd come to them and they acted like she was a goddamn criminal.

The arson guy asked a few more questions, but Officer Kuhns put a stop to it after two minutes. "This is a waste of time, Jimmy. I'll handle it from here."

Plunkett stood and tucked his hands into his pockets. "I want to make a few calls," he said. "You stay put for a few minutes, Miss Duvall."

The second he left, Kuhns slapped his hands on the table and got right in her face. "And what exactly were you doing there with the judge, Miss Duvall?"

She burned him with a look. "Giving the old man a Hoover."

His lip curled. "You expect me to believe that the next chief justice of the Supreme Court called your pimp and got you to come to his apartment so you could suck him off, and a couple of days later he burned the place down?"

"Believe whatever you want." Coming downtown had been a bad idea. There was no doubt who had the power in this room.

He took another sip of his coffee. "We'll file your report, Miss Duvall. You can leave now."

"That other guy wanted me to wait."

"We're done with you."

Prick. She stood and smoothed her skirt, the nice one she'd worn to meet the Higgie guy. "Whatever. I did what I had to do."

"Yes, you did. And now you can go home, Miss Duvall."

Before Plunkett came back, she was out the door and standing on the street. What a waste of time. She should have taken the job Jarell called her about. It wasn't in a very nice hotel, but he was giving her a chance at the better johns. She could have made a couple hundred instead of getting shit on by some cop.

All right, she had to just forget about the whole thing. Forget about the nasty-ass judge and the look his wife had given her. Forget about the fire pictures she saw on TV. *Just go home, Delaynie.*

She stopped for cigarettes and took the long way back to Crapsville, her little apartment that backed up to the railroad tracks in North Charleston.

She trudged up the steps, hearing the distant rumble of the next train, which would shake the whole building for thirty-seven seconds. How many more assholes would she have to screw to get a better life?

She stuck her key in the lock and pushed the door open, letting out a little squawk when she saw a shadow by the window.

"Hello again, Miss Duvall."

What the fuck? "What do you want?"

Someone grabbed her neck from behind, snapping it back with a loud crack. She tried to call out, but just stared at the ice cold sliver of steel that flashed in the light, then jerked at the wet, rubbery sound it made stabbing into her skin.

"You talk too much." The words were growled into her ear, the blade twisting up and slicing more flesh. Pain shot from her neck to her toes as her legs turned to water.

She opened her mouth to scream, but the train drowned out any sound.

She hit the floor so hard, her head bounced. The door slammed, and she was alone.

Dying in a pool of her own blood.

The train was in full force now, vibrating the floor, making the windows rattle.

The blood gushed around her face, sweet-smelling and warm. She tried to lift her head, but couldn't. She lay still, feeling the floor tremble and listening to the freight cars thunk over the tracks.

There was no panic. No desperation. This was it. Death. It felt kind of . . . peaceful.

In the light from the street, she could see the black liquid all over her hand. Her face lay on the carpet, but inches away the blood pooled onto the four tiles at the door. With a grunt that sounded more like a gurgle, she managed to slide a wet finger over the tile.

The train faded into the distance. It came and went so fast. It all went so fast.

She had only a short time left to live. Time enough to do something right with her miserable, pathetic mess of a life.

CHAPTER
THIRTEEN

JACK OPENED HIS eyes and saw black. Sleek, smooth, endless black.

Lucy's hair was just about the most beautiful thing on earth. And it was everywhere. On the pillow they shared, draped over her back, falling onto the white sheets.

The first time they'd made love, it was soaked, like her soapy skin. The next time, it was damp under his hands when he held her head and she took him into her mouth.

He closed his eyes and rode the wave of arousal that memory took him on.

The last time, before dawn, it was dried to a silky sheen. That had been his favorite. Lucy on top of him, her hair hanging down around his face.

She liked that position, too. Running the show, having control. But if she had *all* that much control, she wouldn't be in this bed.

She stirred and turned her head toward him, her eyes still closed. On the left side her blue-black hair had an inch-thick streak of white, painted by nature and caused by something that had changed much more than her hair. Something that had changed her very essence.

He touched the streak, lifting it from her cheek, making her long lashes flutter.

"Your hair," he whispered, "is like liquid sin. You know that?"

She peered at him through ebony slits. "I sleep for the first time in ages and you wake me up with bad poetry?"

"I think this whole insomniac thing is a ploy for sympathy. Every time I'm in bed with you, you sleep fine."

She lifted her head, probably to make sure he got the full impact of her dirty look. "*Every* time? Twice, total. And I sleep because you wear me out."

"See? I'm good for you." He slid his leg over the backs of her thighs, and higher. "Do you have a head-ache this morning?"

"No." She rocked her rear end against his thigh. "The ache is a little lower. I'm out of practice, I guess."

He lifted his head to look down at her. "Why don't you have a lover, Lucy?"

She didn't answer.

"Or do you?"

"I vant to be alone," she said in a lousy Garbo imitation.

"You like sex."

That made her laugh softly. "Contrary to popular opinion, I am human."

He slipped his hand under the covers to stroke the satin skin of her back. "So beautifully, perfectly, deliciously human. And a female human, too." His hand kept going, over her bottom and between her legs. "The best kind."

She moaned softly, arching her back and giving his fingers access to the moist, soft place between her legs. Already his body ached. His hands and mouth and balls and every inch of him ached to get back inside her.

How the hell could he survive this? The last time she shut him out, it almost fucking killed him.

"Would you like a warm cloth? A bath? A kiss to make it feel better?"

With a sigh, she turned on her side, giving him her back and spooning her body against his, her bottom pressed directly against his cock. "I want to go back to that heavenly sleep I was just enjoying."

He slid against her curved flesh, fitting nicely, getting harder. "This probably isn't the best way to go, then." He curled his arm over her waist and stroked one of her breasts, kissing the sweet flesh of her neck.

She moaned softly, but he didn't slide inside her. It wasn't sex he wanted right then.

He nestled into her hair, burying his face in it, his mouth finding its way to the slope of her neck for a nibble.

God, she smelled so sweet, and tasted like cream. And every inch of skin felt like warm velvet. She turned slightly, offering him more of her body to explore.

He did, stroking her as he admired the curve of her cheekbone, her straight, smart nose, the sweet pout of her lower lip.

"You talk in your sleep, did you know that?"

She turned a little more, indignant. "I do not."

"How would you know?"

"Because I had that trained out of me in the CIA. No operative could ever take that risk, so agents are trained in mind-over-matter and self-hypnosis."

"Well, your mind gave in to my matter, and you talked."

"Last night?"

"No."

She faced him. "That night in Malaysia?"

He shook his head. "In the car. On the way to see Eileen."

She frowned. "I barely went deep enough to have REM, let alone chatter any secrets."

"I didn't say you were revealing secrets." He smiled. "But you're worried, aren't you?"

"No."

"You shouldn't be," he said. "I think I've proven I can keep your secrets."

"And some of your own."

He brushed a hair off her face, and cupped her cheek. "Who is Cilla?"

She paled visibly. "Don't, Jack."

"I will never stop. I will never give up. I will never, ever quit until I have what I want."

"What do you want that I haven't given you? You've turned me inside out, made me scream, made me crazy, made me eat chocolate, for God's sake. Do you need to get right into my soul and see every dark corner?"

"Yes."

"Why? So you can have power over me?"

"Is that what you think?" He let out a soft laugh. "That's why you hold it all in, so you can make sure you have control?"

For a long moment, she didn't answer. "I don't know why I hold it all in. It's . . . too much to give in to."

"I understand pain."

"No, you don't," she said. "Not this kind."

His hand cradled her cheek. He stroked her swollen lower lip with the pad of his thumb, a little bruised from all that kissing.

"Do you remember when we met, Lucy?"

"On a yacht in New York Harbor," she said. "You were working a security detail for the president of a pharm company, and I was trying to snag his company as a Bullet Catcher client."

"You walked into the salon of that boat wearing gunmetal gray silk and a look in your eyes that was like . . ." He let out a soft grunt. "Man. I thought, this is a woman who will take no prisoners, no mercy, and no shit from anyone."

"And you liked that."

Liked? She *so* didn't get it. "Yeah."

"Gunmetal gray." She smiled, shaking her head. "You remember the strangest things for a man."

"I remember everything." About her, anyway. "I

remember your first words to me. You walked right up to me, looked me in the eye, and said—"

"'I'm taking this man's business,'" she quoted herself. " 'Prove that you're worth it, and you can stay on board.' "

He grinned. "For one minute, I thought you meant on board the ship. I thought you were going to toss my ass right over the starboard side if I didn't meet your demands. I . . ." *Careful, Culver.* "I really liked that."

She just looked at him, a hint of a smile in her eyes. "You know what I thought about you?"

He shook his head.

"I thought you were great-looking, but also . . . you didn't care what I thought."

That's where she was wrong.

She slid one leg around his, let their bodies meet. "It was a huge turn-on. I knew . . ."

At her hesitation, his whole chest constricted. "You knew what?"

"I knew it was just a matter of time until . . . what was that lovely phrase you used last night? Until you fucked me stupid and blind?"

He smiled and caressed the dip of her waist and the rise of her hip. "That's right, honey. Anytime you want to lose your brain and your sight, I'm your man."

She rocked her pelvis against him. "Now would be good." She closed her hand around him, sliding down his semiaroused cock to stroke his balls. "Really good."

"I want to talk."

She drew back. "If I didn't have this in my hand right now, I'd wonder if you're really a man. *Talk*?"

"My masculinity isn't in question, Ms. Sharpe. But seeing as we're so close to this breakthrough, why don't you just tell me what happened? You'll feel better. You'll be liberated. Then we'll make love, and you'll come sixteen times and beg for more."

She squished up her face in disbelief. "Is that what you think? First of all, sex is a temporary fix. Second of all, this is precisely why I don't have a lover. Because exchanging body fluids does not give you access to my life or my . . . issues."

"Exchanging body fluids?" His jaw dropped open, and something in his chest plummeted down to his stomach with a thud. "Are you kidding me?"

"Jack, don't make this out to be more than it is. I don't want that. I had that."

"You did?"

"I did. I had a husband."

He sat up on one elbow, stunned. "You did?" he repeated. "What happened?"

She narrowed her eyes, lifted the streak of white hair, and let it flutter slowly over her face. "I killed him."

She threw back the covers, rolled out of bed, and walked to the bathroom, snagging the Saks bag on her way. She closed the door gently, the sound barely covering her sigh.

He fell back on the pillow with a sigh of his own.

I killed him.

So she wasn't kidding when she told Eileen that. He

turned on his side and stared across the room, his gaze landing on the antique cabinet that held the minibar.

He felt the old pull in his belly, the lure of liquid anesthesia.

She used sex. He used booze.

Swearing, he pushed himself out of bed and stepped into his boxers. Her vice was a helluva lot better than his.

A soft tone beeped across the room—his cell phone. He found it on the desk, read the ID, and tried to keep any smugness out of his voice when he answered.

"Hey, Gallagher."

"I'm looking for Lucy. Avery said she's using this phone right now." In other words, he would never have called Jack Culver at seven in the morning looking for Lucy.

"She's in the shower. Want me to get her?"

"Yes." He didn't even hesitate or sound surprised. "I have critical information on the case you're working on."

Jack opened the bathroom door and tapped on the steamy shower glass. She popped it open and he handed her a towel and the phone. "Dan Gallagher. Looking for you."

Her eyes narrowed; then she wiped her hands and took the phone.

"Hey, I've been wondering when I'd hear from you."

He ignored the little kick of defeat, leaning against the doorjamb and crossing his arms, making no effort to hide his open appraisal of her wet, slick body.

So she'd been waiting for him to call? *He* was the one who'd been with her last night, not Dan.

She listened to him for a minute, and her eyes brightened as she looked at Jack. "Really? When? Wait a sec, Dan. Let me put you on speaker. I want Jack to hear this."

Jack straightened, surprised. Dan had information that was that good?

"Go ahead, Dan."

"I called in a few favors in Washington when Lucy put out the call for some information on the death of Kristen Carpenter," he said.

Jack ignored the prick of resentment that Dan was on his case. If it helped, who cared? "What'dya find out?" he asked.

"Some interesting stuff, about her brother."

"Theo," Lucy said. "What about him?"

"He used to be a D.C. attorney and has very deep connections in the Department of Justice. He's helped quite a few people through the Witness Protection Program, and knows all the tricks of falsifying an autopsy and creating new identifications for people who need them."

Lucy and Jack looked at each other.

"You've seen the autopsy, right, Jack?" she asked.

He nodded. "It looked legit. But all I was really looking for was evidence of the tattoo that her sisters had."

"So, Theo's background makes it interesting that he was the one who ID'd her at the morgue. Not her mother."

"And someone has been taking money out of Kristen Carpenter's various bank accounts on an almost daily basis," Dan added.

"From what location?" Jack asked.

"Charleston ATMs, and one in Columbia fairly recently. We have pictures."

"Is it a man or a woman?" Lucy asked.

"It's a woman," he responded. "A perfect match with a shot from the fund-raiser. A woman with curly dark hair who entered the party just minutes after you did."

Definitely support for his theory. From Dan, of all unlikely allies.

"Anything else?" Lucy asked.

"Not on that end," Dan said. "But I got a strange call last night from a guy I got to know when I investigated the fire at Willie Gilbert's condo a few weeks ago. Might be a connection to the fire you were in yesterday."

"What is it?" Jack almost grabbed the phone from Lucy's hands. Willie Gilbert, the police officer who'd arrested Eileen the night of the murder and subsequently elicited her confession, was a key piece of the puzzle. In the past several months, Jack had learned Gilbert had been on the take, living far too well for any retired cop, and that he was a scum with secrets.

Then his town house had burned to the ground, with Willie and plenty of secrets in it.

"Apparently a woman named Delaynie Duvall with a record of four prostitution arrests voluntarily visited the Charleston PD last night, claiming to have recently been on a job in the apartment that burned. She said it belonged to the man who paid her for sex."

"No surprise there," Jack said. "We already know Theo Carpenter is scum."

"Actually, she said her john was a judge she recognized from the *Good Morning Charleston* show, who was in town for a fund-raiser. She said he lived in that apartment. She saw his picture on the wall, with family."

He blew out a low whistle. "How do we find her?"

"Well, here's the kicker. The report she made is gone from the system. The guy called me late last night, and left a message. When I called him back this morning, the entire record of her visit to the PD and her record of arrests were wiped from the computers."

"Higgie's signature move," Jack said.

"I got Sage to find her address in North Charleston, and she's e-mailing it to you now."

"We'll go straight there," Lucy said, pressing a button to take the phone off speaker. "And Dan, thanks. This is good information."

She handed Jack the phone and towel and stepped back into the spray, dropping her head to let the water rinse her hair. "So, what do you think of that?" The utter nonchalance of the gesture and the way her raised arms lifted her breasts kicked him hard.

He reached around the shower door and set the phone and towel on the counter. "I think he's the last person I would have expected to help my cause."

"Why?" she asked, turning from him to raise her face to the spray. "We're all on the same team."

He watched the water cascade down the veil of black hair, so long that when she dropped her head back like that, the ends grazed the dimples right above her perfectly shaped ass.

In his boxers, his cock grew hard.

"I had a feeling his Washington connections would help us," she said, patting the wall for the soap. "And you should be glad. It supports your theory that she's alive."

He stripped off the boxers and let them fall to the floor, getting right up behind her under the water.

"I am glad," he said in her ear, over her slight gasp of surprise as he reached around and closed his hands over her breasts, his palms aching at the sweet hardness of her nipples. "That you are the woman in this shower, and I am the man with you."

She turned slowly, blinking away water. "Just in case there's any question, Jack, the man we just talked to on the phone is and always has been my friend. That's all." She put her hands into his wet hair and pulled his face a little closer to hers. "And I have never shared anything with him about my life. Or my past."

Relief and need shot low in his belly. "Good," he growled as he lowered his mouth to kiss her. "I want to be the only one."

He pushed her against the shower wall and seized her waist, gripping her ribcage to lift her off the tiles. "You got that, Luce? The . . . only . . . one."

"Jack—"

He shut her up with another kiss, lifting her high enough to position his erection between her legs. *The only one. The only one who kisses Lucy, and fills Lucy, and loves Lucy Sharpe.*

Biting her lip, sucking her tongue, he pressed her higher against the wall, the water sluicing down his back, adding heat to what was already incendiary.

He hissed a breath between clenched teeth as the head of his cock wedged into her swollen flesh.

She writhed against him, arching her back, taking him deeper with a sweet, strangled plea.

The only one.

Holding her under her arms, he braced his legs on the slippery tile and plunged to the hilt, his back bowing as he howled to the ceiling, crazy and helpless and lost in the pleasure.

The only one.

Opening his eyes, he met her scorching gaze, her lips parted around desperate breaths. He devoured her mouth, clutching her ass, forcing her legs to wrap his hips, pumping her right into the wall, both of them lost and desperate and on the very edge of insanity.

The only one.

Her legs clutched him as she came, her beautiful, sweet womanly envelope pulsed, and every drop of anything in him slammed his balls into a knot.

The absolutely only fucking one. Ever. *Ever.*

He grunted as the first blast of wicked hot release gripped him and squeezed. Water blinded him as he rammed harder and faster, about to detonate.

"Jack. Wait. *Don't.* Not inside me."

Yes, inside you.

"No, please, *please.*"

His grunt turned to a groan of pain as he dug down to the depths for the power to pull out.

Somehow, he dragged his length from her body. Grinding his shaft against her mound, he came hard over her stomach, the water washing away each heavy spurt as he shot and shot and shot until there was nothing left in him.

They slid down the wall to the wet tiles. Their strangled breaths evened out.

And Lucy cupped her hands on his face and looked him in the eyes.

"You are the only one," she whispered, still trembling. "You are."

CHAPTER
FOURTEEN

KRISTEN GRIPPED THE chipped railing of the tiny balcony overlooking the parking lot of the Red Roof Inn, and turned to face her brother as he joined her.

"Why are you packed?" he asked, dangling a bra she'd just added to her suitcase. "You are not leaving, Kristen. You can't."

She snapped it out of his hands and pushed by him into the room. "I can't stay here, Theo. The place costs ninety bucks a night. I'm going to run out of cash at this rate."

"I'll get money soon. Insurance money from the fire."

"That could take months, Theo."

"Not with help from the right people."

She turned away, disgusted. As if her mother didn't have enough heartache.

"Kristen." From behind her, he put his hands on her shoulders and pulled her into his narrow frame. She jerked away, the touch giving her a quiver of discomfort.

"Sorry," he said. "I mean Jennifer. Listen to me."

"I've been listening, Theo," she said. "I listened to you when you dreamed up this plan, didn't I?"

"I'll get money, I promise. And my plan worked, didn't it? I'm going exactly where I want to be. I'll get the cash we need. And then . . ."

"Stop it, Theo." She turned away, not wanting to see his face when he got that way. Instantly, he had her again, but in a headlock now.

"Hey!"

"Are you forgetting what it felt like, Kristen?" His voice was so menacing, chills went blasting up her spine. "Are you forgetting the way it felt to have a stranger hold a knife to your throat?"

She shook him off angrily. "No, and stop it. You're scaring me."

"You'd better be scared. His Royal Higness wants you dead, and when that man wants something, he gets it."

"I know." She hadn't been safe since the day she put all her years of research together on her kitchen table and accepted the truth: Spessard B. Higgins was her natural father. And her biological mother was in prison for murder. And when she drove to the offices of the Supreme Court that afternoon and confronted him, what had he said?

Be careful, Kristen. Be very, very careful.

He'd seemed happy, and told her to meet him when court recessed that afternoon so they could talk and sort things out. Then he'd called and told her that the president of the United States had called him to the

White House. Pretty compelling excuse . . . except that she'd been attacked getting out of her car that very night at her apartment building.

Only serendipity saved her, when Theo pulled up and scared the guy away.

She glanced at her brother, who was staring hard at the clothes, including a few thongs, inside her suitcase. She flipped it closed. "You know, the weird thing is, when I told him that day, I could have sworn he was happy. He cried."

"Of course he cried. The man is a consummate actor."

"It seemed genuine."

"For chrissake, Kristen! He's scared shitless of the power you have. Can you imagine the headlines?" He made air quotes. "Higgie Has Bastard Baby with Inmate."

"I know, I know." She sat on the bed with a sigh. "So when are you leaving?"

"Today. Mom wants to go this afternoon. She just has to meet with some insurance adjusters; then we're off to the races, princess." He grinned at her.

"Don't call me that, Theo."

He looked put out. "Why not? I've always called you that."

"Because it's . . . inappropriate."

He snorted a laugh and sat on the bed next to her. "Like I give a shit about appropriate."

Scooting up higher, she wrapped her arms around her legs protectively. "Well, I do."

For a minute his eyes looked dark and angry; then

he softened. And put his hand on her knee. She tried to move, but he gripped tighter. "You don't like when I touch you, do you?"

That discomfort slid right up and lodged in her throat. "You're my brother, Theo. It's not right."

The dark look came back, along with some color in his cheeks. "I'm not your brother, Kristen. You proved that with all your research. I am *not* your brother."

"Not by blood, but still."

"Still, what?" His voice grew tight. "We don't share a single gene. We don't share a drop of blood. Not a strand of DNA."

What was he saying? "We were raised together as brother and sister, Theo. That's what we *are*."

His fingers tightened on her legs, and she suddenly felt as vulnerable as she had during the knife attack.

"We aren't, really," he said, trying to calm his voice. "That's the cool part. That's the real romance of this movie we're making."

"We're not making a movie," she said.

"Yeah, we are. And it's gotta have everything in it. Drama. Danger. Romance."

She swallowed. "I don't want any of those things with you." God in heaven, didn't he know that?

"Kristen, why the hell do you think I did all this?"

"To save my life?"

"Well, yeah, of course. But the by-product of that is . . . us."

Us?

The realization hit her like a granite boulder to the head. He'd set this up. He pushed her to fake her death and change her identity so she'd be someone other than *his sister*. He could do that with all his connections.

Had he set up the attempts on her life, too?

She pushed herself off the bed, her tongue thickened with nausea. She made it to the bathroom and slammed the door before he reached her, then vomited the sandwich he'd brought her.

She splashed water on her face, then looked in the mirror. She had to do something. She had to go somewhere. Go to the one place in the whole world where he couldn't find her. Where no one could find her.

Taking a deep breath, she opened the door. He was right there, inches away.

"You okay?"

She managed a tight smile. "Yep. Fine. All the fast food is taking a toll on my stomach."

He gave her a doubtful look, but let it go. "I gotta book, princess."

She nodded. "Okay."

Tilting his head to the side, he smiled a bit. Probably like he imagined some actor would do before delivering the perfect exit line.

"I just have one question for you, Jennifer Miller." He leaned closer and she braced herself to keep from recoiling.

"What?"

"Who's Jack Fuller?"

"I don't know anyone by that name."

"Think hard, little sister. Moe's bar. Last May. The night you went out with those trashy sorority sisters of yours."

She frowned. "I never met a guy named Jack Fuller."

He reached his hand up and closed it around her neck. "Don't lie to me. Ever."

"I swear to God, Theo. I don't know anybody by that name."

He let her go. "If you're telling the truth, then there are some loose ends out there in the world. I'll have to tie them up."

"You do that."

He smiled, nastily this time. "Don't worry. I already started, and I won't finish until we're nice and safe." He lifted his brow. "Little sister."

The first clue that something wasn't quite right was the three ambulances that passed them, heading in the opposite direction. Jack barreled the Infiniti SUV into a blue collar neighborhood, watching them fly by with no sirens, no lights, but definitely traveling in a pack and on their way to somewhere.

Or maybe *from* somewhere.

The next clue didn't even take any cop experience. He scanned the crowd that had gathered outside the run-down apartment building that was the prostitute's last known address, taking in the yellow crime-scene tape and the number of cops in the vicinity. There was only one conclusion.

"Homicide," Jack said softly as they drove by and checked it out. "If it was anything else, the buses would have had their lights and sirens on. They were probably headed to the morgue."

"Let's not make assumptions. We need facts, Jack."

"Facts are nice. But I have this." He smacked his chest. "A very bad feeling that someone has taken care of the talking hooker."

"Let's verify that."

"I will. You stay here." At her look, he added, "You're in canary yellow. You're damn near six feet tall with two-tone hair halfway down your back and a G-23 on your hip. And while that is a smokin' hot look that I happen to adore, you don't blend in. Let me handle this."

For the second time—maybe third—that morning, she surprised him and acquiesced. "Park where I can observe everything. Who are you going to talk to? That guy over there looks like he's a detective. Although the uniformed officer with security duty is probably more willing to tell you what's going on."

"Nope." He pointed to two groups of locals gathered across the street, then a group of young black men huddled in front of the next building, peering out from under the protection of hoodies and baseball caps.

"You think those guys know what happened?"

"They know plenty. But it's the ladies to their right I'm going to start with. A much richer target. If our Delaynie is the victim, they knew her, and they'll talk about her boyfriends, her johns, and they probably know her pimp."

The cluster of a half dozen women included both blacks and whites, a young mother with a baby on her hip, an older woman with her hair in curlers, and a very heavyset mama who was exchanging insults with the boys behind her.

He left Lucy with the keys and ambled across the street, nodding to the brothers as he passed them.

They mumbled something, and the one with the hard stare raised his knuckles. "What up, the man?" He grinned, baring a grill. "I ain't guilty."

Jack met the knuckles with his own. Then he continued toward the women, who turned to him. "Ladies."

A twentysomething girl shifted a toddler from one hip to the other. The lady with the curlers narrowed her eyes at the stranger and a third, a weary-looking blonde, gave him a thorough up and down.

"What's goin' down, gorgeous?" she asked.

"Not too much." He nodded his head toward the other building. "You know her?"

"Hell, yeah." The giant black woman put her hands on her hips. "They call her Double D, and now they can add one to it. Triple D. Delaynie Duvall is dead." She swung her hips with each syllable and bared some gold teeth at the boys, who hooted behind him.

She also earned a vile look from the woman with the baby, and the other blonde.

"You the lawyer lookin' for Mr. K?" the baby girl asked. "'Cause they got him in that cruiser already. They pinched his ass big-time."

"It's just plain stupid," the blond woman said. "He'd never hurt one of his girls."

"Mr. K is her, uh, broker?"

Big mama whooped. "Yeah. He brokered her pussy all over Charleston."

The boys cracked up.

The baby got flipped to the other hip, and the young mother practically spat on the other woman. "Shut your mouth. Jarell Kite is a straight up dude. He don' slice nobody. He gets his girls rich white men with big money."

The other one hollered something back, and the insults flew. Jack walked away, having gotten all he needed from this crew. Delaynie was dead, found by her pimp, who was being questioned by the cops.

Now he'd do better with the uniformed cop than a detective who'd get all turf-crazy when Jack started asking questions. He'd certainly never let some stranger talk to his suspect at his past scenes.

When Jack reached the cop, he took a chance that his street information was accurate. In his experience, it usually was. "Where can I find Jarell Kite?"

The cop lifted his eyebrows. "Depends on who you are."

Jack reached out his hand. "Jack Culver. PI. I was on my way to talk to a lady named Delaynie Duvall but it looks like someone talked to her first."

"Some asshole stuck a knife in her carotid. I'd say he didn't like what she had to say." His gaze moved beyond Jack and over the crowd. "What case are you working on?"

Jack shrugged. "Domestic relations. My client's husband got the clap."

"Well, you'll have to wait for the autopsy to find out if the deceased had VD. Body's gone. Scene's clean. Why do you want Kite?"

"Because he knows if the victim screwed my client's husband. Can I talk to him?"

The cop snorted. "Not likely."

Jack wandered through the area, picking up bits of conversation, circling the cruiser, considering how to get to the crime scene. He could do it, but not easily.

When the cruiser door opened and a tall, handsome black man stepped out, obviously free to go on his own accord, Jack decided that talking to Kite was more important than seeing the scene that had already been compromised.

Delaynie's pimp was far more Ralph Lauren than Snoop Dogg. Jarell whipped out a cell phone, and in seconds a black Escalade pulled up and he climbed in. As it rolled down the road, Jack hustled back to his own SUV, his plan formulating.

He filled Lucy in as he pulled out, following the Escalade.

"They let him go?" Lucy asked, surprised. "Her pimp found her murdered and they let him walk away? That's unbelievable."

"Not really. They probably have a reciprocal relationship with him. He's not pushing heroin addicts on the downtown street corners; the guy is high end. You know, politicians and judges."

"Still, it's hard to believe a pimp would call the cops when he found one of his girls killed."

Jack nodded, turning right when the Escalade did and checking the rearview mirror to see if any of the plainclothes were following. There was enough traffic that it was hard to tell.

"He had to have a reason, and an alibi, or he wouldn't have called," he said. "I want to know what it is. And who he set her up to see, if and when she serviced the justice in that apartment on King Street."

"He's pulling into that 7-Eleven," Lucy said. "Let's talk to him."

When the Escalade stopped and the driver got out with the engine still on, Jack pulled up on the passenger side. Lucy got out and followed the driver into the store, while Jack lowered his window and knocked on the black glass.

In a moment, it rolled down and Jarell Kite looked out, the cell phone still pressed to his ear. "I ain't talkin' to no fucking media."

"Not the media, not the cops," Jack said.

"Then get lost." The window started to roll up.

"I'm a friend of Delaynie's."

The window stopped just under angry dark eyes that assessed him. "She had a lot of friends. Talk to the man. I'm not interested."

Just before the window sealed shut, Jack said, "How about Higgie? You interested in him?"

Five seconds passed, then the window rolled down. "Who are you?"

"Is he a customer of yours?"

The window went down all the way, and the barrel of a 9mm Parabellum pointed directly at Jack. "I asked first. Who the fuck are you?"

He casually put both hands on the door to show he wasn't armed. "Private investigator."

"Who you work for?"

"I'm working on the fire on King Street yesterday. You sent her there a few days ago, didn't you?"

"So what? That don't tell me who sliced her."

"Maybe it will."

"I'll tell you if she was there." The phone was still pressed to his ear as he leaned forward and spoke in a menacing whisper. "If you tell me how I can find this Higgie brother."

"I thought he was a client of yours."

"I never heard of the dick." He narrowed his eyes. "And now his name keeps comin' up."

It did? "The cops mentioned him?"

The question was met with a half snort.

"Is that who she met at the apartment on King Street?" Jack asked.

"I don't know who she met," Kite said. "I third-partied that one."

"Then how do you keep hearing the name?"

His eyes tapered to black slits. "I ain't hearin' it. I saw it. She wrote it with her own fucking blood on the floor."

Jack stared back at him. "She wrote 'Higgie' in blood?"

The store doors opened and the driver, a stocky black man, stopped at the sight of the two vehicles and the gun.

"You don't believe me?" Kite challenged, lifting the gun. "Those fuckers didn't believe me, either. Thought I made it up to get the heat off me." He gave a half-nod to the driver, who instantly pulled out his own weapon and aimed it at Jack.

Jack lifted a hand. "We're cool, man. It's okay. I want to help you. What do you mean, they didn't believe you? Didn't they see it?"

"*I* saw it," he said. "I called the cops and met them downstairs. Next time I went up there, it was gone. But I saw it." He leaned out the window and lifted the gun. "Now you tell me who this motherfucking asshole Higgie is, or I'm gonna put a hole in your head in the front, and my man's gonna get the side view."

Kite's driver's door popped open and Lucy appeared inside, her G-23 aimed squarely at the back of Kite's head. She must have come out the back of the store and hidden behind a dumpster to hear the whole conversation.

Canary yellow or not, she was stealth itself.

"Put your gun down," she said calmly. "And tell your friend to do the same. Now."

Kite's nostrils flared, but he gave a look to the driver and let the gun fall on his lap.

"Did you get what you wanted?" she asked Jack.

He nodded. She backed out of the seat, turning off the engine and pulling out the keys with one hand, keeping the gun aimed at Kite's head with the other. When she saw Jack raise his weapon, she got out of the car and came around the back, shifting her aim toward the guy who stood between the two bumpers with his hands raised.

Without a word, she got into the car and Jack backed out, one hand aiming his gun at Kite, the other on the wheel. As soon as they screeched onto the street, Lucy threw the keys far enough away that they could get away before Kite followed.

"Did you get all that?" he asked, slamming on the accelerator and heading due south.

"Enough."

"Enough to know that bastard's involved up to his eyeballs."

She laid her gun on her lap, watching, as he did, out the side-view mirror. "He didn't kill Delaynie, Jack."

Jesus. What was it going to take to convince her? "Wanna bet?"

"Oh, come on. He's in a wheelchair and couldn't leave that compound without the Bullet Catchers knowing about it."

"So she wrote his name in blood. Why? Her favorite john before she died?"

"You believe that guy?" she asked, incredulous. "He would have killed you in a heartbeat."

"Yeah. Did I say thanks?"

"No need." She slipped out her phone. "Maybe Dan's friend in arson can get access to the crime scene photos."

He listened to her bring Dan up to speed; then she called headquarters and ordered a background check on Jarell Kite. Then she called the Bullet Catchers' HQ at Willow Marsh.

"Owen, it's Lucy. Quick question for you. Did Justice Higgins leave the compound at any time in the past twenty-four hours?" She waited, listening.

"Okay, thank you. We'll be there in under an hour, or however long it takes to get from North Charleston to Kiawah Island." Again she listened, then added, "Jack and I had to interview a woman who knows our principal."

Higgins was the *target,* not the principal. Jack

swallowed the thought as she settled into her seat, satisfied.

"Don't tell me," he said. "Mr. And Justice For All was safely tucked in bed all night with nothing but his loving wife and the Bible by his side."

"Everyone was in and accounted for."

Disgust roiled through him. "Whose side are you on, anyway, Lucy?"

"The side of justice. Whoever or whatever that is. I want the truth, and you want revenge. Big, big difference." She gave him a dry smile. "See what happens when you share too many secrets? The opposition uses them against you."

"In just one hour I go from the flavor the month to the opposition? My, how the mighty have fallen."

She lifted his hand to her lips for a kiss. "And fallen hard."

His hand burned where her lips touched, and he forced himself to remember: nothing Lucy said or did was arbitrary.

CHAPTER
FIFTEEN

RESTLESS TO DIG into the secrets he believed were hidden at Willow Marsh, Jack left Lucy to work in her room and wandered the compound.

He started down a long asphalt path that led to the marshland surrounding the estate, to check out the boathouse and dock that jutted into a narrow, winding river. Halfway down the path he reached a brick wall with a gate and realized that this whole side of the estate was dedicated to a huge private garden designed and cultivated by someone with true talent.

Drawn to it, he entered, passing a large shed as he continued to a circle of live oaks around a blue and white gazebo.

There, bent over a table, Marilee Higgins clipped piles of fresh flowers, quietly arranging them in various vases while she hummed.

He didn't want to startle her, so he cleared his throat and said hello.

She turned gracefully, not the least bit startled. She

smiled as if she'd been expecting him, exuding Southern hospitality as palpable as the sweet fragrance of her flowers.

"Oh, hello," she said, taking off her gardening gloves to reach out her hand. "You're Jack, right? I am so sorry—I forgot your last name, but I remember meeting you at the aquarium."

"Jack Fuller," he supplied, the lie easy as his handshake. "We barely had a chance to say hello that night."

"Well, it was chaotic," she said brightly. "Welcome to my home, Mr. Fuller. And"—she made a sweeping gesture around the garden—"my private piece of paradise."

"It's gorgeous," he said. "You obviously have a knack for gardening."

"It's in my blood," she said, picking up her gloves and indicating a bench across from her. "Have a seat. Unless you'd rather help me make the centerpieces for tonight's dinner."

"You make them yourself?" He nodded with approval, moving around the table to check out the flowers, but just as interested in the woman who ran Willow Marsh—undoubtedly a force to be reckoned with.

"I do most everything myself, especially when it involves my flowers. I'd rather no one else handle them."

"Are these camellias?" he asked, lifting up a stem of a peach blossoms.

She nodded enthusiastically. "Oh, yes, those are my darlings. That's a *Prunus mume,* also known as the flowering apricot. Isn't that color spectacular? I'll mix it with white, like this . . ." She took the stem and added it to a crystal vase full of similar flowers in various shades of white.

"We're having salmon in a light white wine sauce for dinner, so this will go nicely, don't you think?"

He crossed his arms and studied the bouquet, and the woman—who, for all her delicate sweetness, struck him as someone with a titanium backbone.

Why would she stay married to a cheater for so long?

"Most people think camellias are native to South Carolina," she said, obviously trained to continue the small talk and let no awkward pauses arise. "But they originated in the Far East. South Carolina does grow the prettiest and the strongest, though, I think."

"Like its women."

She looked up and smiled. "Thank you. I'm a native, you know. My family can be traced all the way back to my great-times-at-least-seven grandfather, who landed in the mid-1700s. He went on to be one of the businessmen who formed our county's first chamber of commerce, right down on Broad Street in Mrs. Swallow's Tavern." She gave him a wide smile of pride. "The first in a long line of active and successful political and involved figures, as you can see."

"Or wives of such men."

She nodded. "Absolutely, and it's a great honor to the family name."

That's why she stayed married to a cheater? Southern honor? But would she stay married to a killer?

"Mrs. Higgins, can I ask you a personal question?"

She lifted another peachy-colored bloom and held it up to block her face from his. After a moment, she leaned a little to the left and refocused on him.

"I fully expect you to," she said with another sweet, unreadable smile. "After all, you're here to capture the emotional subtext of Spessard's life, aren't you? If you don't interview and understand me, then you really can't understand him."

"That's true," he agreed, grateful for the open door. "So tell me, to what do you attribute the success of your long marriage? The ability to compromise? Giving each other space? Having no secrets?"

She smiled and shook her head. "I don't know the meaning of compromise, my dear, and space is a concept that means nothing to old people like us. Secrets? No, we don't have a one. I know everything about him, and vice versa. A long and happy marriage is the result of one thing, and one thing only."

"True love?"

She laughed softly. "God, no."

"You don't love him?"

She turned the white and peach arrangement, frowning. "That's not quite perfect, after all," she said softly.

He waited, his question hanging in the air as she removed the apricot-colored bloom.

"The secret to our marriage is simple," she said, picking up some shears. "If anyone tries to hurt him . . ." She snipped high on the stem, decapitating a perfect flower. "Oh, I didn't mean to do that."

He doubted that, though. She struck him as a woman who did nothing without a purpose—very much like Lucy.

She lifted the flower. "Here, Mr. Fuller. We're formal tonight and I'm sure this will look lovely on your suit jacket. Which reminds me, I'd better get back to work. Our dinner is in just a few hours. It was so nice to talk to you."

Obviously dismissed, he took the flower and left, sniffing the heady perfume all the way back to his room on the second floor of the guesthouse. As he passed Lucy's room, conveniently located next to his, he paused. She'd said she wanted to rest and work before dinner, but he knocked anyway.

"Hey, it's Jack."

"Alone?" she asked.

That was promising. "Yep."

She opened the door but showed only her face. "Just wanted to be sure." Glancing beyond him to the hall and seeing no one, she opened the door a little wider to let him in.

"For me?" She reached for the flower with a smile.

"Maybe." He extended it and used his other hand to tug the tie of her silky short robe. "For me?"

Before she could answer, the robe opened, revealing the soft, smooth rise of her breast. Jack pulled the door closed and locked it.

She sniffed the flower as she crossed the room, settling on the wide window seat. "I thought that was you in the canoe I saw go down the river."

He looked out over the acres of wheat-colored

marshland, the winding rivers golden brown in the afternoon light.

"Not me. I was in the garden with Mrs. Higgins. Must have been one of your men."

"No, they're all in and accounted for. There are guests coming for dinner, I understand. Some names have been sent down to HQ for checks." She curled against the wall, the robe still gloriously open, stretching her legs along a window seat, placing the flower under her nose.

"I love these," she said softly. "They grow in Pohnpei, where my mother was born. I went there once when I was little, and the trip was dreamy, meeting all my little Micronesian cousins." She closed her eyes and sniffed deeply, then set it lovingly on the corner of the bureau next to the window. "Thank you. I'll wear it in my hair tonight."

He hadn't the heart to tell her that Marilee had given it to him to wear in his jacket. Instead, he lifted her legs and sat on the window seat cushions, placing her calves on his lap.

Leaning closer, she laid a finger on his lower lip, tracing it. Then she slid the tip into his mouth.

The gesture kicked him in the chest and he closed his eyes, parted his lips, and tasted her finger. She slid it out and drew a line down his chin, over his throat, playing with some hair at his open collar. Then she inched toward him and opened her mouth, breathing into a long, lazy kiss.

Sometimes she just surprised the hell out of him.

"While you were picking flowers," she said, pulling

them both down to lie face-to-face on the window seat, their bodies completely sealed together, "I was making plans."

His hard-on pushed at her, and she lifted her leg over his hip to lock them into place.

"God, I hope your plans include being late for dinner." He kissed her again, dipping his fingers into the robe to tweak her hardened nipple.

"I have a plan for every minute of the night."

"Of course you do." He lowered his head and kissed her breastbone, moving the silk robe out of his way to lick her nipple. "And if it doesn't include this, I'll be breaking with plan."

She lifted his face to meet hers. "Don't you want to hear my plan first, Culver?"

"Don't call me that. I'm Fuller. Jack Fuller. And can we be open about our relationship tonight? Because there's no way I'm going to be with you all night and keep my hands off your body." He underscored that with a stroke over the smooth skin of her thigh, closing his eyes like he'd been shot with delight.

"Higgie told me he wants to get me alone at some point to give me the names on his short list for potential assassins and enemies from his past."

"He's just taking you in circles, Lucy. This is his way of keeping you from finding out anything at all. I'm only interested in two things. Did he know that Kristen Carpenter was his biological daughter, and does he know she's still alive? That's my goal for tonight."

"What about the vault?"

"I'd like to find that."

"So after dinner, when I have him alone, I'll get him away after he's shown me something in the cottage. I'll forget something, go back and get it, and be sure the door is unlocked. You can go in and dig around the back rooms. If he has such a vault, I think it's back there somewhere."

"Works for me." He stroked her thigh again, slipping his hand between her legs. His erection grew, pressing against her. "And so does this."

He nuzzled closer, kissing her hair, her eyes, her cheeks, and finally, closing his mouth over hers for a long, wet exchange of lips and tongue and sweetness.

"What else have you been up here planning?" he murmured, moving his fingers higher, aching to touch the soft, wet center of her.

"I thought that maybe, after all that spy work is done, you and I could get in bed . . ." She kissed him again, nibbling his lower lip and flicking his tongue.

"I like the way you think, woman." He dipped a finger inside her. Wet. Very wet.

"And that we could talk."

He froze. "Yeah?"

"Yeah."

"You want to tell me something?"

She touched his face, rubbing her thumb on his cheekbone. "I want to tell you everything."

A weird tingling zipped through his veins. A sense of anticipation. Of disbelief. Of something he couldn't quite describe. "Why?"

She smiled. "Because of something that Eileen said."

He tried to remember what Eileen had said, but he'd gotten so stuck on Lucy's revelation that he'd missed anything after that. "I don't remember what she said."

"She said you loved me."

The tingle turned to ice.

"And you didn't deny it."

For a long minute, maybe two, he didn't say a word. He didn't even think a word. He just stared into pools of midnight black eyes, seeing his own reflection, imagining all of the possible reactions when she knew the truth.

The most likely? She would send him far away again.

"Do you love me, Jack?"

"Love is a pretty broad concept, Luce." How could he possibly manage this without losing her? Sex was fine. Lust was fine. Shared secrets of dark pasts, fine.

But the way he loved her? She'd recoil and run, if she even believed it.

Sex was the only answer. Slowly, with as much heat as he could produce, he stroked the moist folds between her legs, slipping the very tip of his finger inside her.

"Do you love me?"

Oh *God,* yes. "I love touching you." He pushed a little farther, adding a second finger. "I love being way, deep, completely inside you." His thumb stroked the nub of her clitoris, and he lowered his mouth to hers. "Let me make you come. Let me make you lose all that sweet control and come right here in my hand."

Instead of rocking toward him, Lucy pulled back. All the way back, her gaze unrelenting.

"Don't change the subject. Don't distract me. And, please, don't lie to me. I have to know this. Do you love me?"

He exhaled softly. "Why do you have to know? Is it that you can't share what you need to share unless you know I love you?"

She shook her head slightly.

"Then why does it matter so much?"

"Because." She touched his face, slid her fingers into his hair, and for one unbelievable minute, he thought she was going to tell him she loved *him*.

He waited, suspended, terrified, hopeful.

"Just because," she finally said, stopping any more conversation with a kiss and a touch that showed him she was every bit as adept at using sex to cover her feelings as he was.

"Where's your boutonniere?" Marilee marched up to Lucy and Jack when they walked onto the patio for cocktails, her gaze sharp but teasing.

"I gave it away," he said, putting a possessive hand on Lucy's back.

"And I didn't have time to pin it in my hair," Lucy said smoothly, pretty certain that Marilee was astute enough to pick up the electricity that probably still arced between the two of them. "But Jack told me what a beautiful garden you have."

Marilee looked from one to the other, a knowing little smile pulling at her lips. "So Spess is right about you two."

Marilee was *very* astute.

"I'm always right." The drawling baritone came from behind Lucy, accompanied by the low hum of his wheelchair motor as Higgie joined them. "You look absolutely beautiful, Ms. Sharpe, and hello again, Mr. Fuller. Welcome to Willow Marsh."

Jack responded to the offered hand with a shake, a very insincere smile on his face.

"I have great news for you about our book," Higgie announced, full of enthusiasm. "I have a title. Isn't that the perfect place to start a book?"

Higgie flashed his world-class smile at Jack, ruthlessly assessing and no doubt judging the man Lucy had brought to write his book.

Jack merely nodded.

Come on, Jack. Fake it. Lucy brushed his hand in silent support.

"Would you like to hear it?" the justice asked Jack.

"More than life itself."

Only someone who knew Jack as well as she did could have picked up the sarcasm in his reply. And maybe someone who had a lifetime of experience judging people.

"Justice is, you know, a blind woman," Higgie said. "And last night, while reading Samuel Butler's poem *Hudibras,* the title came to me. *Painted Blind.* I've taken it from my favorite line of the poem. 'For justice, though she's painted blind, is to the weaker side inclined.'"

"Are you?" Jack asked, the smallest note of challenge in his voice. Lucy knew it masked his real question. *Were you really home reading poetry last night, or out killing prostitutes?*

"Am I inclined toward the weak?" Higgie tilted his head as he considered the question. "History will be the judge of that. And after our interviews, perhaps you will, too, Mr. Fuller."

For one millisecond, Lucy thought they were busted. Maybe it was the starched tone he used, or the wise gleam in his eye. That might just be Higgie's style, or . . . he knew more about what they were doing than they thought he did.

Jack had been at the prison many times. If Higgie closely monitored Eileen's visitors, he could know Jack Fuller was really Jack Culver, which is why they'd given him a new identity. Could he have pictures of Jack?

Looking over Lucy's shoulder, Marilee's face suddenly lit up. "And look who's here. My dearest friend in the world."

Lucy turned to greet the next guest coming onto the patio, watching Marilee usher in a heavyset woman deep into her sixties.

"Higgie, our darling Bernie is here."

The woman entered cautiously, as if she were truly in awe of the overwhelming surroundings of size and wealth.

"Hello, Justice," she said softly. "It's nice to see you."

"Bernadette," he replied, holding out both hands and shaking his head. "If I could stand up from this damned chair I'd give you a hug. I'm so sorry to hear about what happened."

Lifeless brown eyes, the same color as her hair, closed. "At least no one was hurt. That's the miracle, I guess."

Marilee made introductions. "Bernie, this is the head of our security detail, Lucy Sharpe, and her friend, Jack Fuller, who is going to ghostwrite Spessard's memoir."

Lucy stepped forward to shake the woman's hand. "Bernadette—"

"Is my closest childhood friend," Marilee said. "We've known each other since we were no more than little girls in grammar school."

The other woman smiled and shook Lucy's, and then Jack's, hand. "Something like that. It's nice to meet you." Sadness, almost a bone-deep depression, rolled off the woman in waves.

"Bernie has just suffered the most incomprehensible tragedy," Marilee explained to Lucy and Jack. "Her Charleston apartment burned yesterday. Did you hear about the fire on King Street?"

"Yes, I did," Lucy said, not glancing at Jack but sensing his whole body suddenly on alert. "Did you live in the building?"

"I live in Virginia," Bernie said. "But I've kept that apartment for ages, and, of course, Marilee and Spessard use it when they're in town and don't want to drive all the way out here."

That explained a lot.

"Were you there when it happened?" Jack asked.

"No, thank God. No one was, and no one in the building was hurt. But I had to come down from Roanoke to deal with the investigators and insurance people."

Someone was in the apartment, Lucy thought, her

focus on Bernadette. Wasn't *Roanoke, Virginia* the childhood home of Kristen Carpenter?

"I'm sorry to hear about that," Lucy said to Bernadette, taking in the lines of unhappiness, the black circles under her eyes. "That is a tragedy."

"It's not a tragedy to lose some stuff in an apartment," Bernadette said, her voice as sharp as the look she gave Higgie. "A tragedy is losing a child."

Lucy swallowed hard. "It certainly is," she said carefully, noticing that Bernie's gaze remained on Higgie. "I hope you never have to endure that."

"I already have," she said, protectively wrapping her arms around her girth.

For a moment, no one spoke.

"I'm so sorry," Lucy managed.

"Uh, you left me in the driveway." A man's voice, rich with irritation, came around the corner.

"We're out here, honey," Marilee called, then added, "It's Bernie's son."

A tall, lanky man with thinning black hair and beady eyes stopped in the doorway, seemingly surprised at the gathering of people. He scanned the group, flickering over Jack, but landing on Higgie.

"Hello, Uncle Spessard. You look well for a man who just defied death."

"Hello, Theo."

CHAPTER
SIXTEEN

THROUGHOUT THE COCKTAIL party, and a multicourse dinner, Theo Carpenter barely acknowledged the presence of Lucy and Jack. Either he was a brilliant actor or dumb as dirt.

Jack tended to think the first. He'd tried to get near the guy but wasn't able to. Several other couples had arrived, and the table for twenty was full of lawyers, legal clerks, and a smattering of Charleston's social registry members.

Since he couldn't talk to Theo, Jack watched the young man, sizing him up. All he gleaned from conversation was that he'd given up his law career to follow a lifelong dream of making films, a passion that was met with a tolerant smile from his mother and a flat-out eye roll from "Aunt" Marilee.

The way Jack put it together, Higgie had pulled Kristen from the foster care system—probably killed the couple who adopted her from Sapphire Trail—and planted her close enough to home to keep an eye on her. When she realized her life was in danger, she had her brother cook up a fake death.

But she couldn't know she had sisters. Did she even know that Higgie was her father? He had to get to Theo for some answers.

Dessert was served on the patio, but when the guests rose to move that way, Theo slipped out a side door and disappeared. Jack shot Lucy a look that said he refused to be stopped, and followed Theo in less than two minutes.

He was out to the lawn by the time Lucy caught up with him. "Breaking with plan already? You're going into the cottage when I get Higgie away."

"Screw the plan. I want to talk to Theo."

"Jack, the justice just promised me some time to go over a list of people in Charleston from his past," she said. "He's getting it from his office. Then I'll convince him to go outside to discuss it, then you can get in. That's your window. It's all I can promise you tonight, and maybe for longer."

"Theo's my priority." He lowered his voice to a whisper. "He knows where Kristen is. He tried to kill you. I don't want him getting in a car and driving away tonight. You've figured out what happened, haven't you?"

"With Kristen?"

He urged her deeper into the shadows, as quiet as he could be. "Higgie arranged that adoption. Remember, she was with a family in Virginia, and they were killed in a car accident? Then she lands on the doorstep of his wife's best friend, where he can keep a close watch on her."

Lucy nodded. "I can see where that's a possibility."

Irritation shot through him. A possibility? "And that guy"—he pointed in the general direction Theo had gone—"knows where she is now. So as much as I want to stick with our plan, my number one goal has *always* been to find Eileen's daughters. All three of them. Then I'll nail that bastard for ruining her life."

"All right," she agreed. "But don't lose touch with me. It's ten-thirty. By eleven-fifteen, I'll have him out of the office. Don't lose the opportunity; I don't know when we'll get it again."

He nodded and stepped away, but she grabbed his arm. "Be careful. He's dangerous."

"I'm armed." He brushed her lips with his thumb, then followed it with a kiss. "You be careful with that bastard. I don't trust him."

"I can handle myself with a seventy-four-year-old man."

Jack gave her a hard look. "Don't underestimate him, Lucy."

"I won't."

He turned toward the path that led to the marsh, his fingers already grazing the gun under his jacket.

The delay cost him, because Theo was gone. Jack circled one side of the house, jogged through the garden, ran the perimeter of the guesthouse, and ended up at the long asphalt-covered path that led toward a marsh river. It was lined with thick live oaks and willows, and barely any moonlight seeped through as Jack moved soundlessly on his mission. Near the dock, he caught a flash of a light shirt and dark pants disappearing around the front of the boathouse.

Got him.

Taking out his Ruger, he racked the slide and positioned it comfortably in his left hand. He approached the structure silently, examining the dock that led to the river, then checking out all four sides of the building, the high windows, and the stone-sided foundation that sank deep into the marsh.

He had him. Jack lifted the weapon with two hands, braced himself for a shot, and shouldered the big door with all his strength.

It opened easily to a dark, deserted single room, with a few canoes and kayaks hanging neatly on huge hooks in the wall. The only light came from thin bands of moonlight streaming in from long, horizontal windows that ran along the rafters, revealing plenty of shadows, canoes, and tools, but no Theo.

"Carpenter!" Jack called.

Nothing. Not a molecule moved. He looked to his right, where a table ran along the whole wall, under rows of fishing rods, tackle, and cleaning gear. Straight ahead, the canoes and kayaks hung with the hulls open, so no one could be hiding in them. On the third wall were hooks with wading boots, life jackets, and more hardware.

There was no other door. Had Theo gone around the boathouse, not into it? Out to the marsh? The river?

He headed outside to the end of the dock. Beneath it, the water was shallow enough that the grass reeds jutted up all around the dock, so even if Carpenter had balls of steel and no fear of alligators, he couldn't have tried to swim away. Jack looked up and down the length of the narrow river and along the swampy sides.

A loud splash of water came from behind him and he whipped around, aiming his gun. But only a long, curious gator skulked at the surface.

Jack started a slow, thorough inspection of every inch of the property, the surrounding marsh, and the other two buildings, finding nothing but the occasional security guard. None of the Bullet Catchers had seen Theo.

Finally, he checked his phone to see the time: eleven-twenty. This was his window to get into Higgie's office.

On the way, he passed Owen Rogers, headed toward the small carriage house the Bullet Catchers had turned into an impromptu headquarters.

"Have you seen Lucy?" Jack asked.

"She went canoeing with the justice."

She went *what*? Canoeing in gator-infested water in the dark with that murderous son of a bitch? And Theo on the loose?

"Where you going?" Owen asked.

Wasn't he in on the plan? Lucy always told the whole team everything. But maybe she hadn't had the chance.

"Just looking around," he said vaguely.

Jack headed in the direction of the office when something in his gut made him stop.

Sometimes plans had to be broken.

"All right, this is . . . unorthodox."

Higgie laughed softly as Lucy wheeled the chair over the asphalt path and reached the dock and boathouse.

"Orthodox is for pussies." He grinned over his shoulder at her. "And I'm guessin' you're not one of those."

She ignored the rudeness, chalking it up to his happiness at being out of the house and getting someone to take him for what he'd told her was his favorite pastime—a midnight paddle.

"At least there's moonlight," she said, looking up at the nearly full moon that bathed the marsh grass in silver, turning the golden sweetgrass into a sepia-toned carpet that stretched for miles, and the rivers into ribbons of twinkling white light.

A very light fog hung low over the marsh, and night creatures ticked and hummed and rustled in the reeds.

"The tide is high," he said. "Good thing, 'cause it's little more than a mudflat when it's low. The canoe's in the boathouse. You can easily drop it in the water and pick me up at the end of the dock."

Beyond the boathouse, a long, narrow dock led to the strip of water.

"We can get out there simply enough," the justice said, following her gaze.

"Out where?"

He pointed. "God's country, Lucy. Lowcountry. It's a magic place, and the only place on this whole damn compound that no one will hear us talk."

A chill lifted the hairs on the back of her neck, but she was armed, and she'd told Owen and Donovan what her plans were. She had a cell phone with GPS and a system that allowed the Bullet Catchers to track her every move. And this would give Jack plenty of time to explore Higgie's office.

"Now I understand why they call you the most focused justice to ever sit on the bench. You want something, you don't even let a wheelchair stop you, do you?"

"'Course not. Wheel me down to the edge of the dock and drag that canoe out. Can you handle that, young lady?"

She'd changed from her dinner dress into sneakers and jeans for the adventure, but she hadn't used the time to call Jack. If he was tracking Theo he'd want to be totally quiet, and the last thing she wanted to do was endanger him with a ringing cell phone.

She left the justice at the end of the dock and headed to the boathouse, considering texting Jack to let him know.

"Come on, Luce!" Higgie called. "Marilee'll be down here in ten minutes to have my ass in a sling. Let's get going."

She'd almost said no to this wild plan, but then he'd whispered some magic words over bourbon-drenched strawberries and cream.

There was a trial, many years ago. There were discrepancies. There was tampered evidence. I want to talk to you about it.

She'd asked him if he was referring to a trial he judged, and he shook his head. "But I was there in the courtroom, Lucy, just the same."

She surveyed the inside of the boathouse for the right canoe, spotting a two-person Kevlar. Hoisting it off its hooks was easy due to the lightweight material. Beside it was a small motorized raft that was totally illegal to use in these heavily protected, environmentally sensitive waters.

Though she would have preferred the raft to paddling, she carried the canoe to the water and pushed it until she could jump in and row to the end of the dock, where Higgie waited.

"All right, Mr. Justice," she said with a smile as she climbed out to give him assistance. "Let's take a midnight boat ride."

"Oh, I like the sound of that." He pushed the armrests, stood, and took the three steps with perfect ease.

"Surprise, surprise! The man walks. Something tells me the docs wouldn't like it."

"Screw the docs," he said with a hearty laugh. "My motto is do first, ask questions later."

With remarkable ease, he let himself down into the canoe, maintaining his balance as it wobbled while he settled into the bow bucket seat, facing her. She took the middle bench, sliding a paddle out from its Velcro fastener at the bottom.

With one good push, they were out into the narrow river.

"Not very deep here, is it?" she said.

"Nope. Probably just a little over waist high in the middle."

"So we won't drown."

He chuckled. "That's not how you die out here, Luce." He made a giant jaw with his hands, letting his palms slap together. "'Bout a hundred thousand of them in mating season, but plenty out there in the fall, too."

"I'm sure it's against the law, but if I have to shoot one, I will."

He chuckled. "Or I will."

She glanced up to read his face. Had he come out here with a gun? "Ever kill one, Justice?"

"Nah. They're pussycats if you leave them be."

"How about anything else?" Or any*one*.

He thought about that for a minute. "Fish and game don't count, I imagine. Never sent anyone to the electric chair. No, with the exception of a few punchlines, I never killed anything of note."

Maybe Wanda Sloane wasn't *of note* to him.

Or maybe he didn't kill her.

She took a few long strokes, her paddle rubbing the bottom two or three times until she maneuvered them into the center of the seven-foot-wide river.

"You have, haven't you?" he asked.

"Oh, yes," she replied easily. "But never a gator."

Something splashed softly nearby and they shared a quick look.

"If he gets too close, you have my permission and we won't tell the natural resources people." He winked at her. "And you can get a nice new belt out of it, too."

She laughed softly, floating them along in silence, waiting patiently for him to feel comfortable enough to talk.

The brackish water mixed with a pungent odor of sulfur that permeated the marsh. The moon was bright enough to see at least fifty feet in any direction, and the marsh grass low enough that Lucy felt safe, regardless of their vulnerable position.

"Do you do this often, alone?" she asked.

"Every chance I get."

"Well, speaking as your personal security specialist, don't. Armed or otherwise."

He didn't answer but looked around comfortably, surveying his land and the silent beauty of the marsh at night.

"I don't think the person who wants to kill me is at Willow Marsh," he finally said.

"Then where would we look for this individual?"

"I don't know. I don't even know her name."

Lucy stilled her paddle, letting the water drag them. "Her?"

"My daughter."

She let the boat drift. "You have a daughter, Justice?"

He nodded. "Somewhere. And that's why I couldn't risk talking about this where prying eyes and ears could be."

He didn't know that Kristen Carpenter, who'd probably called him "Uncle Spessard" like her adopted brother did, was his daughter? Then . . . he hadn't killed her?

Or maybe he was referring to one of the other triplets? Maybe he *did* know about all three of them.

All she wanted was the truth. Whatever it was.

"Why do you think your daughter would want to kill you?"

"Well, probably because I let her mother take the rap for a crime she didn't commit."

Holy God, was this a total confession? "Who did commit it?"

"I sure as hell don't know."

Not a confession. "But you know your daughter's mother didn't commit the crime?"

He closed his eyes and inhaled deeply. Lucy balanced the paddle on the side, letting the slow current carry them, focused on eliciting the truth from Spessard Higgins.

"I know because I was there. I was in an alley, with a . . . woman." He gave her a look. "Not my wife. She was shot, and I ran, and another woman was arrested for the crime."

"The woman arrested is the mother of your daughter?"

He gave her a shaky smile. "I was a little wilder in my younger days. But those days are gone. I don't cheat on my wife."

Apparently he didn't count prostitutes as cheating. Or maybe Delaynie had lied to the arson investigator.

Everything in her, keenly trained to read people, said he was telling the truth. But Eileen hadn't lied when she told Lucy that Higgie had fired the gun. Lucy was equally as certain of that. Which one was telling the truth?

"Tell me about this woman, this crime. How was she convicted?"

He snorted. "That court was a joke. Tampered evidence. Piss-poor defense. Shoddy investigating. Christ, the DA didn't even do an investigation."

He sounded bitter and resentful, not like a man who'd orchestrated it all.

"Why didn't they investigate?" She decided to go for bluntness. "Because of your involvement?"

"Because Charleston was a mess back then, with a corrupt PD and an even more corrupt legal system. I'm not proud of those days, Lucy. I wasn't a whole lot better than the rest of them."

The wrong question could give far too much away. She had to remember that, to him, she knew nothing of this.

"Is this the trial you were referring to over dessert?"

"Yes." He looked at her, his hair even whiter in the moonlight, his still-dark brows knitted in a single line. "But that's not why I brought you out here, Lucy."

The chills that had crawled up her spine earlier returned at his tone, and she set the paddle down again so she could reach for the gun at her waistband if she had to.

"Then why are we out here?"

"To find my daughter."

The crack of a bullet bounced off the Kevlar side of the canoe, rocking them sharply. Lucy threw herself across the boat at Higgie, pulling him down into the center where the sides offered the most protection, and covered him with her whole body.

She had her gun out in the next move, staying as low as she could to search the shadows and grass for any possible movement, ready to shoot.

"Don't move!" she ordered. "The boat's bulletproof, so stay as low as you can."

With her right hand still aiming the Glock, her finger on the trigger, she pulled out her phone with her left and hit the speed dial for the Bullet Catcher HQ on the estate.

"Lucy, where are you?" Donovan Rush answered.

"Shots have been fired at the principal," she announced. "In the marsh. I need a team down here fast. We're about a quarter mile south of the dock and boathouse. Hurry."

"I told you she was out here," Higgie said, sitting up in the wobbling canoe. "She wants to kill me, and I know why. I need to talk to her."

Another bullet smacked against the side, rocking the boat.

"God damn it!" Higgie tried to stand. "I want to talk to her!"

The canoe tilted dangerously sideways, and Lucy worked to right it. "Don't!" she screamed, using all her might to pull him down. "My men are coming. Stop it!"

He jerked out of her grasp. "I need to explain something to her."

"Not now!"

Higgie started to lift his head, but she elbowed him back down again. Then she saw the gunshot flash as another bullet whizzed overhead, missing her by inches.

Higgie managed to push himself up again, struggling to a full stand.

"No, Justice!"

She fought him, pushing his sizable frame back down, which made the canoe tip sideways. They rolled and grappled as Lucy tried to use her weight to right them, but it wasn't enough.

Just as another shot cracked the night, the canoe capsized with a loud splash. Her gun and phone went flying as she slammed into the soft bottom of the riverbed, her knees going right into Higgie's chest.

She seized him and tried to pull him up through the four feet of water, but he was dead weight.

She stood, seized a lungful of air, and shot back into the murk, grabbing under his arms and using her legs to push his head above water.

Was he unconscious? Shot? She planted her feet firmly and used all her strength to push his upper body straight to get him into a stand.

The process sank her feet deep into the muddy riverbed, the muck literally sucking at her shoes.

As their heads popped up out of the water, she spat water and hair out of her face, squeezing the judge to get him to take a breath. There was a loud splash a foot to her right and she turned, half-expecting the shooter to be right there.

A pair of glassy eyes set in a long, narrow head peeked up from under the water. The alligator's jaws opened wide, his sharp teeth white in the moonlight, his massive mouth a black hole.

Lucy didn't move. Higgie grunted and started coming to.

She tried to back them away slowly, but the gator followed.

"Lucy . . ." Conscious now, Higgie tried to stand on his own, but his injured leg gave way.

She supported him as best she could, but his weight forced her down, taking her under again for a second. Her feet sank even deeper into the mud, and she tried to dislodge them, but they were buried well past her ankles. She managed to stand up, but Higgie's weight was pushing her deeper with every moment.

The alligator inched closer, his curious stare growing more predatory.

In the distance she heard a rumble, and the sludge around her feet vibrated. The motorized raft.

"We're here!" Lucy called, her gaze on the gator, her arms holding up Higgie, who was drifting out of consciousness again. Her left arm was completely exposed, holding Higgie across the chest, her wide stance submerging more with every breath.

"Here!" she hollered again.

At the sound, the alligator attacked, and Lucy whipped her arm away a nanosecond before its jaws snapped where her wrist had been, instead getting the soggy fabric of Higgie's shirt. She threw Higgie backward, tearing the shirt and barely getting his chest away from the teeth as they clamped down again.

The throw tilted her backward, her head just inches from the water now.

The animal sensed the fear and danger and death. It shot forward ferociously, its jaw stretched in a gaping bite as it popped out of the water and lunged at Higgie's shoulder.

Lucy threw herself at the beast, her fingers closing over slick scales as she managed to toss it backward. It hit the water with a loud splash that splattered muck in her face.

Before she could wipe her eyes it lunged again, missing Higgie's arm by a fraction of an inch, then opening wide with its snout pointed to the sky, preparing for a huge and deadly mouthful. The deafening sound of a gunshot splintered in Lucy's ear, and the alligator's nose exploded into a million bits of skin and teeth.

Lucy whipped around to see Jack standing wide legged in a kayak, bathed in moonlight, his gun still extended, his left index finger firmly on the trigger. He leaped from the kayak and took two long strides through the water to grab them, one arm around Lucy and the other pulling Higgie up as he dropped into the water again.

Then the motorized raft roared up, Donovan at the controls while Owen jumped out to assist.

"Take him," Lucy said, indicating Higgie. "We're stuck in the mud."

Owen righted Higgie, pulling him out of the mud, while Jack did the same to Lucy.

"Someone was out there, taking shots," she told him.

"Yeah, I heard from the boathouse." He righted Lucy's canoe and pulled her closer, putting his mouth to her ear. "You're not going to believe what I found in there."

Behind her, Owen said, "We'll take him inside, Lucy." He and Donovan had gotten Higgie, who was waking again, into their raft.

"Keep him low, under cover." She peered around, still on guard for the shooter. "I'll be right there."

"No, you won't," Jack whispered. "We're going to the boathouse."

She gave him a questioning look. "What did you find? Theo?"

He shook his head. "The vault."

CHAPTER
SEVENTEEN

"GOD, TELL ME you don't believe his crap, Lucy." Jack threw the fiberglass canoe hard enough to make the wood floor of the boathouse tremble and cause the hanging tools to clatter.

She closed the boathouse doors and turned to him, hands on soggy hips, her hair matted with mud, her filthy white T-shirt molded to her body. The look in her eyes told the whole story.

She'd fallen for it. She'd gotten under Higgie's spell, and now she was on his side. How the hell had that happened?

"Jack, I've been studying people for a long time. I know a lie when I hear it. And I know the truth, too."

Oh? He'd lied to her to get a job, and she hadn't sniffed that out. "Then prepare to find out you're wrong this time. Dead wrong."

"You aren't thinking straight. Eileen hasn't told you what happened or what she saw that night. I just heard a very different version from the one you painted—from someone who doesn't deny that he was there."

"Eileen didn't kill Wanda Sloane," he ground out.

"Well, someone did. And, frankly, I'm not worried about that murder right now. I've got a principal to protect and he was just shot at, and attacked by an alligator on my watch." She shook her head, clearly disgusted with herself. "He thinks his daughter is out to kill him."

"Maybe she is. Wouldn't that be sweet if she was right here?"

"Yeah, sweet. Listen, Jack, there's someone out in that marsh with a gun and an agenda, and I've got to stop him. Or her. Whatever it takes. That's what I committed to do when I took this assignment—not try to accuse my principal of a thirty-year-old crime that's already been solved."

"Jesus Christ, Lucy!" He kicked the corner of the kayak and whipped around, marching across to the opposite side of boathouse. "You committed to help me when you took this assignment. To bring the bastard down, not make sure he's safely tucked in bed every night. You committed to help a woman falsely accused of a crime, a woman who sacrificed her whole life so her daughters could be safe. Does she come in second now because she isn't paying for your goddamn protection services?"

Behind him, he heard her draw in a slow, steadying breath. "Whatever you think you found, Jack, show it to me quickly, Because I don't have a phone and I assume yours is soaked, too, and I need to know what's going on up at that house."

He pulled his phone out of the pocket of his shirt. Bone dry. "Call whoever you like. Then come and look at this."

She crossed the plank floor, leaving a trail of water in her path, her black eyes blazing at him. Taking the phone, she pressed a few buttons while he went to the three-foot-high door he'd found behind one of the canoes.

"All right," Lucy said, giving him back his phone. "He's in the cottage, requesting to sleep in his private suite. Marilee says they don't need a doctor; he just needs to rest. Owen is being posted outside the cottage doors and the whole compound is in lockdown. Donovan and Roman are taking the motorized raft out to look for the shooter." She pointed to the door. "Storage?"

"Did you see how this place was built, underneath?"

"There's a stone wall around the foundation of the boathouse, so I assume there's storage space built into the marsh."

"Come on." The door had no handle or lock, just a metal grasp that he yanked open. "My flashlight's still down there. I dropped it when I heard the gunshot, so you have to feel your way."

"What's down there, Jack?"

"Something to change your mind." He put a hand on her shoulder to lower her and guide her in. "It's a narrow opening until you reach the stairs on your right. There are about five of them, then a landing and five more. You want me to go first?"

She shook her head and dipped down, close enough for him to smell the sulfur and sweat on her skin and in her hair. She slipped into the hole and he followed, closing the door firmly behind them.

"There's the steps," he said when she stopped at a brick wall. "Be careful," he warned. "They're steep."

He followed her down the steps and stood next to her on the landing.

"Now what?"

"One more set of stairs, but they're wider." He put his hands on her shoulders and inched her forward into the open area he'd found at the bottom of the steps.

He used the flashlight to illuminate a five-by-five-foot cellar, with a cement floor and brick walls. It was completely empty except for a square, industrial type of air filter built into one of the brick walls.

"What is this, other than a cellar hole?" Lucy asked.

"It's a way in and out of the compound."

She frowned at him. "How?"

He crossed the cement to the filter, sticking his finger into the insulation and wiggling it to make a hole big enough to peer through. He moved aside and let her look, adding the beam of the flashlight to help her see.

"It's a long tunnel or duct," he told her. "I figure it goes many, many feet, probably ending under the cottage."

She rocked back on her heels. "Interesting. Maybe there's an access to it from Higgie's room. I swore I saw someone inside, but they got out without ever leaving through the door."

"Precisely."

She squinted in. "Not exactly a vault full of damning, submittable evidence, Jack. This tunnel is probably a duct for heating and cooling. There's probably a fan at one end to push the air and make it the temperature of the soil or water. Unusual in salt marsh country, but obviously doable."

"Heating and cooling? It goes under the garden."

"It might be part of the irrigation system, a dual function thing. I've seen that in big waterfront houses. That's why it's clay. And, look, there are valves and openings for water to run through."

"I saw that," he said, already working on loosening the filter. "I'd have gone in there to explore, but I heard the gunshot."

She put a hand on his arm. "Wait. Let's go get proper tools. Let's look at the blueprints. Let's make a plan."

He closed his eyes. "Let's not, and go find what I came here for."

"Jack, I want to help you, I do. I wouldn't have gone to all this trouble if I didn't believe in you and your cause." She turned his face so he'd look at her. "But he's no good to you dead. And if Kristen Carpenter is alive and trying to kill him, then she's our target, too."

He let the common sense sink in and override his need to act. "All right. Let's go back up, look at the blueprints, get a team in place, make a goddamn unbreakable plan."

She smiled. "Now you sound like a Bullet Catcher."

He rolled his eyes, but she didn't see, since she'd already backed away and headed toward the stairs to the boathouse. They'd just cleared the tiny door, closing it behind them, when something clunked on the dock outside.

They shared a quick look.

Jack pressed his finger over her lips before she spoke. "Let's hide," he whispered. "Could be our shooter."

He pulled her to the darkest corner, where he'd moved an old wooden canoe when he'd been searching earlier. "Get in," he ordered.

She did, and Jack adjusted the angle of the hull so they could hide, yet peek over the edge.

As the doors opened, they heard a woman's voice and saw a figure dressed entirely in black, wearing a dark knit cap, a cell phone pressed to her ear.

"I swear to God, I'm right where you left me." She pulled the door closed behind her, and Jack and Lucy inched up to look. "I never answer the hotel room phone. It's too dangerous."

Her back was to them, so all they could see was a dark hooded jacket, jeans, and the back of a knit cap. She turned, her attention to the ground, her concentration on the phone, her face still impossible to see.

She took the phone and rubbed it hard against her chest. "What? Theo? You're breaking up." As she spoke, she covered and uncovered the speaker with her thumb. "Theo? Are you there? Can you hear me?" Then she snapped the phone shut, walking straight toward them.

Ten feet away from them, she whipped off the cap and shook out a mane of blond hair and gave them a perfect view of her face.

He peeked to see Lucy's expression.

With one quick move, Kristen was on her knees, through the cellar door, and gone.

Jack practically leaped from the canoe. "Let's go. Let's get . . ."

Lucy wasn't moving.

"Don't tell me you still don't believe she's alive."

"I do. I'm thinking. I'm considering our options."

"You go right ahead, Luce. Consider until you turn blue. But I am going in that cellar and getting her."

"No, you're not." She climbed from the canoe, giving him the deadly look that reduced grown men to tears and instilled confidence in clients and fear in enemies. "This is my show, this is my company, and this is my job. It will take less than ten minutes to pull the team together, create a plan, and do this right. We'll capture her, we'll find evidence if it exists, we'll get to the bottom of it—but we'll do it right."

"Lucy—"

"If you bust in there, guns blazing, accusations flying, taking matters into your vengeful hands, the wrong person could die." Her expression softened just enough to keep him from moving. "And if that is you, Jack, I couldn't bear it."

The soft catch in her voice cut through his heart.

The only thing he wanted more than retribution and revenge and justice was Lucy. And he was so close now, even he couldn't be stupid enough to lose that.

"Lead the way," he said quietly. "Let's make a plan and let's get them both."

When Marilee and the bodyguard finally left, Spessard reached into his mouth and removed the pill she'd made him take, folding it into a tissue and hiding it behind his Bible. When his fingers touched the book, he lifted it absently. Marilee had left one soft light on across the room, barely enough for him to read.

He opened the book anyway, to look at the picture of Kristen he'd tucked there the week she'd died, with the silent prayer he'd said for her. Opening the page, he ran his fingers along her photo and thought about the few memories he had of a bright little girl who'd occasionally spent summers at Willow Marsh.

He'd had so little time with her. And he never appreciated it when he did. But that day, when she'd walked into his chambers, that serious look on her face, that challenge in her eye, she'd reminded him very much of a woman he once knew and . . .

Well, no need to get melodramatic. He'd never loved that secretary, although he enjoyed screwing her on his desk. And in his car. And in his chambers.

It was fun while it lasted, but then she'd gotten pregnant, and the balance of power shifted to her. She could have ruined him, and he couldn't have let that happen.

Thank God cooler heads had prevailed.

Or had they?

Thirty years later, the past continued to haunt him.

He smiled, running his hands over the newspaper clipping. Kristen had a bit of her old man in her, didn't she? Faking death took some piss and vinegar to pull off. No doubt she had help from that smarmy brother of hers.

But she couldn't be that smart or she wouldn't have shown up at the fund-raiser in that pathetic disguise. He was going to ask her to dance, and torture her, but then she'd shot him . . . and turned the tables on him one more time.

As soon as he was able, he'd go back to Washington. He *owned* the Department of Justice; nobody would refuse if he was asking the questions.

He'd find out how she did it. And he'd find her.

If she didn't kill him first.

He fluttered the pages of the Bible, opening to a random passage.

Ah, Romans. Quotes about the wages of sin, and what is a law unto itself.

His heart was so heavy it hurt.

This was his punishment for all his selfishness, for his pride, for his sexual appetite, forever unfulfilled by an icy woman he'd married because her ambition matched his, and her wealth guaranteed open doors. A wife who couldn't give him the legacy he wanted—children. He was forced to watch the one child he had from afar, and when she finally came close, she disappeared like a ghost on a mission to haunt and kill him.

He closed his eyes and pictured her, but instead, the pale, bloodless face of a woman lying dead in an alley burned in his brain.

Another private hell.

A thud at the foot of his bed pulled him right out of that bad memory; then he heard the slow, grinding noise of the secret door opening.

Holy God, someone was *in* there.

He pushed up on his elbows, his heart racing. This was it. This was death, surely. Whoever was in the marsh had found his secret cellar and . . .

He saw a halo of honey blond hair and the outline of a slender woman.

"I'm not a ghost," she said, as if she'd read his thoughts.

"I know." He put the book aside. "I saw you at the aquarium. I know you're alive. And that you want to kill me."

"I don't want to kill you. In fact, I'm here to protect you."

He sat up a little straighter. "Why did you disappear and pretend to be dead? You didn't even give me a chance to explain anything."

"I thought you tried to kill me. I thought you saw me as a threat."

"You're my *daughter*."

"I was wrong," she said simply, walking to the side of the bed. "It was Theo, and he was the one who convinced me I had to do this. He's very close, Uncle Spessard. He wants to kill you. He shot at you in the marsh."

"There's plenty of security here. He won't get me." He patted the bed. "Please sit down. Please let me tell you what happened."

"I know what happened. You had a child out of wedlock, I was given up for adoption, my parents were killed, and you placed me with Bernadette Carpenter. I have a lot of information that could end your career."

"You're wrong." He closed his eyes. "I'm not that ambitious, child."

"Well, I am." The voice rose from the floor, shocking them both. Theo's head and shoulders appeared first, his gun aimed directly at Kristen. "And you two sound a little too cozy to suit me."

"Theo, why are you doing this?"

"Did you think I'd forget the secret passage we discovered when we were kids?" He laughed. "But no one else knows it exists, so it's the perfect place to get rid of you two. Get in there." He raised the gun to Kristen's heart. "Now."

Lucy took less than ten minutes to pull a crew together and lay out a strategy for combing the compound to find the shooter, while she and Jack gathered the tools necessary to go through the duct that ran below the house.

Owen was alerted that there could be a security breach inside the cottage, and the rest of the men took off in various directions, linked by satellite phones.

Next to her, Jack's whole body thrummed with the need to move, yet he maintained his composure, helped create the plan, and stayed completely focused on the task as they headed for the boathouse cellar.

"I appreciate that you're being such a team player," Lucy said.

He held up a hand to stop her. "I'm not doing anything for the team. This is for one person, and one person alone."

Eileen? "You really love her, don't you?"

He snorted softly, but Lucy's phone rang with a 911 beep. "It's Owen. There's a problem." She flipped the phone open.

"Seven's gone," Owen said immediately. "When I went in to check the security breach you told me about, the room was empty and the wheelchair was sitting there."

In the background, she could hear a female sobbing and muttering in horror. "Who is that?" she asked.

"Mrs. Higgins. She's certain he's been killed."

Maybe he had been. Maybe Kristen worked faster than she did. "Calm her down. I know where he is."

"You do?" He was stunned. "Where? I'll tell her."

"Are you in his private rooms now?"

"Yes."

"You need to find the underground entrance some-where in the—"

The crying got louder.

"Just get her out of there," Lucy said. "Get her out of the cottage and hand her over to someone who can calm her down. I'll come over there."

She flipped the phone shut and looked at Jack. "Marilee's losing it and I'm going to go to the cottage. I can find the way into that cellar, if we're right, and I think we are."

"Fine," Jack replied. "We can get them coming or going."

"I'll meet you down there. If there's any problem, call me."

"I might not have satellite service underground. We're going to be blacked out for a few minutes."

"I'll find you."

"Perfect." He started to jog away, but she grabbed his T-shirt and pulled him close.

"Jack." She narrowed her eyes. "Do not fire a gun unless your life is on the line. Do not make a move until we have each other in sight and we are in sync. Do not break with plan and try to worm your way into that cellar and hammer out Jack Culver's version of justice."

He just smiled. "I'd have preferred a kiss for luck."

She yanked him closer and put her lips on his, then she gently pushed him toward the boathouse. "Go."

She ran at top speed toward the cottage. The fastest way was to cut through the garden, if the gates were open. If not, she'd jump the wall.

The first gate was not only unlocked, it was wide open. She slipped in, peering into the shadows. Every light in the garden, which had been lit since she'd arrived at Willow Marsh, was off. The heavy perfume of camellias permeated everything, mixed with jasmine and something she didn't recognize.

She darted through the middle of the garden, her soaked sneakers barely touching the grass as she headed for a gate she knew was there, swearing softly when she found it locked.

She had holstered her gun and reached out to grab hold and jump it, when she sensed someone in the shadows. Before she could react, he attacked her, taking her to the ground, slamming his hand over her face, and giving her neck a good twist.

Her attacker was strong and thorough and trained . . . like a Bullet Catcher.

She grunted hard as he pressed her face into the ground, denying her the chance identify him. She felt her gun removed from its harness. Then her phone.

Oh, yeah. Her men knew exactly what would cripple her. She slammed an elbow and hit a rock-hard abdomen, her brain clicking through one man after another.

He was rough, yanking her up, his hand still on her mouth as he pinned her forward so she couldn't see who it was. He hadn't said a word and had no distinctive smell. More furious than scared, she tried to jam the top of his foot with her shoe, but he was too fast.

Bullet Catcher training.

Without a word, he pushed her into the shadows of the garden, away from the gate.

Who would betray her, and why? This had never happened before.

A gun prodded her back as he pushed her. She didn't think about where she was going or why, because in the back of her mind, she kept hearing a phrase Jack had used over and over.

He can do anything.

He could even buy a Bullet Catcher.

CHAPTER
EIGHTEEN

JACK KEPT THE flashlight off as he went down the cement stairs, staying close to the wall with his gun drawn.

The tiny cellar was empty, but the filter that led into the duct was askew and there was about an inch of water on the floor, which he didn't think had been there before.

With the flashlight in his teeth, he started to work on the air filter, easily finding the mounting clips. In a few moments he had it off and climbed into the four-foot-round tunnel to crawl under the garden.

He moved quietly but fast, keeping the flashlight straight down so the beam didn't announce his arrival to Kristen. The duct was ingeniously built, allowing air to heat or cool the cottage, and to move water when irrigation into the garden was necessary.

He crawled about a hundred feet, the sulfury smell of the salt marsh strong, then stopped at the sound of a whining, ticking motor and a man's shout. He turned off the flashlight and crept forward, stopping when the duct ended with a fan separating him from another cellar.

This cellar was larger and lit by a single bulb on the wall, casting a yellow light over stacks of large plastic storage bins against the walls and near the bottom of a curved metal staircase.

And sitting on top of two bins, aiming a gun at Higgie and Kristen, was Theo Carpenter.

The fan's whir was deafening in the tiny space, and the blades turned too fast to see clearly or to get a clear shot.

Theo said something and Higgie replied, both voices harsh, but the words were impossible to make out over the fan's noise.

Jack slid out his cell phone and pressed a button to text Lucy, but there was no signal down here.

He had to warn her. She'd be coming down those steps any second, not knowing what to expect.

Theo looked more than a little unstable, and Jack had no doubt he'd shoot before he asked questions.

There was no way to turn the fan off from this side, and no matter how straight his shot, he'd never get a bullet through without hitting a blade, risking both a miss and ricocheting the bullet back at him.

Higgie leaned forward and said something, and Theo put his head back and laughed.

"Stop it, Theo!" Kristen's exclamation was clear and loud, and she stood, hesitating when her brother lifted the gun higher.

Jack traced the edges of the fan to figure out how

it was connected. Since Kristen had been able to take it out and climb through the opening, the bolts shouldn't be that tight.

He found the edges of a chunky hex nut and started to twist. It released easily, but the fan was still solidly in place.

Kristen sat back down, her shoulders hunched. She spoke to Higgie, who leaned closer and put his arm around her, patting her back.

Phony bastard.

Jack felt for the next bolt and got his fingers on the edges, twirling easily and checking to see if that loosened the fan enough to push it out.

Not even close. Watching the three of them, he went to work on the next nut, then the next.

Where was Lucy? He crouched to get to the bottom of the fan, and water soaked the knee of his pants.

There hadn't been any water when he got in here. If water was coming through the irrigation valves, he couldn't see it or hear it over the fan.

But there was at least two inches of water around his knees now, and the electrical fan in his hands made for a deadly combination. He hesitated, hoping like hell he didn't hit a live circuit and fry.

Something hit his calf and he peered down to see the flashlight, fully submerged. Swearing mentally, he moved faster. If he didn't get this thing out and soon, he would be electrocuted.

It looked like Kristen was crying, as her brother spewed incomprehensible words. Higgie kept his arm firmly and protectively around her, until Theo lunged and physically threw the older man away from his sister.

Jack didn't understand the dynamics, and he didn't care. All he wanted to do was get the fan out and take a shot at Theo.

But where was Lucy?

He deftly unscrewed three more bolts, sweat soaking his back as the water rose closer to the lip of clay that surrounded the fan. With one solid shove, the fan would pop far enough from the hole to give him room to take a clean shot.

He pulled out the Ruger, positioned it in his left hand, got a grip on the fan, and aimed for Theo.

But the light went out. The fan sputtered. Kristen screamed, and Theo's feet hit the concrete as he jumped off the storage bins and hollered, "Shut up, K!"

"Hey!" Kristen cried, the sound of her voice moving as she did.

Jack couldn't see a damn thing, and one wrong shot would take out Kristen.

He stopped moving, still holding the fan and the gun.

Where in hell is Lucy?

By the time Lucy was shoved across the garden and pushed into the pitch-black shed, she'd identified her assailant as Owen Rogers. He stuffed a filthy rag into her mouth, bound her hands and feet, and tossed her in a corner, her backside smacking on hard cement.

The son of a bitch was a credit to her elite training.

She didn't try to fight him; she didn't want to get hurt, or worse. He was working for someone, and until she learned who she was up against, and why, she'd save her strength.

Alone on the cold hard floor, Lucy inhaled, getting a noseful of fertilizer—and camellias.

"He told me your men call you Ms. Machiavelli."

Marilee Higgins's soft Southern drawl came from across the small shed. Lucy could almost make out a shadow as her eyes adjusted to the complete darkness.

"Is it true?" Marilee asked. "Do they call you that?"

Lucy didn't give her the satisfaction of a grunt, which was all she could have managed with the rag in her mouth.

"It's a compliment, don't you think?" Lucy heard rustling silk as she imagined Marilee shifted her position, still wearing the navy Chanel dress she'd had on at dinner. "I think it's the highest of praise."

Lucy could barely make out Marilee's light, expensive perfume over the heavy smells of the shed, but she definitely smelled danger. Marilee was likely armed.

"I'm a bit of a Machiavellian personality myself," she continued. "But I suppose you've figured that out by now."

Yes, she had.

"I'm a different breed than you are, though, Lucy. I'm a stay-in-the-background kind of manager, content to pull strings not for the thrill of power, but for the total peace that comes with knowing I am utterly in charge of my destiny."

The last statement was punctuated with a soft sigh. Lucy shifted on the unforgiving floor, checking the strength of the cord that bound her wrists. As soon as her eyes adjusted, she'd scan the shed for possible tools and weapons.

"I'm a big believer in the concept of destiny," Marilee continued, as though they were sipping wine on the patio. "And mine, it seems, is inexorably tied to a man named Spessard B. Higgins."

Was she doing this for Higgie? Was she his puppet? Or could Higgie be oblivious to what his wife was up to?

Maybe *she'd* shot at him in the marsh.

"There's a threat to my destiny right now," she said, "and it's not whoever tried to shoot my husband at the fund-raiser. Do you know who I'm talking about, Lucy? You should; you're sleeping with him."

Lucy stayed perfectly still, her eyes wide to speed up the process of getting her night vision.

"And," Marilee added smugly, "I believe you're falling in love with him."

She couldn't know that. Lucy barely knew it. And Jack still had no clue.

"You should have told him this afternoon, you know."

Stunned, Lucy straightened, blinking in surprise as she started to make out Marilee's pale skin.

"If you had admitted how you felt while he was so busy admiring your underwear, he would have said he loved you, too."

She'd *heard* that conversation? Impossible. Lucy had checked for bugs herself, they'd used a scanner on the room, and she'd kept it locked and used five different systems to detect if someone had been there while she was gone.

"But your other plans interested me more," Marilee continued. "It was always my strategy to get your dangerous lover close to me, so I could get a little more control over him. The assassination attempt helped, but I would have had you here without it."

She certainly was a master manipulator.

"But then you mentioned one thing, and it bothered me, Lucy."

What had they talked about? Eileen?

"You told your boyfriend that Spessard wanted to give you a list of some sort. Something from his past. Remember?"

Lucy kept her face blank and fearless, sure that Marilee's night vision was fully functioning.

"That revelation was worth the loss of that dear and perfect camellia."

The flower—*that's* how she put a listening device in the room.

Lucy remained still, her only goal to keep Marilee talking for as long as possible. Jack would tear Willow Marsh apart until he found her.

"And I must thank you, Ms. Machiavelli, for delivering my nemesis directly to my door. Although he would have shown up eventually, of course. He's tenacious, that one, and I've known it was just a matter of time until he zeroed in on my husband in his quest to save that wicked, evil woman in jail. He's kept me quite busy these last few months."

All this time, Jack had thought Higgie could do anything, but the truth was, *Mrs. Higgins* could.

"It has to end." The statement was made with hard,

cold finality as Marilee stood. "And in true Machiavellian fashion, I'm going to end it by using other people to do my dirty work. In this case, you."

Marilee knelt in front of Lucy, where they could easily see each other. "Because I think you are smart, fair, and extremely ambitious, Lucy, I would like to make you an offer that can get you out of this situation with fame, glory, and money. And, of course, your life."

Lucy lifted her chin as if to say *Bring it on.*

"Stop your boyfriend's quest for whatever version of the truth he is after. Use any means you like, but I suggest something permanent. In return, I will make sure that the world knows there was a brutal and horrific attack on the next chief justice of the Supreme Court, and the owner of the Bullet Catchers singlehandedly thwarted it, making you a national hero. Or . . ."

Marilee stood and walked to a small cabinet on the wall. She opened it, revealing an electronic panel. Her fingers grazed some buttons. "I've just started letting the water seep in, but . . ."

Lucy's throat tightened as she realized what the box controlled.

"A flick of a few switches, and that tunnel, and the two cellars that it connects, will flood like the proverbial Red Sea. The way I built it, the end in the boathouse has a safety panel, ensuring that the water stays in the duct. If I choose to, I can do the same on the other side."

Without her being able to talk to Jack, he might go back into that tunnel, and die. Owen could convince him that the plan had changed, and tell him she'd instructed him to stay. With a rogue agent out there and no way to warn anyone, that flip of the switch could kill Jack.

Marilee fingered the panel. "He thought he was so brilliant, hiring a builder I didn't know, but the man is a fool. I know, and I control, everyone. I let him think he was the only one who knew about his little safe room. But if anyone is safer because of it, it's me."

Lucy just stared at her.

"And here's the part of our deal that I like the best, Lucy." Marilee turned, leaning casually against a worktable. "I have such good friends all over Washington. All over the world, actually. Some right in the CIA, where you used to work. Mostly wives of powerful men—women who like to stay in the background, like me. Women who come from powerful families, who want to keep them that way. Women who know secrets, and keep them. Even from their husbands. *Especially* from their husbands.

"Secrets can be very useful," she continued. "I understand there's an incident in your past that has been conveniently eradicated from your file. Something about a man named . . ."

Lucy's heart dropped.

"Roland. An unusual name, Roland Grosvenor. I'm sure you remember it, Lucy."

Information was so much power, and right then, Marilee's was impressive.

She looked down at Lucy. "There's quite a bit of hush surrounding his untimely demise. He was shot, it seems. When another man was supposed to have been shot—by you. Instead of killing the Al Qaeda lieutenant running a terrorist training facility in Kosovo, the facility discovered by Roland Grosvenor, you took your shot a little . . . off target."

Lucy didn't move.

"That was a fairly costly form of revenge on your husband, wasn't it, Lucy? It seems you put your own emotions above the mission. And how many people— no, how many *children* died because of that little bit of vengeance you had to have?"

Many. Lucy tried to swallow, the old black hole of pain threatening to suffocate her.

"But you are quite adept at rising like a phoenix from your ashes, aren't you? And you could rise again, if you work with me on this," Marilee said. "You can be the golden girl once again. A victor against evil, the ultimate Bullet Catcher and hero."

Disgust rolled through Lucy, but she stayed perfectly still.

Marilee tapped the top switch. "Which one, Lucy? Devil or angel? What are you made of?"

Still, Lucy refused to let Marilee know her words had made any impact.

"Ah. You've moved to the side of the angels, then. Fine." Marilee snapped the first toggle switch down. "It's going to get very wet in there for your poor Jack."

CHAPTER
NINETEEN

FOR A SPLIT second, Jack thought the sound was a generator. There was a clunk of metal, a roar of power. Then the rushing, gushing sound of water echoed through the clay tube where he hid. All hell was about to break loose.

This time Jack couldn't wait and observe.

He pushed the fan out and launched into the cellar, the pitch darkness covering him, while Kristen screamed and Theo hollered.

Jack followed Theo's voice, stepping closer to him. The second Theo saw his shadow, he lifted his gun and shot, just as Jack swatted it out of his hand.

Higgie moaned in pain.

"He's shot!" Kristen screamed. "You shot him, Theo!"

Theo had already backed away, slinking behind a stack of bins like a cornered animal without a weapon.

Kristen jumped to help Higgie, evidently unaware that Jack had entered the cellar. Water gushed onto the ground as the duct overflowed.

Jack squinted into the dark, using every sense to find Theo. One of the plastic bins moved and he whipped in that direction, still too blind to take a shot.

Higgie moaned in agony.

"Oh my God, he's shot in the stomach! He's dying, Theo!" Her voice rose into a panicked scream.

Was Theo headed back to the stairs? Jack positioned himself at the bottom, waiting, ready to kill.

Kristen screamed Theo's name again, leaving Higgie to find her brother, her voice coming straight at Jack. He held out his hand and it hit her chest.

"Don't move," he ordered quietly, hoping Theo wouldn't hear him over the gushing water.

He felt her inhale for a big scream, so he pressed his hand on her mouth and pulled her closer with the other one, still holding the gun. "I'm going to help you get out of here. Don't say a word," he whispered.

Her whole body was shaking, but she managed to nod.

Slowly he let go of her mouth.

"And him?" she murmured, her arm reaching back toward Higgie.

"Go up the stairs." He pushed her. "Get help. Find Lucy."

"Lucy—"

He pushed her harder. "Go!"

She did, quietly enough that Theo probably didn't know she'd left. The water was two inches deep now, and rapidly rising. All he had to do was climb up the stairs after Kristen and get to safety.

Higgie would die. Theo, too.

But Eileen would die in jail if he didn't get proof from that son of a bitch who put her there.

Jack stepped into the water, knowing that too much movement would give away his location. He heard a noise, and smelled the fear a split second before something hard and sharp slammed down on his shoulder.

It knocked him to the ground but he flipped over, his gun already aimed to shoot whoever had walloped him. Something long and silver sliced through the air, whooshing straight toward his head. He rolled to his side and metal clanged mercilessly on the concrete, inches from his body.

Jack *thwacked* it, his arm slamming solid iron, but managed to knock it away as he popped to his knees and raised his gun, found the center of the shadow, and pulled the trigger.

"Fuck! Ooooh." Theo slumped to the ground.

Jack inched closer, his gun straight out, squinting into the darkness.

"Who are you?" Theo groaned. "Who the fuck are you?"

Jack leaned closer, ready to shoot again if he had to. But Theo could barely breathe. Jack saw the whites of his eyes as they rolled back.

"Help!" From above, Kristen banged on something. She wasn't out yet?

Jack could make out Higgie, slumped on the floor, bleeding from the gut. He had the answers. But he needed proof to unlock Eileen's jail cell.

"Let me out of here!" Kristen hollered again, pounding on the trapdoor.

Jack hoisted himself up, the water calf deep now, and ran up the circular stairs.

"Kristen," he called. "I'll push it open."

"It's locked," she hollered back. "We're locked in here."

She was on the top stair, shaking, crying, and looking at him with a mix of confusion and hope. "How do you know who I am? Who are you?"

He moved her down a few stairs. "I'm a friend of your mother's."

"Bernadette?"

He shot once, then again at the flat panel above them, certain he was firing into the floor of Higgie's bedroom. Six shots and he could push the door open like a manhole. He did, using all his might until light poured down into the stairwell.

"No," he said, stepping aside to help her up. "Your birth mother. Eileen."

She froze and looked at him. "You're Jack. Her guardian angel. She talked about you."

He nodded with a tight smile, just as Owen Rogers's head poked over the hole.

"What the hell's going on, Culver?"

"Get this woman to safety," he ordered. "Where's Lucy?"

"Lucy?"

Jack narrowed his eyes. "Sharpe. The woman you work for."

"She's fine," he said, reaching his arm down toward Kristen.

Irritation punched his gut. "I didn't ask if she was fine. Where the hell *is* she?"

"She went with some men after Seven, in the marsh."

Every cell in his body screamed *Impossible!* Lucy broke with plan?

From below, a loud, miserable plea for mercy reverberated up the stairs.

"Is that the justice down there?" Owen asked as he pulled Kristen out of the opening.

"Yeah," Jack said.

"You'll never carry him up alone," Kristen said. "He's been shot in the stomach. He's dying."

"Get her somewhere safe," Jack told Owen. "Then send a team down here to help me get two wounded men upstairs—fast. And get Lucy."

He headed back down the stairs. Just as he reached the bottom, he heard the enclosure slam back into place.

Did that son of a bitch close him back up in here?

Before he could react, he realized that the water was already covering Higgie's hips. He had to lift him off the ground so his wound wouldn't get wet, wring out some answers—and then decide if the bastard deserved to be kept alive.

Lucy watched as Marilee flipped switch after switch.

She hadn't been serious about the deal; she just wanted to show that she had ultimate control.

"It won't take long for that duct to fill with marsh water. I've basically just opened a dam. A shame to ruin all those papers and valuable documents," she said, her face, which Lucy could now easily make out in the dark, pinched with displeasure. "But I probably have enough to open Spessard's library posthumously, if I have to. Even if he doesn't get out of there, his reputation will be intact."

She flipped the last two switches. "In the end, that's all a man leaves behind, you know—"

The banging on the shed door silenced her.

"It's Owen. I've got someone you want, Mrs. Higgins."

Jack? Lucy's heart clutched as the deadbolt slid to the side and the door opened.

But it was Marilee who gasped as Owen shoved another woman into the small space, just as viciously as he had Lucy.

Marilee stumbled back, clearly shocked at seeing Kristen. "Let her go, Owen."

He did, sliding a defiant look at Lucy.

"I'm not dead, Aunt Marilee," Kristen said, her blue eyes bright as she reached for the other woman. "I realize this is a shock, but I had to do it . . ." She looked at the floor where Lucy was, and instantly Owen stepped inside and slammed the door behind him, cutting off all light.

"Hey! What's going on?" Kristen demanded.

"You're supposed to be dead," Marilee said coolly.

"That's what I'm trying to tell you," she said. "I'm not."

"Then we'll remedy that."

Owen's cell phone rang, and Lucy recognized the personalized tone of Roman Scott. They all had their own ring so they could ID the caller without looking at the phone.

Was Roman in on this, too? She closed her eyes in despair.

"Sorry, I haven't seen her," he said to Roman. They had to be talking about her, which meant Roman hadn't turned traiter.

"She could be anywhere," Owen said defensively. "Last I heard, she was off with Jack somewhere."

Had she missed all that attitude from this guy, or did he just assume she was as good as dead and it didn't matter?

"I don't need to be there. I'm in Seven's office, where Lucy told me to stay." His voice was heavy with exasperation, revolting her. Regardless of what happened to her, her men would piece it together.

And they'd hunt him down and rip him to shreds when they figured it out. She hoped she was around to help.

"Take Kristen down to the marsh," Marilee said calmly when he hung up. "Take her all the way out to the mound. It's about half a mile away, an island in the middle of the river. Make it a clean kill, then let the alligators destroy the evidence. Hurry."

He seized Kristen's arm behind her back and pulled her against him with a gun to her head. As he slipped out the door, Lucy got a glimpse of the gun in Marilee's hand. A small one, a simple street gun . . .

A Raven Arms that she handled with a great deal of familiarity.

The very type of gun that killed Wanda Sloane.

No—the *very* gun.

She shifted her gaze to the panel of switches. Would Jack die without ever knowing the truth? Or had he died already?

Her heart ached as the impact hit her as hard as . . . as . . . Cilla.

Now she'd loved twice, and lost them both.

The wound wasn't fatal. Jack could tell that instantly, but Higgie was old and already injured, and he was losing blood fast. The only humane thing to do was drag him up the stairs and get some other Bullet Catchers to help pull him out of the hole and get him to the ER.

Then he'd live.

Higgie moaned as Jack hoisted his rock-solid body to a storage bin that was high and dry. It wouldn't be for long, though. The muddy, smelly waters were pouring in.

Theo was dead, and Jack could get out alive easily. But Higgie?

"Please," he pleaded with Jack. "Help me upstairs."

"I was just thinking about that. Not sure I should do that, Higgie."

He managed a deep breath, cringing at the pain. "What do you want? Money?"

Jack snorted.

"Name it. Name whatever the hell you want, and get me out of here."

"I want Eileen Stafford to be free."

Higgie stared at him.

"And I want you behind bars for the murder you committed, with a public apology to her and her daughters."

"I didn't kill her."

Jack gave a dry laugh. "You don't have a lot of bargaining power here, Justice. You're going to bleed out or drown in less than an hour. I don't give a flying crap if you do both. But you stole that woman's life and I am giving you the opportunity to give it back, save your own, and give something to all three of your daughters."

Higgie frowned, and not from pain. "Why do you keep saying daughters? She's . . . Kristen. She's my daughter."

"She's one of them."

His eyes grew wide. "One of . . . what?"

He really didn't know. "Triplets. Your mistress gave birth to three babies at Sapphire Trail. Didn't they tell you that?"

He closed his eyes. "Three babies. Oh, Lord, what have I done?"

"Precisely what I'd like to know. Time's running out, Justice. A full confession, and a promise to write it down, give it on tape, and set that woman free. And you live."

"Are they all girls?"

"Yep. An anthropology professor, a stockbroker, and Kristen, whom you obviously know."

A tired, pained hand reached out to Jack. "I didn't kill Wanda. I was with her. I ran after she was shot, but I didn't kill her."

"Yeah, then who did?"

He turned his head toward the duct, where water rushed over the broken fan. "This is the work . . . of our . . . irrigation system."

What? Jack stared at him.

"Run by . . . my wife." He tried to breathe through the pain. "Everything is run by . . . my wife. She can . . . do . . . anything. *Anything.*"

"Your wife killed Wanda Sloane?"

"I've always suspected as much . . . but preferred not to think about the truth. She's . . . the one you want, Jack. She's the one . . . with your answers." He looked up. "I swear to God, on the Bible, and on the life—lives—of my children. I am innocent of that crime."

"Prove it."

"I . . . can't."

"Then you die."

"I don't have proof. There is no proof. Only my word against Marilee."

If what he was saying was true, she wouldn't be the first woman to kill to save her husband's reputation and future. She was certainly tough enough, smart enough, rich enough, connected enough.

"Marilee is a manipulator," Higgie rasped. "She is very shrewd."

A low burn of bad feeling rolled deep in Jack's gut.

"Shrewd enough to pay off jurors, cops, lawyers, and reporters?"

Higgie snorted. "Even the nurses. She had one with her in the hospital, already getting her information, whispering. I wasn't asleep, I heard her talking to this Risa. She gets everybody to do—"

"Who?" Jack jerked up. A nurse named Risa on Marilee's payroll?

If Risa was at the hospital, then Marilee knew exactly who he was. They'd never revealed to the nurse that Miranda and Vanesssa were Eileen's daughters. But if she knew who he was, then she knew . . .

Lucy.

"Wait here," he said, launching up. "I'm getting help."

At the top of the stairs, he threw his full weight at the trapdoor, grunting when it didn't budge.

Owen *locked* him in here?

He couldn't have—Jack had shot it open before. He pushed again, Higgie's moans floating up the stairwell almost as loudly as Jack's curse of frustration.

Don't die, Justice. Not now. I need you.

Owen hadn't locked him in there, Jack realized. He'd put something over the opening. The bed or a dresser.

"Hurry . . . please . . ." Higgie called from below.

"The door's blocked," he yelled back.

"It slides," Higgie managed. "It slides on a track. Hurry. I'm not going to make it."

If the old man died, he'd never, ever prove Marilee's guilt. And Lucy . . .

With strength he didn't know he had, he tried to slide the door into invisible tracks, but it only moved an inch.

Owen had placed that monster of a bed on top of the opening to trap him down there.

Jack pushed again, letting out a howl of fury with the effort, and getting only one more inch for the work. Enough to slip two fingers through. If he could get a good grip, he might be able to slide it out from under the bed, into the rails built between the floor and the ceiling of the stairwell. He was going to get out of here, save Spessard Higgins, free Eileen Stafford, and spend the rest of his life with Lucy Sharpe. Because no shit piece of wood was going to stop him.

He slipped his finger into the crack and pulled. Slowly, haltingly, it finally slid into the tracks, freeing it from the weight of the bed and allowing Jack to push it all the way open.

Weapon aimed straight up, he took the last few steps and aimed two-handed, spinning around ready to clear the room just as the bedroom door burst open and Donovan Rush ran in.

"Where's Lucy?" Jack demanded, no longer ready to trust anyone.

Donovan looked at the gun and held up his hands. "Easy, Jack. I'm not the one you want. We can't find Owen or Lucy."

Jack narrowed his gaze at Rush. Could he trust him? "Where's Marilee Higgins?"

"MIA also."

Damn. "Go down there and get Higgins. Bring him up alive. Get him to the hospital. Fuck it up and you're dead."

Donovan gave him a seething look. "I'm on your side, dude."

"You'd better be. Owen isn't—watch out for him." Then he took off to find the only thing that really mattered.

Lucy.

CHAPTER
TWENTY

As soon as the door closed behind Owen, Lucy managed to reposition herself and lift her legs, trying to use her knees to squeeze the rag out of her mouth.

Marilee heard the sound and got right down in front of her face.

"What are you doing, Lucy?" She plucked the rag out but held the gun in her face. "Trying to say something to me?"

"You killed her."

"Owen will. My hands are clean."

"Your hands are filthy. You killed Wanda Sloane, with that gun."

Marilee stood, glancing at the gun. "I did indeed, which should tell you that I'm an excellent shot and quite good at getting away quickly. Why are you looking at me like that? It was a brilliant plan. Three birds with one shot."

"Three?"

"I eliminated Wanda, who was not going to go

quietly. I shut up Eileen and kept her bastard daughter under my thumb, and I scared the living daylights out of Spessard, who agreed to no more affairs. Although there's nothing I can do about those distasteful prostitutes he uses. Our deal is no intercourse, and he's been very good about following that."

Lucy imagined how close Kristen was to the marsh by now. How a bullet—one of her very own—would kill her.

Fury and fear rocked her as she forced her fingers to reach up into her wrists to try to untie the binding.

"Then why did you ask me to investigate him?" she asked, keeping her voice calm.

"I wanted you and your friend Jack under my watch. You know the old adage: Keep your friends close, your enemies even closer."

Lucy got a thread of twine between two fingers and yanked, making the tie tighter. *Damn.* "And you killed one of those prostitutes, didn't you? That's why she wrote your name. Your last name."

Moving easily in the dark, Marilee pulled something off the shelf. "I didn't cut her throat, if that's what you're implying. But I must say, you've done an excellent job with Owen. He's deadly."

And she'd been worried about Jack going against plan?

"I let other people handle the dirty work—but that's what money and power are for," Marilee continued. "I've used quite a bit of both keeping tabs on Eileen Stafford. Risa wasn't cheap, but she's on a very short list of people whom I don't need anymore. Like that distasteful Officer Gilbert who arrested Eileen. He just turned too greedy."

"And Howard Porter?"

Marilee shot her a look. "A visitor at the prison, as I recall. Risa said Eileen was far too talkative that day. Who was that man, anyway?"

Vanessa's father. She really didn't know about the other girls. Could that information be disarming enough to get Marilee to make a mistake? Lucy watched, considering her enemy.

Jack had been so right . . . yet so off the mark. He'd spent all his energy on the wrong Higgins.

Where was he now? Had he made it out in time? Or would he die not knowing the truth? And not knowing just how she felt about him.

But she couldn't let herself go anywhere near emotion now. She had to put all her focus on Marilee, who hoisted a large bag onto the small table. Using a gardening scoop, she filled a large plastic jar as calmly as if she were sifting flour.

The acrid smell of ammonia and fertilizer filled the shed.

There was only one thing she could do with ammonia nitrate fertilizer, other than grow flowers.

"You can't possibly think you're going to get away with this."

Marilee laughed softly. "First of all, the place is crawling with security that I hired, so I'll look innocent. Secondly, the media will be so focused on my husband's death that one of the bodyguards dying in an explosion won't make headlines. We'll make it part of a big, dramatic story that paints my husband as a hero."

Lucy tried again to work her hands under her hips, but the twine just sliced into her flesh and she didn't have enough space between her arms. Sweat tingled her neck, and her body ached with frustration.

"There will be an investigation," Lucy said. "You can't stop that."

She tried one more time to break the twine, not caring that it cut her skin.

Marilee looked up from her work, a small bottle in her hand. Many liquids could cause an explosion, but gasoline would be the most efficient.

"Evidently you've forgotten something, Lucy." She smiled, opening the bottle, releasing a whiff of gas. "I can stop anybody I want from doing anything. Even you."

Lucy had only one card left to play. One piece of information that might surprise Marilee into making a mistake. "You can't stop Vanessa and Miranda. They know everything."

The other woman frowned, looking around for something. "I don't know who they are, so I doubt they matter very much."

"They're Kristen's sisters. They're Spessard and Eileen's other daughters."

Marilee's look was sharp and vile. "What?"

"Kristen was one of triplets."

For a moment Marilee said nothing, her head tilting quizzically as if Lucy were speaking a foreign language. Then she started to laugh. A soft, ladylike trill at first, then a true guffaw.

"You are very, very good, Ms. Machiavelli. You had me—you really did. Triplets." She nodded with approval. "Brilliant."

She picked up the rag that had been in Lucy's mouth, holding it gingerly with two fingers. She sprinkled the rag with gas, then slid the smaller bottle into the large jar full of fertilizer.

Once she lit that rag, Lucy had only seconds to stop the inevitable. Because as soon as the plastic bottles heated and melted, the fertilizer and gas would blow this shed to the marsh. She'd throw herself on top of the flames if she had to; she'd rather be burned than be blown to bits.

But she still had the weapon of information.

"You *haven't* paid all the right people enough, if you don't know about Miranda Lang and Vanessa Porter. Put them all together and read their tattoos."

"What?"

"They were tattooed by a nurse at Sapphire Trail. Miranda has an *h* and an *i*. Vanessa has two *g*'s. And Kristen? I bet if you stop Owen and take a good look at the back of her neck, you'll find the last two letters of a very famous nickname."

Marilee stared at Lucy. "I don't believe you. There was only one baby born in Sapphire Trail," she continued, opening a box of huge nails. She eyed the wall behind Lucy, then gestured with her gun. "Stand up."

"Are you willing to take that chance?"

"I don't believe you. Stand up."

Lucy didn't move.

She raised the gun. "Stand up or I'll shoot you, and you can explode with a bullet in your heart. It makes no difference to me how you die, but I need to make sure you can't move."

If she stood, she'd have some leverage.

Lucy slowly pushed herself to stand on her bound legs as Marilee looked around.

"This should work." She grabbed a heavy canvas apron from the wall and stood in front of Lucy. "Move one centimeter and I shoot."

She curled one of the strings around a hook next to Lucy's head, then did the same with the other, flattening the waistband of the apron against Lucy's neck so she couldn't move. Then Marilee reached for one of the nails and used the butt of her gun to hammer the thick tie into the wooden wall.

"There." Marilee stepped back, surveying her work smugly. "Go ahead, try and move."

Lucy did. If she moved forward or tried to duck down, the apron pressed against her windpipe. If she used any amount of strength to tear the apron from the nails, she'd choke herself.

From the pockets, an array of tools stuck up toward her face. Lucy dipped her chin to see what she had—a trowel, a weeder, some gloves. A pair of gardening shears completely out of her reach. The only thing she could grab with her teeth was the plastic handle of some tool, she couldn't tell what.

"As much as I like to delegate," Marilee said, "I get a certain joy from handling you and Jack Culver myself."

"You won't handle Vanessa and Miranda, or my entire company. You can't pay them off."

She rolled her eyes. "I can if I want to. But I believe there was only one baby born in Sapphire Trail. And right about now, she's taking a bullet to the head."

"You're wrong, Marilee. Those girls will not rest until they have you." Lucy had to press against the wall to keep the apron from strangling her.

"If you *are* telling the truth, and I don't believe you are, those girls will rest just fine. They think my husband killed that woman, don't they? And he's gone, and your Jack is gone, and in about two minutes, you'll be gone, too." She shrugged and turned to the table, totally confident that she didn't have to watch Lucy anymore.

Big mistake.

"What about Eileen?"

Marilee let out a soft snort. "That unfortunate being will die where she belongs, in prison."

Lucy clamped her teeth over the plastic tool handle and yanked it up, dragging out something with a round blade that looked like a pizza cutter.

With Marilee still turned, Lucy twisted her neck, forcing the tool over her right shoulder, the sharp blade cutting her T-shirt and the skin underneath. She opened her mouth and let it fall into her hand, wincing as the blade sliced her palm.

Marilee turned and Lucy erased all expression.

"You might have been able to outsmart my husband, Ms. Sharpe, but not me. Haven't you heard?" Marilee struck a match, the fire flaring brightly in the little shed. She held the flame over the cloth. "I can do anything."

Well, so can I. With the handle in her left hand, Lucy rolled the blade over the twine. One cord snapped.

Marilee dropped the match.

The other cord snapped.

Lucy swung her hand free and whirled the cutting tool around her, throwing it with mighty force straight at Marilee's neck the instant she turned.

Marilee ducked, and the blade went directly into her eye.

Behind her the fire ignited, and Marilee's scream reverberated through the shed as she fell back to the table, dropping the gun and struggling for balance above the fire. Lucy reached her hands under the apron belt and used every drop of strength she had to tear the fabric from the nails, but it wouldn't move.

Marilee shrieked, rolling on the floor with her hand over her eye as the rag burst into flames.

She managed to get to her feet, then stumbled again, wild with shock. Inches from her, the table caught fire and flared in a giant roar of orange flames cracking in the middle and falling with a loud crash, the whole container of explosives slamming on the ground.

Lucy rammed her hands against the canvas ties, her veins popping with the effort, the slash on her palm scorching with pain. Marilee crawled toward the door, inches from the flames, howling in agony.

The jar slipped to the right with the first softness of a melt.

They had only seconds to live.

Lucy lifted her feet to brace against the wall, pressing and choking, the flames so hot and close, she felt her hair heat up.

Marilee was nearly to the door, clawing her way toward safety.

Helpless, Lucy watched the plastic container shift again.

"Lucy!"

Jack! He was out there!

There was a loud bang, and Lucy braced for the pain of being blown apart.

But it was Jack, shooting down the door. She flattened herself against the wall as bullets blasted through the wood and metal; then Jack kicked the door open.

He stepped right over Marilee as he charged in, giving the apron one furious swipe. Free, Lucy almost fell against him.

"Jack, get the gun! On the floor. Get the gun!"

"We don't need it." He started to drag her out.

"Yes we do! It killed Wanda!"

He turned and reached down to grab it, then flipped her over his shoulder and tore from the shed at full speed. They weren't ten feet away when it exploded with a deafening blast. The impact threw them to the ground, and Jack covered her completely as debris and sparks and metal poured over them.

She felt his mouth on her head, heard him repeating her name like a litany, like a prayer. His body was soaked and he was shaking as much as she was.

"I thought I lost you. I thought I lost you, Lucy." His voice was desperate, raw. "Oh my God, I love you. I *love* you."

Everything in her wanted to respond with relief and love, but she had only enough strength to say one thing. "Owen has Kristen. He's going to kill her."

He rolled off her and grabbed a shard of hot metal, then sliced the ties at her feet.

A gunshot echoed over the open marshland. Without a word, he took her hand, and they ran.

At least she could reason with Theo, Kristen thought. Attila the Hun was a whole different story. He pushed her to the marsh, threw her into the canoe, then paddled with one hand, his pistol aimed at her with the other.

"Please don't kill me," she whimpered, getting a quick, dismissive look in return.

He rowed toward the mound, the island where she and Theo used to race, each taking one of the two rivers from the boathouse to see who could get there first. Where Uncle Spessard taught her to do the Eskimo roll. Where she was about to die and be eaten by alligators.

"I'm already legally dead," she tried again. "No one in the whole world knows I'm—"

A fiery explosion tore a shocked gasp from her throat, lighting up the sky and all of Willow Marsh.

The shed. Where Marilee had that woman tied up.

That woman who was now burned to bits. Kristen's stomach roiled.

"Who was she?" Kristen asked softly.

"Just some bodyguard."

In the distance she heard sirens scream and alarms blare. Hell had broken loose, and the place would soon be crawling with U.S. Marshals and FBI agents. And no one, not a single person there, would know to look for her.

Because she was already dead. And her brother was dead. And Uncle Spessard was probably dead, too.

Maybe Jack, the guy who knew her birth mother, would wonder what happened to her. But maybe not.

They were a hundred yards from the mound when Owen stopped for a moment, his gaze on the water next to him.

"Look at that." He shifted the gun, squinted to aim, then fired at a four-foot gator.

Blood instantly darkened the moonlit water, which would only attract more. They'd find her dead body on the mound. They'd eat her.

Hot tears welled in her eyes, spilling over. "Please," she begged, a sob cracking the word. "Just leave me. Don't shoot me. Please."

"Shut up." His look said the rest. *Or I'll shoot you now.*

How had she gone from her normal life to . . . this?

She'd gotten curious. She wanted to know who gave birth to her. She wanted to know her medical history and her gene code and her DNA. She wanted to know what the tiny mark on her neck meant, the thirty-one or *ie* that she'd had since birth.

It turned into a mission, and now she was going to be dead for the second time.

The sickening irony was that Uncle Spessard was really happy with the news. He didn't care about the media; they loved him. So he had an affair thirty years ago. This was America, and he was Higgie.

Theo had made it all up just so she would no longer be his sister. He was sick. In love with her, and sick. And now he was dead.

Giant tears rolled now, wetting her face, sliding into her mouth.

She stared at the fire in the distance. Maybe that controlling bitch Aunt Marilee didn't get out in time.

Twenty more strokes, and they'd be there. Not many heartbeats left until they reached the raised hill of grass in the widest part of the river. The gators were all around it. They loved that spot—especially at night.

Ten more strokes.

She looked over her shoulder and saw the mound of tall grass, with two cypress tress that the birds loved to nest in. Moss hung heavy from the long, low branches, silver in the moonlight.

She used to hide in those trees when she came here in the summer as a kid. She would climb in the trees and wonder who she was. Who was her real mother, her father? Did she have more brothers . . . a sister?

Her killer studied the mound, probably trying to find the best place to shoot her.

Was there anything at all she could do?

There was! Uncle Spessard had taught her the move when she was ten, and she was pretty good at the Eskimo roll. All she had to do was throw herself forward, yank the canoe hard, and it would flip. But would it throw a two-hundred-pound man into the water?

She knew what to do if she succeeded. She'd curl up underneath the hull and kick away, underwater but with air. Gators didn't usually bite unless you threatened them—or you were dead meat for dining. He might shoot at her, but would his gun work if it got wet? Could it shoot through the canoe? It was metal, so maybe not.

But she had absolutely nothing left to lose.

As he turned to look behind him at the mound, she took a deep breath, clenched her fists, and dived forward.

"Hey!" He stood instinctively, as she hoped he would, and she threw all her weight to one side. Just as the canoe flipped over and landed upside down on top of her, she heard a gunshot. And another and another.

Was he shooting at her from underwater?

She kicked up from the mucky water, expecting the burn of a gunshot wound, but nothing hurt. Using the sides of the upside-down canoe, she yanked herself into the hole of the hull, sucking the pocket of air and paddling her feet madly to get away.

He'd have to dive into the murk and get under there to shoot her—which he might.

She kicked like a crazy woman, her breath loud in the hull. Then she heard . . . a woman yelling her name. And a man.

She froze for a second and closed her mouth to stop the sound of her breathing.

"Kristen! Stop!"

Was this a trick?

She kicked again, moving rapidly down the river, when she felt the canoe rock in her hands.

He had her. He was a ruthless killer who was about to dive into her upside-down canoe and get the job done.

She saw a shadow underwater; then he burst through the surface under the canoe.

But it wasn't him.

"Kristen," the man gasped. "You're okay now. He's dead. You're safe."

"Jack?"

He nodded, his black hair dripping. Then he reached for the side of the canoe, and she let go as he flipped it upright. He helped her in, then climbed in behind her, and they just sat there for a moment, staring at each other.

"Your mother," he said with a deep gulp of air, "made very resilient girls."

Girls? "Did you say *girls*?"

The motorized raft appeared from the other side of the mound driven by a tall, dark-haired woman—the one who'd been on the shed floor?

Attila the Hun lay prone in the back, and yes, he was dead.

The woman tossed Jack one oar, then another, as she pulled up next to them. "Are you okay?" she asked Kristen.

Kristen nodded, then looked at Jack. "Did you say girls? Plural?"

"I'll meet you there," the woman said to Jack, pointing ahead to the dock. "And by the way, nice shot, Leftie."

"Below the neck," he hollered as she drove away. "That's what I win!" Then he smiled at Kristen. "Yes, I said girls."

As he rowed back to the dock, he told her the most amazing, mind-blowing, unbelievably wonderful story.

She had sisters.

CHAPTER
TWENTY-ONE

FOR THE FIRST time in more than thirty years, Eileen Stafford was dressed in yellow—the color of sunshine. Only Jack would know just how much that meant to her, and she'd cried when she'd opened the package he'd sent her. She reached up and touched the simple blond wig that had come in the same box.

She'd promised him she'd wear it all today: the day they all arrived and the process that Jack called "securing her freedom" would begin. She would meet with the girls first, then some lawyers, then the prison board.

He'd said it would take a few weeks, maybe months, but it would happen. And when it did, she would wear yellow that day, too.

It was the color of happiness.

And she was so deeply, truly happy. Jack Culver had solved the crime, found the real murder weapon, saved her life, and given her back her daughters. Her joy was total.

Her feet, in pretty brown shoes that had come with the suit, made sweet little tapping noises on the linoleum as she walked down the hall. She paused at the room where she'd been instructed to go, took a deep breath, and opened the door.

They were all there but hadn't heard her enter, their backs toward her as they watched a TV set, mesmerized.

"It is with great anguish that I announce my resignation from the highest court in the country."

The voice, familiar and frightening at the same time, filled the stunned silence.

Eileen listened to a reporter ask a question, the booming answer, the spin on some version of the truth. None of it mattered anymore. All that mattered were the three—four, counting Lucy—young ladies in this room, and the men they loved.

She had a family now, and nothing could ever take it away again.

The thought was so thrilling she sucked in a little breath, and instantly Jack turned and saw her. His smile was wide and as real as the joy in her heart.

"Hey, Sunshine."

Her eyes filled. She could never repay him for this.

He reached to bring her into the room and then everyone realized she was there, and they greeted her with a shower of exclamations and congratulations, and so much warmth and love that she couldn't shut off the tears.

The man on the TV was forgotten as, one by one, her girls kissed her cheek.

"I guess I'll have to call y'all by your real names, now," she said as they guided her to a chair and seated her like a queen, her girls surrounding her.

"Call them anything you want, Eileen," Jack said. "They're your daughters."

One of the girls put her hand on hers. "You can call me Anna, if you like."

"No," Eileen said, reaching out to touch her china doll face. "You are Miranda, the first one to find me."

"That makes me the oldest," she said with a laugh.

Eileen turned to her left. "And you're the lifesaver, Vanessa—the one whose blood cells cured me."

Vanessa winked. "Happy to make the donation to a good cause."

"And you"—she looked up at the third—"are the wily one who stayed alive by pretending to be dead."

"Alive is better," Kristen said with a dry wit that reminded her of Vanessa. They looked alike, and they had a lot of the same mannerisms. They were twins, she decided, and Miranda was a bonus who'd grown alongside.

But they were all sisters, and they were hers.

Wade and Fletch placed possessive hands on the shoulders of the women they obviously adored. Behind them, Jack stood close to Lucy, no arm of ownership necessary when a man looked at a woman like that.

"And you," Eileen said to Lucy, beckoning her with a finger, "can be an honorary daughter of mine."

"I'd like that," Lucy said, coming closer.

"You are the one I used to fantasize would come

swooping down from heaven and make me feel all better inside."

Jack put his arm around Lucy and looked right at Eileen. "That's funny. That's exactly what she did for me."

Eileen beamed, pleased. Well, now. Maybe she'd paid Jack back after all. He certainly looked happier than when she first met him.

They all started to laugh and talk again and Eileen just listened, loving them all, and looking forward to the rest of her life with her family.

When Lucy and Jack returned to her imposing mansion, she brought him to a suite of stunningly beautiful rooms full of warm colors and soft textures—and a heavenly-looking bed. Then she disappeared into the bathroom.

Jack strolled the rooms, getting comfortable with his surroundings. Since Willow Marsh, they'd been inseparable and he expected that to continue.

Throughout the briefings with the FBI and U.S. Marshals, discussions with the Charleston PD, and the press conferences about the death of Justice Higgins's wife, Theo's accidental shooting, and Kristen's admission to orchestrating her own death, they'd stuck to each other's side.

They'd handled the aftermath as a team, including the debriefing of all of the Bullet Catchers on the assignment to determine together that Owen Rogers had indeed been a rogue agent working alone for Marilee.

They'd visited Eileen, then flown back to New York

on the Bullet Catcher jet, always holding hands, kissing, touching, loving.

But Lucy had not yet kept her promise to talk.

And something about her silence on the drive up to her estate told Jack the pressure to do so was getting too great for her.

So he gave her space. Instead of joining her in her bathroom, he found another to shower in, then strode naked through the hall to her bed to wait for her.

Did she think there was anything at all that she could admit to that would end his love for her? Didn't she know by now?

In the master bath, he heard the sound of the hair dryer.

He turned all the lights off but a dim bedside lamp, then slid into sheets as smooth and creamy as her skin, just as the bathroom door opened and Lucy stepped out.

He couldn't speak. He couldn't breathe.

She actually looked a little shy. Hesitantly, she walked across the room, then touched the front of her hair self-consciously.

Her entirely black hair.

He opened his mouth to speak, but couldn't. She looked so different. So completely . . . free.

She approached the bed, sat on it, and looked directly at him. "I decided it was time to let go of the past."

Somehow, he managed to drop his gaze from the stunning sleekness of her newly darkened hair to drink in what she was wearing.

A black lace bra, trimmed in a million ebony pearls.

"You got a new one," he said with a smile. "For me?"

"I found one in every color," she said as he ran his fingers along the little pearls. "But do me a favor and don't destroy them all with your teeth. They cost six hundred dollars apiece."

He whistled. "I'll just lick them." He reached up and stroked her shiny, black hair. "And you. You're so beautiful, Lucinda."

"I love it when you call me that. No one ever has."

"Most people don't know you the way I do."

She closed her fingers over his hand. "The way you're about to."

He reached for her, pulling her to his chest. Inhaling her spicy scent, he cuddled her body into his.

"Tell me everything. Tell me your story."

She rubbed her cheek against his hand, then finally looked up at him. "Her name was Priscilla Joy Grosvenor, and she was . . . miraculous." She hesitated, her voice tight. "She was bright and adorable, and . . . she was my baby."

A single tear slid down her cheek. He wiped it away, and listened.

"We were living in London, working for the agency, when she was about to turn three. Roland, my husband, was on a very sensitive assignment, developing a critical high-level contact. He learned that someone from a previous assignment had tagged him, blowing his cover and putting him in serious jeopardy.

"I was in Paris for two days, and I . . ." She took a long, unsteady breath. "I trusted him with Cilla. Because he was her father, I thought she was safe."

"What happened, honey?"

"He used her. Took her out and used her as a cover, certain these people wouldn't hurt him if he had a baby. When he got into his car and started the engine, he realized immediately that they'd planted a bomb. He threw himself out, and saved . . . himself."

Jack tightened his arms around her. "But not the baby."

She shook her head. "Not Cilla."

After a moment, she turned to face him. "We divorced, because I couldn't even be in the same room as him. But I . . . I . . . festered and grew . . . ugly. I wanted revenge."

"I hope to God you killed the fucker."

She smiled. "Culver justice. Yeah. I did. But . . ." She closed her eyes. "It didn't turn out that well."

"Why?"

"I arranged an opportunity a year later for us to be in the same place at the same time. I was dropped in with instructions to take out a very high-ranking terrorist in Al Qaeda with ties to the center of the organization. A huge hit, one that mattered a lot to national security." She averted her eyes for a moment. "I threw the assignment, broke with plan, and killed Roland instead."

Jack lifted a brow. "The ramifications?"

"Were massive." She tried to swallow. "The target escaped, the agency investigation folded, numerous covers were blown—"

"Not the end of the world."

"And the organization bombed a schoolhouse in Kosovo."

"Because you shot your ex-husband?"

"That bullet had a domino effect."

"Do you think that wouldn't have happened if you hadn't screwed up the operation?"

"I have no way of knowing, Jack. But I do have plenty of guilt."

Guilt and pain—a deadly cocktail he'd drunk many times. "I take it you were disciplined. Is that why you left the CIA?"

"No," she said. "I was put into seclusion, and under psychiatric care."

"For how long?"

"Long enough for the powers that be to discover that Roland had traded secrets to Korea, and was a rogue agent."

"So you were a hero for taking him out."

"I had no idea he was a traitor when I killed him, Jack. I was a vigilante. I wanted retribution, and some kind of peace in my heart."

"Did you get it?"

She laughed bitterly. "I got a silver streak in my hair, and an endless fight for a solid night of sleep. The only way to dull the pain was to devote every waking moment to saving lives, instead of taking them."

Jack gently traced her cheek. "And you became a believer in plans, and you despise anyone who takes matters into their own hands."

"I don't despise you," she said pointedly. "But loving you is . . . ironic."

"But you do."

"Love you?" She smiled. "Deeply."

Deeply. That was good. That was so good.

He kissed her tenderly, easing her onto her back and trailing a finger over her cleavage and her sweet pearls. "That night, the first time, do you remember why we had to go out to the jungle?"

"It wasn't exactly a military maneuver, as I recall. The client was Reed Consolmagno, the Formula One driver. He was in Kuala Lumpur for the Grand Prix."

"And he had a sudden, burning need for water from the *hutan*. Couldn't race without it, remember?"

"I remember. I wanted you to go get it alone, but of course you coerced me into coming with you. And we got stuck in that downpour and had to spend the night in a mud hut."

"I orchestrated that whole thing."

"You made it rain?"

He leaned very close and put his mouth on her ear. "He had six gallons of *hutan* water. I emptied them all."

"Just to get me alone in the jungle?"

"Exactly. I took you there to tell you something, but then, we . . ." Realization dawned. "We saw those schoolchildren and you fell apart."

"Now you know why."

He held her tighter, wishing he could do something to erase her pain. "Let it go, Lucy. You have to let it go."

"I know. I'm trying." She looked up at him. "What did you want to tell me out in the jungle?"

"That I loved you." He threaded his fingers through her hair and looked into her eyes. "I love you so much and so naturally, it's like breathing or eating or wanting to be in the sun. I love your strength and your beauty and your soul and your wicked need for control." He kissed her face, her throat, the rise of her breasts. "I love you, Lucinda Sharpe, and I will never, ever stop."

"I love you, too, Jack."

"Good." He nestled her closer. "Because we're going to have a wonderful life together. You, me, and all . . . these . . . pearls."

She gave a half sob, half laugh, curling her leg around him to pull him closer.

"I want you inside me now," she whispered, closing her hand around his erection and leading him to the warm, wet spot between her legs.

"Are we skipping foreplay because you're afraid I'll wreck your six-hundred-dollar bra?"

"We're skipping foreplay because I want you where you belong: deep in my body. Here." She guided his hard-on past her silky thong.

"Aren't we forgetting something?"

"Not a thing." She arched her back and he entered her unsheathed, his lips meeting hers.

Tight and hot and wet, she took him with nothing at all between them.

Absolutely nothing Lucy Sharpe ever did was arbitrary.

He smiled into the kiss, and she smiled back.

Deeper, faster, sweeter, he lost himself in Lucy. When she climaxed, she whispered his name, over and over. Watching her, loving her, he let go and gave her everything, all his love and life with each aching burst of pleasure.

Hours later, the light still burned. And Jack lay staring at the ceiling, stroking Lucy's hair, listening to her steady, satisfied breaths, thinking about a baby named Priscilla Joy, and what they'd just done.

"Lucy?"

She just breathed softly, completely and deeply asleep.

EPILOGUE

"THEY'RE GOING TO kill each other!" From her office window, Lucy watched the game of touch football under way on the lawn below.

That last "touch" had Max Roper's knee in Alex Romero's chest, with Alex's wife, Jazz, screaming foul from the sidelines. Johnny C had wisely opted out of the game, instead barbecuing something delicious for the party celebrating the engagements of not one but two of the Bullet Catchers. Their fiancées had talked them into Christmas weddings, so there'd be many more parties over the next few months.

The house teemed with life, such a change from Lucy's usual solitary Sundays. She was used to a crowd on Saturdays, when almost the entire staff showed up for meetings, briefings, food, and some no-holds-barred football.

Smiling, she watched Fletch annihilate Jack with a full-body tackle, only to have Jack roll, flip, and almost take the big Aussie down. A testosterone free-for-all.

She turned from the window, when the sound of a car roaring up the driveway pulled her back. The black

Maserati drove around the fountain and parked directly in the spot where they all knew she couldn't see the driver from her office window.

But she knew who owned that car. And she'd known he'd come back eventually.

Dan Gallagher had found every imaginable excuse to avoid the Saturday staff meetings, so she certainly never expected him here on a Sunday. In the past two months he'd only come to the estate once, when his assignment in the city ended and he needed to file his report. But he'd chosen a day when Lucy was in Miami at a client meeting with Alex and Jazz. Since then, he hadn't come in for another job, and she hadn't contacted him.

She watched him greet Fletch and Wade with warm handshakes and manly back-pounds of congratulations, taking a few minutes to speak to Miranda and Vanessa, saying something that made them laugh.

That was his gift: laughter and light.

He stopped to talk to Sage and Johnny, plucking something from a platter and popping it into his mouth, giving Johnny some knuckles in appreciation. He glanced around as he talked. Looking for her? Or Jack?

Then he looked up at her window, and she saw him wink.

So it would be today. She turned away and considered the most comfortable place to have this conversation. At her desk? Too much like work. On the settee? Too intimate.

It didn't matter where they sat or stood; she was about to hurt him.

"Can't you even stop working during a party?" Dan's voice, a warm rumble that still carried a note of happy confidence, floated up the stairs.

She leaned against her writing table and folded her arms. "I'm not working," she called back.

"Liar. You are on that BlackBerry lining up—" He froze in the doorway. "Whoa." He literally had to snap his jaw closed. "Of all the rumors that circulate about you, Juice, I was pretty sure this one was a big fat lie."

She slipped her hands under her cut and colored hair, fluffing the black locks over her shoulders. "Like it?"

"It's . . . different."

"That's damning with faint praise."

He grinned as he ambled in, his jeans and T-shirt suggesting he planned to stay for the barbecue. And that alone made her want to weep with relief.

When he reached her, he put his arms around her in a warm hug.

"You know what else I heard?" he asked.

Her heart stuttered a little. *You and Jack Culver are in love.*

"I can't imagine," she said, delaying the inevitable.

"I heard some bitch nailed you to a wall."

Lucy laughed. "I hope they mentioned that I got out of it with my hands tied behind my back."

"And a little help from your new boyfriend."

Here we go. "Nice to see the Bullet Catcher rumor mill is in perfect working order."

He stepped back, sitting on a chair's armrest to study her. "Yeah, I guess I do like your hair. You look great."

She smiled her thanks. "All is well, Dan. Excellent, in fact."

"I heard that, too."

She crossed her arms and shrugged. "So, you don't need to talk to me. You know everything already."

"I keep my ear to the ground. Anyway, I'm not really here to talk. I just dropped by to tell you something."

His serious tone caught her. "What's that?"

"I've decided to . . ." He looked down, then back up, his grass green eyes dark, his jaw clenched. "Take a leave of absence."

"Oh." The soft exclamation was out before she could stop it. "Don't leave, Dan. Please. You don't have to."

He looked at her like she was crazy. "I know I don't have to. I'm not going off to lick my wounds, Juice. I'm okay with change."

Was he? "What are you going to do?"

"I'm going to . . ." He hesitated and Lucy held her breath. "I have a bit of business I have to finish up. I'm going to take care of that."

They just looked at each other, and a lump started to form in her throat. He was leaving. He was leaving the Bullet Catchers, and her. Her closest friend in the world, her sounding board, her dependable right-hand man.

"Are you going to tell me what this unfinished business is?"

"It's personal."

"Dan, we've known each other too long for that. Where are you going? How long will you be gone, and what will you be doing?"

He shook his head. "You don't need to know."

"Yes, I do."

"Then let's put it this way: you don't have the right to ask. I'm on leave, and off the payroll."

She let out a soft breath. "I'm asking as a *friend*."

"And as a friend, I'm not telling you."

"Something or someone?"

"You *really* don't have the right to ask that." He covered the gentle reprimand with that signature smile, revealing those two ever so slightly overlapped teeth and a gleam in his mossy eyes. "Sorry I can't stay for the engagement party—or parties, as the case may be."

Jack appeared in the doorway. "Don't leave now, Gallagher. We're just starting the next game." His dark hair was tousled, the ends damp from sweat, his ancient New York Jets T-shirt streaked with dirt. "Max is looking for another pretty face to mess up down there."

"Hey, Culver," Dan said, heading right toward him with an outstretched hand. "Nice work in South Carolina. Great to have you back on board."

Jack shook his hand, his own smile genuine. "Come on down; I'll tell you about it."

"I can't, but thanks. Listen . . ." He glanced at Lucy, then gave Jack's shoulder a friendly pat. "You take care of her, okay?" His smile didn't falter, but Lucy heard the slight catch in his voice. "Don't let her eat chocolate. It gives her headaches."

Jack smiled. "I know."

Dan narrowed his eyes. "And God knows she'll have
enough of those with you around."

Jack laughed, not bothering to disagree.

Dan gave Lucy another keen look, his eyes narrowing as he pointed at her. "You know, Lucy, you are
actually . . . glowing."

"I'm happy," she said simply.

"I see that." He tapped his forehead in a casual salute. "See ya, Juice."

As Dan walked out, Jack strode to Lucy, holding
her close, smelling like earth and sweat and grass. She
kissed his shoulder, and rested her head there.

"You should have told him," he said.

"He knows."

"Good. Then let's go make the announcement."

She drew back with a smile. "We're going to wait a
few months until we know for sure, remember? Will
you never learn?"

He laughed, nuzzling into her neck, pulling her so
close she could feel the beat of his heart. "No. And
won't that make for a fun and unpredictable ride?"

"I don't like fun and unpredictable." She closed her
fingers over his shoulders, as though she could actually
hold on for that ride.

"Yes you do. You love it." He kissed her cheek, her
hair. "You love me," he said with wonder and blissful
contentment.

"I do." And she was ready to tell the Bullet Catcher family just how much. "All right. Let's tell them now. Let's break with plan."

He gave his most insolent grin and winked, sliding a familiar hand against her belly to rest it there. "I already broke every plan you ever had, Lucinda."

She covered his hand and squeezed. "You didn't break a thing. You fixed it."

INTRODUCING
THE BULLET CATCHERS

from the first two books in
Roxanne St. Claire's new and exciting trilogy . . .

Meet Adrien Fletcher in
FIRST YOU RUN

and

Wade Cornell in
THEN YOU HIDE

Now available from Pocket Books

First You Run

Suddenly the heckler bounded toward the front of the room, and Miranda instinctively backed up. She hit a wall of man and spun around to come face to face with wide shoulders. Higher, she met amber eyes that had gone from flirtatious to dead serious.

He gripped her upper arm and in one move had her two feet from the podium. "Go. Now." He held her firmly, walking her to the railing that overlooked the first floor.

"Wait a second!" She tried to yank out of his grasp, but it didn't loosen.

He leaned close to her ear. "I'm going to help you. *Move*."

The store manager ran up the stairs, horror on her face at the chaos in the room. "What's going on?" she demanded, breathless.

The man steered around her. "Dr. Lang needs a safe place to go. Now."

Without questioning, the young woman thrust out a huge ring of keys. "The silver one will get you into the stockroom downstairs. It's right past the—"

He seized the ring. "I'll find it." With a gentle push, he urged Miranda forward. "Move. Fast."

She managed to free her arm and glare at him. "Who are you?"

"At this moment, house security. You want to stay and be eaten by the natives or get somewhere safe?"

Her linguist's brain stalled. His voice was richly, beautifully accented with the distinct sheared sounds of Australia, and it matched him perfectly. A voice with purpose, with poetry in every vowel. She glanced over her shoulder, to where the instigator ranted on, standing on a chair and flipping flyers to the crowd.

"Go to this Web site," Wild Eyes called out. "Find out the truth. Find out how to avoid the inevitable." He paused to meet Miranda's gaze with one full of hate.

Holding on to her rescuer's powerful arm, she flew down the steps, turned a corner behind a stack of reference books, and hustled toward a door in the back. After stabbing the key into the lock, he threw open the door, stuck his head in, and checked it out.

"All right," he said, pushing her into the closet-sized room jammed floor to ceiling with cardboard boxes and the gluelike smell of freshly printed books. "In you go, luv."

Was he leaving her there? Locking her in? The wave of panic subsided as he stepped into the room and closed the door behind him.

"Are you all right?" he asked, the concern unmistakable in that lyrical voice.

She nodded. She would be as soon as her heart stopped pounding her ribs. "I'm fine. I just . . . didn't . . ." She blew out a breath and forced her shoulders to relax. "Thank you. I didn't see that coming."

He guided her to a cracked vinyl chair. "Quite a unique crowd you draw."

"I never dreamed the crazies would be here."

"The crazies? Who are they?"

She looked up at him—way up, since he had to be more than six feet tall—and searched his face. Who was this lifesaver who swooped in from nowhere? Was he one of them and this all a ploy to ruin her first event?

But she didn't see anything crazy about him, only intense whiskey-colored eyes framed in thick lashes the same shade as his too-long hair and the shadow of a soul patch on his chin. Dangerous, yes, but not crazy.

"Who are the crazies?" he repeated.

"A group of zealots who call themselves the Armageddon Movement. Who are *you?*"

He smiled, adding attention-grabbing dimples to his growing list of attributes. "Adrien Fletcher." He held out his hand, and she shook it. His palm was wide, strong, and masculine.

"Miranda Lang," she replied.

"The famous author." *Fie-mous oh-thah.* Oh, that was pretty. And just in case the accent weren't endearing enough, he added a little wink, as if they shared an inside joke.

"Not so famous." She released her hand. "No one's ever heard of me."

He pointed over his shoulder, in the general direction of the second-floor reading area. "Evidently those people have."

"Fans like that, I don't need." She frowned a little. "Why are you here? You don't look like a regular at readings."

"I just wandered in a bit ago. I saw there was an author reading, and I was curious. Didn't expect I'd have to work tonight."

"Work?"

"I'm a security specialist."

"Whoa." She drew back, a half-laugh caught in her throat. "Talk about serendipity."

"Talk about it," he agreed, unleashing another blast of dimples.

They made her heart beat even faster than the rough crowd. She stood and smoothed her skirt. "I think it's safe to go out now."

"Not entirely, but we'll check and then duck out."

Disappointment dropped her back onto the chair. "My first signing, totally ruined. I won't sell a single book."

"Don't be so sure." He reached for her hand and tugged her up. Despite Miranda's five-foot-six-plus-two-inch-heel height, they weren't eye to eye. More like eye to soul patch. "Controversy is usually good marketing."

Outside the stock room, only a few people meandered about, the commotion now over. Toward the front of the store she spied her table, the stack of books as tall as it had been when she'd walked in. A bottle of water sat in a ring of condensation, two pens next to it.

"Maybe I should just sign a few stock copies," she said wistfully.

He nudged her forward with a shake of his head. "Not a good idea. Anyone could be waiting to renew their heated debate."

"You're right." She walked with him to the front of the store. "Anyway, the night is spoiled, and over."

"It doesn't have to be over," he said, his voice rich with implication.

At the cash register, the clerk held out a plastic bag to him. "Here you go, sir. The book you purchased."

He nodded thanks, took the bag, and led her out to the dimly lit sidewalk. Then he opened the bag. "Would you sign it for me?"

"You bought my book? Before you heard me speak?"

"I thought they might run out."

"Yeah, *that* was likely." She found a pen in her purse and opened the cover, thinking of the right words to thank him and maybe impress him. She looked down at the open page, the pen poised. But all she saw was a piece of white paper with stark, dark letters across it.

Have dinner with me.

She stared at the boldly written words. All confidence, all flair and total command. And no question mark at the end.

"For an expert in the nuances of language, you sure are taking your time," he said.

She slowly lifted her gaze to meet his, drinking in the smile, the dimples, the twinkle of invitation and attraction in his eyes. "When did you write this?"

"When I saw you walk into the store." He lifted one eyebrow. "C'mon, Miranda. At the very least, I can keep you out of harm's way for a few hours."

Under all that hair, an earring glinted. Under that tight T-shirt, a tattoo peeked. Under that lyrical voice, a man who had targeted her before she knew he existed.

He *was* harm's way.

And for some reason, that appealed to her. "Yes. I'll have dinner with you."

THEN YOU HIDE

TRIPLETS. *TRIPLETS?* For the second time in one day—hell, in one hour—Vanessa was dumbfounded. "Nobody even *had* triplets thirty years ago, did they?"

Wade laughed softly. "They had them, it was just a surprise on delivery day."

"How could I not know this?" After all the research she and her father had done, it didn't seem possible that a fact as monumental as *there are two sisters* slipped by some of the best adoption investigators Daddy's money could buy.

"Very few people do know about this," he said.

"No shit, Sherlock. Where are we going?"

"You look like you're going to faint," Wade said as he ushered her to the same patio restaurant she'd been at less than two hours ago.

"I don't *faint*," she shot back. "It's a thousand degrees out and you shocked me and I—I'm *reacting*."

"Gotcha. Well, you look like you're about to react, so let's sit down in the shade here, under this umbrella, and have a cold drink and talk about it, okay?"

His patronizing drawl infuriated her, but the suggestion had definite appeal. She needed something cold—and potent—to make sense of everything that had happened since she got off that boat.

"Two iced mineral waters," he said to the waitress.

"And a vodka tonic," Vanessa added. "But skip the tonic. And no lime."

One side of his mouth lifted in a half smile. "You drink like you talk and walk. Tough."

"I hate limes. And tonic." *And you.* She crossed her arms. "You'd better have proof."

"There's no actual paperwork."

She slammed her hands on the tabletop and pushed back in the chair. "I knew this was totally bogus."

"But I have a picture." He placed a photograph on the table between them.

Wasn't that a fine twist? For the first time in three days, *she* was being shown a picture instead of the other way around. Though she wanted to be a complete brat and refuse to look at it, curiosity won out. She squinted at the photograph, half expecting—and half dreading—to see a reflection of herself.

"Oh." The word was a note of pure wonder, matching the sensation that rocked her. "She's beautiful." Then she shoved the picture back at him. "And she doesn't look a thing like me."

"You're beautiful." He slid it forward.

"Thanks, but I'm blonde—natural, by the way— and my face is longer, my mouth is wider, my eyes are shaped differently." Unable to resist, she took one more look. "She's really . . . delicate looking." Willow-thin and fragile. No glasses. No boobs. No cleft.

No dice.

"We don't even look related." She gave the picture a good shove.

"Triplets aren't always identical," he said. "Some-times two are, and one is from a different egg. That might explain the difference in your looks, and makes it possible that you're a match for the marrow, when she's not."

"She's not?" That hit her hard. If this alleged sister had been a match, would Eileen Stafford have dispatched an investigator to find *her*? Or would she have let Vanessa go to her grave without ever initiating contact? Of course she would have. God, she despised the woman right down to her last bad cell.

She turned toward the bar, lifting her hair with one hand to get a nonexistent breeze on her neck. "Where is that drink?" This was so ugly, so complicated, and so *not* what she wanted to be doing with her time in St. Kitts. Or anywhere, for that matter.

With impossible purpose, Wade inched the picture back across the table, like a gambler willing to risk a decent card for the remote possibility of a better one.

"Her name is Dr. Miranda Lang."

Something slipped inside Vanessa. *Miranda.*

She didn't care what her name was. She didn't *care.* Didn't he get that?

"What kind of doctor?" she asked, so casually it couldn't be interpreted as anything but small talk.

"An anthropologist. She has a book out that's been getting some media coverage, about the Maya calendar and the myth that the world is going to end in 2012. Have you heard about it?"

She lifted an indifferent shoulder. "Unless it moves money, changes the Dow Jones Industrial Average, or otherwise generates cash with at least seven, preferably eight, figures involved, no." She fanned her sticky neck, the heat pressing hard on her chest. At least, she thought it was the heat.

Finally, a drink tray landed on their table.

"Thank Christ," Vanessa mumbled, her gaze sliding over the much-needed vodka only to land on the much-hated picture.

Wavy auburn hair. Wide smile. Pretty. An anthropologist.

She grabbed the ice-cold glass and plucked out the damned lime. "There's obviously been a mistake. I'm sorry she's going to be disappointed. But my father and I did exhaustive research and there were no sisters."

She put the cold glass to her lips.

"I have another picture."

She didn't drink. She couldn't. She watched as he slowly reached back into his billfold, methodically drawing out another picture. Part of her wanted to kick him into faster action and get this hell over with. But it was easier just to watch his stunningly masculine hands as they moved to find something she just knew she didn't want to see. Nice hands. Sexy fingers. Bad, bad news.

"I think you'll be real interested in this one." He burned her with a look that might have been a warning, or might have been something else. It was hard to read this man, hard to get past the eyes and the body and the face.

Was that a calculated move by Eileen? *Send an irresistible hottie to sway her. I need bone marrow.* Her stomach tightened and she pressed the cold glass on her cheek.

"This picture," he said, his voice as measured as him movements, "is actually of the back of Miranda's neck."

Her choke sent vodka splashing over the rim of her glass. Oh, no. *No.*

"Right here." He reached a hand around her head, making a tiny circle with his fingertip, right above the nape, a million little hairs rising up at his touch and sending shivers down her back.

"She has a tattoo right here, and all three babies were marked with them. You have one, don't you?"

The drink slipped out of her grasp and clunked on the wooden table, drenching her shorts and legs with ice and vodka.

She pushed back from the table and swiped at the spill much harder than necessary. "Screw you."

He instantly grabbed a napkin and started swabbing her soaked thighs. His hand was hot on her leg and she jumped back, standing up.

He looked up at her. "I'm gonna take that as a yes on the tattoo."

Catch up with love...
Catch up with passion...
Catch up with danger....
Catch a bestseller from Pocket Books!

Delve into the past with *New York Times* bestselling author
Julia London
The Dangers of Deceiving a Viscount
Beware! A lady's secrets will always be revealed...

Barbara Delinksy
Lake News
Sometimes you have to get away to find everything.

Fern Michaels
The Marriage Game
It's all fun and games—until someone falls in love.

Hester Browne
The Little Lady Agency
Why trade up if you can fix him up?

Laura Griffin
One Last Breath
Don't move. Don't breathe. Don't say a word...

 POCKET STAR BOOKS A Division of Simon & Schuster A CBS COMPANY

 POCKET BOOKS A Division of Simon & Schuster A CBS COMPANY

Available wherever books are sold
or at www.simonsayslove.com.

17660